*Grace had done the unexpected. She'd won him over.*

"I understand about you wanting the land, maybe needing it—I do, too. It's beautiful, and you've been here all your life, Jack. This is what you know, what you love. It's just, I've never had anything like this. I've never even lived in a house, much less one with all this land." Her eyes looked overly bright. "You've got everything. You've got family and this town, and friends on top of friends. You're so lucky, so very lucky."

Her words almost broke his heart. And they were true about him. He had it all, except a reason to be here, to keep going, to find his way beyond his old life. If there was a woman like Grace in his future... He didn't want to even think like that. He couldn't.

"You're right," he managed to say, and if she hadn't touched his arm, he would have ended it there.

Dear Reader,

In Wolf Lake, family and friends are everything.

So when Grace Evans receives a windfall from her now deceased father, who deserted her and her mother years ago, she takes what is on offer—a piece of land in Wolf Lake, New Mexico, that feels like home to her from the minute she sets foot on the property. But one person's blessing can be another's source of pain.

The story of Grace and Jackson Wolf, the eldest Wolf brother, is of their struggle to make a life that they both want desperately, and to make that life work in spite of what seem insurmountable odds.

But unexpected love has a way of evening out the differences, giving each person what he or she truly needs, and making a high-stakes gamble become a blessing so incredible that hearts are mended and lives are changed forever.

I hope you enjoy the journey of Grace and Jack as they find their home, together, in Wolf Lake.

Mary Anne Wilson

# HEARTWARMING

## *A Father's Stake*

—

*Mary Anne Wilson*

HARLEQUIN® HEARTWARMING™

Recycling programs
for this product may
not exist in your area.

ISBN-13: 978-0-373-36698-9

A Father's Stake

**Printed in U.S.A.**

**HARLEQUIN®**
™ www.Harlequin.com

## MARY ANNE WILSON

is a Canadian transplanted to Southern California, where she lives with her husband, three children and an assortment of animals. She knew she wanted to write romances when she found herself rewriting the great stories in literature, such as *A Tale of Two Cities,* to give them happy endings. Over her long career she's published more than thirty romances, had her books on bestseller lists, been nominated for Reviewer's Choice Awards and received a career nomination in romantic suspense.

**Books by Mary Anne Wilson**

**HARLEQUIN HEARTWARMING**

**HARLEQUIN AMERICAN ROMANCE**

*The Carsons of Wolf Lake

For Emily Vaughn Geisler,
an unexpected joy and blessing in my life ten years ago
and still making everything brighter and more fun.
Love you more than you could ever say you love me!

# CHAPTER ONE

IT HAD BEEN almost two years.

To him it seemed an eternity since his life had been torn apart, and now, it had happened again.

Jackson Wolf Carson sat on the stone step that led up to the porch of the old adobe house, and he could feel that gut-wrenching churning once more. He thought he'd moved past that in the two years since his wife, Robyn, had died. But he was wrong. It had stayed there, hiding, until an hour ago when he'd gone to the family ranch to confront his father.

That shattering encounter had brought those old emotions back to life and this time he wasn't sure how he could get beyond them without giving up…for good.

He closed his eyes and ran a hand roughly over his face, damp with sweat that came from the baking July sun beating down on the fallow three hundred acres spreading out all around him. Life had gone on while he'd wandered through the days and nights of the past two years alone. He'd finally thought he had found an anchor, something to hold on to. But any hope he'd let flicker back to life had been extinguished at nine o'clock that morning, the moment he'd walked into his law offices in Wolf Lake.

The email had come with four attachments. He'd thought his contact in the county offices had sent it, but the moment he started to read the letter, he knew he was wrong. Dead wrong.

Disbelief had given way to a burning anger at his father's betrayal. He almost cringed at his reaction. He'd driven to the ranch, burst into his father's office and thrown the papers at him. He'd yelled, kicked the massive desk so hard it jarred his entire body, but his father just sat behind the desk without saying a word. It was his mother who'd come up behind him, her face filled with horror, and asked what was wrong.

One look into her eyes and he realized she'd been betrayed as badly as he had. Without looking at his father again, he'd touched his mother's shoulder. "Ask him," was all he'd said before storming out, heading for the old ranch adjoining his parents' spread.

He took off his baseball cap, raked his fingers through his shoulder-length, iron-straight black hair, then slapped the navy hat against his denim-covered thigh. He'd been so sure the old adobe house and the land sprawling around it was the connection he needed so desperately in his life. Each brick of the low structure had been handmade by Jack's grandfather, Jackson Wolf, the man he'd been named for. The older man had passed away more than three years back, going quietly at the age of ninety-two, outliving his only wife by almost twenty years.

His grandpa had come down from the reservation with his wife, down from the high country in the foothills of distant mountains to the low valley, all Wolf land. It had been his people's land, generation after generation. He'd worked against the odds to make a life for his family, creating one of the best grazing areas in the state and building a home for his seven children. This place had always been a second home to Jack.

Jack narrowed his eyes and gazed into the

distance, the land shimmering in the oppressive heat. Generation after generation of the Wolf people were embedded in the very soil of this land. The town of Wolf Lake bore the people's name. And Jack had figured out that his only hope for survival was to hold on to that past and try to make a future by taking over this place.

He stood, tugged the cap sharply to shade his eyes, and stretched in an attempt to release some of the knotting tension in his shoulders and neck. He took the steps down to the packed earth and gravel of the drive, where dust motes curled up into the still air. The parched scent of sage and grass only made the place feel more deserted. The ranch had been closed since his grandfather died, and all the joy he'd brought to this land had gone with him. Jack wanted it back with a vengeance.

He kicked at a rock near the drive, hitting it squarely and sending it sailing through the air toward the run-down stables that sprawled on the low hill beyond the house. He'd never seen this coming. He'd never thought his own father could do this. He'd never dreamt, that after every promise and every protestation, his father would damage everything again.

He turned his gaze to the drive that disappeared over a rise beyond the stables then cut down through the grazing land to the main road. The sound of a car engine was barely audible, and when a cloud of dust rose up over the roof of the stables, he knew his phone calls had worked.

He'd made the first of two phone calls fifteen minutes after he'd practically run from his parents' house. Sitting then in his red Jeep at the end of the drive, he'd phoned his brothers; he hadn't been able to move from the spot since.

A police cruiser crested the hill, followed by the billowing dust. He hadn't wanted to pull either brother into this right away, but he needed them. And, realistically, there was no other way this could all play out.

The cruiser pulled in behind his red Jeep, the engine died and the door swung back as Adam stepped out. It still felt odd to see his kid brother in his police uniform, the billed cap shading his eyes. It had only been a month since he'd come back from Chicago, alone. Faith, the woman he'd left with, had stayed there with her father following his conviction in federal court for a series of fraudulent business practices. Adam had quit his job as a detective in Dallas, Texas, before he had gone to Chicago, and joined the Wolf Lake Police Force when he returned, working side by side with Chief John Longbow, a family friend since they were kids. Adam said he'd come back for the job, and he probably had, but Jack knew it was also because his brother was concerned about him. That hurt, to think people altered their lives to try and repair his. And now Adam was walking into another rescue mission, but Jack wouldn't let it come to that.

He raised a hand, and saw the strained look on his brother's face. Before Adam could say anything, Jack cut him off. "Let's talk when Gage gets here. He shook his head. "I can only do this once."

Adam didn't fight him, just nodded and put a hand on his shoulder. "It's your call."

His younger brother stood an inch or so below Jack's six-foot-two, but had the same broad shoulders. All the Carson brothers had inherited the dark eyes, dark hair, and bronzed skin of their mother's ancestors.

Jack found himself saying, "I'm sorry." And he realized he was apologizing for the past two years, for all he knew they'd gone through watching him grieve.

Gage and Adam had known Robyn all their lives, and they'd loved her, but not like he had, and still did. It had always been Jack and Robyn. When he'd graduated from law school in California, and come home, the first thing he'd done was propose to Robyn. That memory still made his stomach clench. It had been the most natural thing in the world to marry the love of his life and the best decision he'd ever made.

They'd built a life together for almost nine years, and then one night, one wrong turn on the way home from the Reservation where Robyn taught second grade, and she'd been gone.

Adam studied him from shadowed eyes, then shook his head. "You're looking bad."

"Thanks."

Adam held up a hand. "Hey, I'm sorry. This day started out rough, very rough. I'm just...."

Jack thought he was going to talk about their parents despite his request to wait, but Adam's next words were about him and Faith.

"I'm not used to being here and Faith being

in Chicago. I mean, she really needs to help her dad adjust to house arrest and what will follow, but I need her, too." A rueful smile touched his lips. "Who would have thought I'd ever say that about a woman?"

"Not me," Jack admitted as the two of them headed for the porch, sinking side by side onto the stone.

"Can't figure out why this place has been empty since the old man died. Makes no sense." Adam turned to rest his hand on Jack's shoulder. "I was really glad that you were thinking of taking it over."

Jack tensed and glanced at his brother. Adam looked away, off to the distance. "What's taking Gage?" he asked as if he hadn't spoken before.

"He said he had a few things to do. Any time now, I'd think. This place belongs here," Adam went on, obviously unable to keep totally silent about the purpose of this meeting. "The folks' ranch is great, bigger and newer, but it doesn't fit into the land like this does. Grandpa knew what he was doing."

His words echoed the way Jack had always felt. Their grandfather's ranch was right where it should be, and he wanted to be here, too. "All I'm going to say until Gage gets here is, I'm sorry." He squeezed Jack's shoulder then drew back, looking out beyond the stables.

The heat seemed to hum in the silence until Jack finally cleared the lump in his throat. "Did you ever bring Faith out to see the place?"

Adam shook his head. "When she was here it was too cold, too much snow and not enough time."

"When is she coming back?"

Adam stood abruptly, flexing his shoulders under the tailored uniform shirt. "I don't know." His voice seemed tight, and Jack had a fleeting thought that maybe things weren't right between him and Faith, that maybe Adam coming back without her had nothing to do with Jack, or with the job.

"Hey, there!"

The loud shout from the west startled Jack and he looked toward the heavy stand of trees in that direction.

"He couldn't just drive over like the rest of us, could he?" Adam said.

Jack watched Gage walk toward the house, leading his black horse, Grenada. "Sorry to be late," he called out, kicking up dust as he got closer. He stopped by an old stone hitching post their grandfather had hewn from a long rock he'd lugged down from the Rez, and secured the large horse to it.

Jack knew if any strangers saw them, they'd see three men who looked like possible triplets, all tall, dark and strong looking. But those strangers would never know how very different all three were. "Day from night," their grandfather had said more than once. And that was true. It was incredible that all three of them were back in Wolf Lake at the same time. That timing was perfect for Jack.

As Gage strode to the bottom of the step, he actually smiled up at his brothers. "Merry soloed this morning." he said.

"I never thought she'd ever get back in a plane after your scare on the mountain." Jack said, remembering the haunted look on the woman's face during the rescue helicopter ride after she and Gage had crashed in the high mountains last February.

Gage nodded. "I wasn't sure, either, but now she's doing great and is even thinking about taking Erin up. That little girl is in love with planes." Another flash of pleasure lighted his face. Gage, Merry and the little girl they were adopting were already a family, even though their wedding date hadn't been set.

Jack felt a wave of jealousy, but blocked it. "Good."

As suddenly as he'd smilcd, Gage sobered. "So, tell me what's going on."

"Let's go inside," Jack said, turning to lead the way to the great room, the ceiling low with heavy beams, the worn tile floor starting to get dusty after the last monthly visit from the cleaning crew. The air in the adobe was at least twenty degrees cooler than outside, the natural insulation of the thick bricks doing a good job against the dry heat.

They passed the massive stone fireplace in the middle of the room, getting glimpses of the well-worn leather furniture where the dust sheets had slipped a bit. All the furniture in the house had been handmade on the Rez by friends of his grandfather's and was still sturdy and usable. They walked into the small kitchen at the back of the house.

An old-fashioned yellow Formica table, its faux marble pattern almost worn away by use, stood by a window that overlooked a stand of huge pines, parted to expose the panorama of the distant mountains. If you knew where to look, you could see part of the Rez from there, a deliberate decision by his grandfather when he'd cleared some of the pines.

Once they were all seated on the high-backed wooden chairs, Jack leaned forward, resting his forearms on the table beside two large manila envelopes that he ignored for the moment. He had to figure out exactly how to say what he had to say. He didn't want that anger to come again. He didn't want to destroy their family.

"It seems like forever since the three of us have been in here together." And he meant it. He hadn't realized how much he'd missed this connection with the past and his brothers.

Gage nodded. "Yeah, it's nice. It's been a while what with Adam catching criminals and me building the complex and you...." His voice died off before he added. "I hear you're doing a bit of law now and then."

"I do, now and then."

Both brothers sat silently, giving him time. Finally, he just started to talk. Whatever he said, he'd live with. "I talked to Mom and Dad a couple of weeks ago. I asked about this place, about me buying it out of the trust, and they said they'd thought about it before and they agreed that they wanted to deed it over to me."

His brothers didn't say anything. After clearing his throat, Jack pressed his hands palms down on the dull yellow table top. He spoke to Gage. "Seems you're thinking of living in town, getting an office going, and that acreage out by Delany's Stables that you bought years ago, you could build on that." He turned to Adam. "And you've always wanted that parcel over by Natchee's spread—word is, he's thinking of heading back up the hill. It could become available."

Adam nodded, but his face was tight. "Yeah, I've had my eye on it."

"And this has always felt right for me." If he'd been able to talk Robyn into coming out here to live, he would have already been in possession of the land. But her teaching position was on the Reservation, and being in town let her tutor the kids more easily. Their loft above his law offices had been right for them until they had their own kids. Kids that would never be born now. "This place feels right for where I am now," he admitted. His heart started to race, as if he was running full tilt.

"Go on," Gage said. "Right after you hung up, and Merry and Erin drove off for town, Mom was there, crying, and said Dad was locked in his office. When I asked what was going on, all Mom said was, 'Ask Jack.'"

"I didn't want Mom to be in on it," Jack muttered. "I really didn't, but I couldn't get her out, and...."

He looked from brother to brother. "Okay, this morning I found out that they don't own this land anymore."

Both brothers looked surprised. Adam said. "But it doesn't make sense."

"Dad lost it," Jack said bluntly. "It's gone." He looked around the house, then back at his brothers. "We're trespassing, in the eyes of the law."

Adam shook his head, took off his uniform cap and hung it on the back spindle of the chair beside him. "It can't be gone."

Jack pushed the papers toward Gage and Adam. Swallowing hard, he finally managed, "Just read these."

Both men hesitated, but mercifully didn't ask any questions before picking up an envelope and taking out the four papers inside. Jack closed his eyes, not able to bear watching them read the words. He didn't open them again until Adam spoke.

"Dad wouldn't have done something like this, he wouldn't." He tossed the copy of the new deed onto the table top. "He couldn't," he muttered tightly.

Gage simply lowered his copy of the enclosed letter from the county offices and met Jack's gaze. "How did you get these?"

"I finally put in the papers to switch the deed on the property. I know someone in the county offices, and she sent them to me, telling me I didn't have any right to transfer it into my name since it wasn't a Wolf property anymore. Dad took the land. He deeded it to a Charles Luther Michaels in June, the tenth to be specific, of this year. All legal. All very binding."

"Just like that? Dad sold this place? That doesn't make any sense. It's a mistake, a county error. It has to be. Besides, he couldn't do that without Mom's signature and she'd never agree, no matter what."

"I checked. He has power of attorney over all their financial dealings," Jack said flatly.

"Why?"

"After everything he's done in the past, she still trusts him!" Suddenly the anger and hurt were there again, and he couldn't stop himself from hitting the table as hard as he could with the flat of his right hand. "It's done. He did it. He took it and gave it away. No money changed hands. And do you want to know why he gave the land to that Michaels person?"

He didn't wait for them to respond. "He was drunk and in a private high stakes poker match, and he put up the deed for this place on a bet, winner take all. It's all there in the letter the clerk faxed to me."

"And Dad told you the same story?" Gage asked, his shock still lingering on his face.

"No, actually, he looked surprised. June tenth was toward the end of his last bender, when he disappeared for two weeks. My guess is, he had one of his drunken blackouts. I doubt he even remembers the game."

Adam looked up at him intently. "Why would he tell you to take the land if it was already gone?"

Jack ran both hands over his face. "Like I said, a blackout. He didn't remember much of anything." He looked at Adam. "At least he found his way to Rick Carter's, his old banking friend who lives in Henderson, Nevada. Two days later, he was back here, refused rehab, but got a grip and seems to have been sober ever since." He grimaced. "But who knows."

"What about Mom?" Gage asked, barely above a whisper.

"I hoped she'd be gone when I got there, but she wasn't, and she knew something was wrong. I managed to get Dad alone in the office, but Mom came in when she heard me yelling." That broke his heart. "I can't believe how many ways he's hurt her and she's forgiven him. I'm not sure she will this time."

Jack swallowed hard before continuing. "She was crying when I left. I should have stayed for her. I should have never left her like that."

"No," Gage said quickly. "No, you shouldn't have stayed. You'd said enough."

Jack felt reproach in the words, but when he looked at Gage, he didn't see any sign of criticism. Just pain. And he felt it too, for their mother. He could barely think about his father, crying, begging for her forgiveness, promising anything it would take to keep her with him. More empty promises, as empty as his vows to never drink again.

Adam sat back, his arms folded tightly over his chest. "Mom and Dad will have to deal with their own lives. We'll be there, and Mom knows that, but we can't change anything."

Jack nodded, feeling an odd exhaustion now that he'd told his brothers about everything. "You're right. For now."

Gage sat back. "So, all we have to do is find this Michaels guy, make him an offer he can't refuse and that's that." He made it sound like a foregone conclusion. "As for Dad, I don't know what to do. He refused rehab when he got back, so that's probably out. But we really need to talk to Mom about rescinding Dad's power of attorney."

"You two do it," Jack said, not having the heart to even see his mother yet. "I'll work on trying to contact Michaels. There's an address from the original deed change, so I'll start there."

"Where is it?" Gage asked.

Adam glanced down at the letter on the table. "It's in New Jersey. While you do that,

Jack, I'll run a background check on Mr. Michaels."

Gage had picked up the letter and scanned it before he looked at one brother, then the other. "The one thing that doesn't make sense to me is, if Michaels has owned the title for about a month, it seems odd that he hasn't made his way out here, from New Jersey or even from Las Vegas right when he got the land. Even if it was just to scope it out and sell it? Wouldn't he at least send someone to size it up and figure out what to do with it?"

Three hundred acres of prime grazing land, with water rights, wouldn't be cheap if it went on the open market. "No one's been out here, I don't think, and we would have heard if someone in town was asking around about the ranch." Jack exhaled as he raked his fingers through his hair. He actually felt a bit more settled now that he'd talked to Gage and Adam. He motioned to the documents on the table between them. "Take what you need, Adam. I've got the originals back at the office."

Gage was the first one to stand. "I can ask around about deals like this going down, and what can be done."

Jack shook his head. "It's too late to call any of this illegal. It's not."

"No, it's not, but that doesn't mean there can't be some leverage brought to make sure, when you find him, that Michaels would be more compliant with your request to purchase it back from him."

Frowning, Jack just shrugged. "I appreciate whatever either of you can do to help out."

"Done," Gage and Adam said in unison.

The three brothers stepped out into the afternoon heat, the sky a true blue overhead. They stopped by Gage's horse, and as Jack rubbed the large animal's silken muzzle, Adam asked, "What about Dad? Are you going to talk to him again? " Jack knew his tone was tight, but he couldn't help it. "I don't want any kind of contact with Dad for now. He can't make up for any of this. I just want this land back from Charles Michaels."

Gage reached for his horse's lead, and with a glance at each brother, walked off toward the trees. Adam slipped into the cruiser and gave Jack the hint of a salute, his forefinger tapping the brim of his uniform cap before he drove off down the dusty driveway, another cloud of dust in his wake.

The slight diminishing of stress was gone as soon as both brothers were out of sight. Jack felt the tension return. He shouldn't have yelled, or threatened his father. He shouldn't have done anything in front of his mother. She didn't deserve that.

He locked the door and then dropped down heavily onto the stone step again.

As his gaze skimmed over the land spread out before him, memories of his grandfather herding cattle and sheep came to him. He could almost see him, the dogs yipping at the heels of the stock, dust rising and his grandfather bringing up the rear. He could hear his sharp whistles to the dogs, altering their patterns, an old-fashioned herder's staff in one hand.

This ranch was their family's heritage and his father had gambled it away. There would be no new memories created for future generations. Jack couldn't let that happen. He wanted to make a life for himself right here. His father had fought for sobriety, and had lost the battle several times, but the war was not over. Win or lose, that part was up to him. All Jack could do was try his best to get the land back. And to make that happen, he needed to find Charles Luther Michaels.

# CHAPTER TWO

THE TRIP FROM Los Angeles to Albuquerque, New Mexico was the first time Grace Evans had ever flown in her twenty-six years. As she stepped out of the terminal with her suitcase and overnight bag, she spotted a tram she was supposed to use to pick up her rental car. Half an hour later, she was in that car, a red compact, and heading out of the terminal parking lot toward her future. At least she hoped it was her future—her daughter's and her mother's as well.

Her world had been turned upside down, and she still didn't know if this trip would lead to something more than a huge wish on her part. It had all started two weeks ago. After a double shift waitressing at the diner, she had been exhausted as she'd headed to the tiny, second story apartment she and her family shared in a less than gentrified area of

Los Angeles. All she wanted was a hot bath after ten hours on her feet.

She'd found her mother in the living room with a stranger. The man probably wasn't much taller than her own five-feet-two-inches and was sitting in the rocking chair. Grace had immediately noticed the assortment of papers spread on the low coffee table.

The stranger stood when he saw her, smoothing the front of his elegant dove-gray suit.

"I am Ethan Vaughn, with the Seals, Silkirk and Vaughn Law Firm." Grace barely had the time to acknowledge her mother's strained expression before he took her hand and said, "I am representing your father in a legal matter that concerns you."

She'd just stared at him. Her father? She looked around, then let go of his hand and sank onto the couch by her mother. Reclaiming his seat in the rocker, he'd leaned forward, picked up a couple of papers and handed them to her.

The first one she read was a deed for a three hundred acre property in New Mexico, outside a small town called Wolf Lake. "What is this?" she asked, then stopped as she saw her name on the deed. She stared at it, certain she was hallucinating.

"A property deed and…." He motioned for her to look at the next sheet of paper.

The hallucination expanded. In her hands was a cashier's check for fifty thousand dollars attached to a verification letter that had her name on it. She'd shaken her head, then turned to her mother. Gabriella Michaels touched her daughter's knees. "It's yours," she said in a shaky voice. "It's all yours."

Mr. Vaughn had spoken then. "Your father wanted me to bring these to you."

Charles Luther Michaels had disappeared from Grace's life when she was about three years old. The man had been there one day, and gone the next. No goodbyes, no arguments, no warning.

"He's restless," her mother had explained more than once. "He needs to be on the move, and he's not equipped to be a husband or a father." The words had meant little to a tiny girl who didn't have a daddy anymore, and though the tears had long since dried up, she had never quite lost that deep longing for a family.

When her own marriage had failed, she

wondered if she'd deliberately picked a man like her father to try and prove to herself that she could make it work. But she'd been wrong. So very wrong. Her daughter Lilly, now six, hadn't even been born when Jerry Evans said he couldn't do the whole family thing. Her mother's mistake had become her own, and the only good thing out of the mess was her daughter. Grace had listened as Mr. Vaughn explained that the deed and money were hers if she wanted them. If not, they could go to charity. She'd almost laughed at that, although she'd recognized that the laughter would have bordered on hysteria. She was close to being her own charity with a child to support.

As she drove now into the afternoon sun, the New Mexico countryside passing by unnoticed, her mind refused to settle. By the time Mr. Vaughn had left the apartment that day, she'd known that no matter what the reason behind this sudden windfall, it was hers, and she could make the life she'd always dreamed of for her little family.

Maybe Lilly could go to a school that didn't require security guards at the doors, even for kindergarten. The air had to be cleaner out here, the streets safer. As the miles flew by, she was getting closer and closer to the end of her own personal rainbow. New Mexico. She'd never thought much about it before, except for the city of Taos far to the south, an artists' mecca. But that had been in her teens, when she'd had dreams of being an artist after she graduated from high school. Instead she'd ended up as waitress at The Table, a down-on-its-heels diner.

She exhaled. The owners were talking about making the diner into a bikini bar, giving the area yet another dive. Now she wouldn't have to figure out how to get another job in the city or worry about how she could make her boyish figure fill out a bikini. She shook her head at that thought. She'd been getting a bit desperate before Mr. Vaughn suddenly appeared in her apartment.

She glanced at her bag on the passenger seat and smiled. If this worked out, she wouldn't ever be desperate again. She had images of rolling pastures and maybe a horse or two, some cows and chickens, definitely a dog and a cat. Everything she'd never had and never would have in her Los Angeles neigh-

borhood. Clean air, clear skies, safe surround-
ings. It all sounded like a fairy tale to her.

She just didn't know why the euphoria
she'd had while planning this trip had de-
flated a bit since she got on the plane. She
felt a tinge of fear now that all this might just
be her own fantasy. After all, her father had
never owned anything, he'd never wanted to.
No money, no land, nothing like that.

That afternoon in her apartment, she'd
looked from Mr. Vaughn to her mother and
voiced her confusion. "I don't understand any
of this. Is he dead?"

Mr. Vaughn had shaken his head immediately. "No, he's not."

"Then why did he send you?"

"Honestly, I believe he didn't want any direct contact, just to make sure you got the
land and the money."

That had brought anger and pain in equal
measure. She hadn't missed the soft gasp
from her mother. No contact. A slap in the
face. But Grace hadn't been stupid enough to
let the attorney take the deed and check back.

There was a note her father had sent with
Mr. Vaughn for her. "It might explain things
a bit," the attorney had said.

The words were burned into her mind, and she could almost see the single sheet of paper with the strong writing on it. *"Never did nothing for you, Gracie, never could. Thing is, I'm no father, never meant to be and it scared me. I knew, as much as you would hate me for it, the best thing I could do for you and your mother was to leave and keep away. I loved you both, as much as I was able to love anyone, but I never could be tied to much of anything. I had some good luck recently, and I have no use for what came with it, so I want to offer it to you. Maybe it can make up in some way for what I never could do for you."* The note wasn't even signed.

Pain still came with the memory, but she realized it was as close to an explanation for all of this as she'd ever get. Mr. Vaughn had tried to clarify things. "Why he did this is the one thing I can't explain to you, but I can assure you that all of this is yours, and it's up to you what you decide to do with it."

Her call. A fortune in land and money, and it was her call. Why her father had done it shouldn't matter. The only thing that mattered was that it could change her life, her daughter's life and her mother's life.

She drove past Santa Fe, barely glancing at the city. Her only thoughts were on getting to Wolf Lake, then driving on to her property. The deed included buildings and water rights. Mr. Vaughn had explained it was near an Indian reservation, but the three hundred acres was totally private, unencumbered by liens or mortgages, and it had been empty for a few years, maybe three or four.

The person her father had received it from was a man named Herbert Carson. The land where the ranch was situated had been part of a land grant in the eighteen hundreds to the Wolfs, then deeded to the Carsons after Jackson Wolf had died.

When she'd looked at her mother, silently questioning what she should do, Gabriella had simply nodded. "Let him do it for you. He owes you that much."

After that, there had been a blur of signings on the dotted lines, making arrangements to have the check deposited in her account, then figuring out how she could go and look at everything to check it out. Now she was close, so close, and nervousness was building in her. Mr. Vaughn had said there was a house on the property, but he had no idea what condition it was in. Even a search on Google Earth had shown lots of land, roads cutting through it, dark stands of trees, outbuildings, maybe a barn. Details were lost in the aerial photo.

She rode in silence as portions of her father's note came to her. "*...the best thing I could do was leave and keep away. I had some luck...make up in some way for what I never could do for you.*" Good luck was all the deed and the money were to him.

She'd been so worried about Lilly's school, worried about saving to move to a better location, worried about her job disappearing. Now she had a place to go, and fifty thousand dollars in the bank. All thanks to her father's luck. That probably meant gambling, though it seemed far-fetched that three hundred acres of land could be payment for a gambling debt. But that was all her father had known about making money. Find a game, get the upper hand and know when to fold.

Her world had always felt a bit unstable, ready to tip upside down in a second. And she'd been holding on for dear life. But now, she had the means to let go and have a life, a stable life. A real life.

JACK GOT HIS horse out of his parents' stable around dawn and rode off before he saw anyone stirring. He'd spoken with his mother on the phone only once since the confrontation with his father, hearing determination in her voice to make the best of what had happened. He'd hated it when she'd apologized to him for the land being lost to them, as if it was her fault.

He hadn't had any contact with his father over the past six weeks, and that was fine with him. He didn't want words and promises. They were too easy to speak and impossible to back up.

He spent most of the day up in the high country, visiting a few friends on the Rez, then headed back down in the middle of the September afternoon. The heat was at its peak, but more mellow than it had been for a while, and the day was bright and clear. When he approached his parents' land, he hesitated, then road past, farther east, and a short time later cut between the worn stone pillars that marked the drive to the old ranch.

He slowly headed up the incline of the packed dirt trail to a smaller rise that hid the old house from view. He wound around, past the stables, and the house appeared. He was trespassing again, he knew it, but he had to come. Just one last time until he could be here legally again.

He drew up by the hitching post, dismounted and secured his horse. Instead of going inside the house, he sat down on the stone step where he'd waited for his brothers back in July when he'd felt as if his world was going to end. It had come darned close, but it hadn't ended. His determination to get this land back one way or the other kept him going,

Now frustration was driving him. The problem was, he'd found out plenty about Charles Luther Michaels, except the most important things—where he was and how to reach him. They knew he was basically a drifter and a professional gambler, moving constantly from place to place. The papers he'd sent to the address listed on the legal documents with an offer for the property had been returned. By the time a private investigator checked out the address, a boarding house in a small city near the Jersey shore, Charles Luther Michaels had been gone for two weeks.

Adam had found a criminal record for the man, a few DUIs, public disorder, minor confidence charges, vagrancy, misdemeanor assault on a casino bouncer, all scattered around the country, one in Canada. But all of them had been more than five years old. Jack and his brothers knew he'd been in Las Vegas in June, but that led nowhere. The game had been "private," which meant big spenders in a private suite in one of the hotels and unreported to any gambling authority. They couldn't find anyone who would admit to him being there. Privacy for big spenders was everything in that city. But it meant the man had enough stake money to get in the door, and he'd walked out with whatever cash he'd won along with the deed their father had thrown into the pot.

Michaels was out there somewhere, they knew that, but the man left no tracks. That frustrated Jack to no end. Somewhere along the way he'd come to believe that healing the tear in the Wolf family heritage by regaining the lost land would mean he could heal his own wounds. But unless their luck improved and they found Michaels, he didn't know what would happen with the land and with him.

He flexed the tension in his shoulders as he glanced at his horse, then over to the stables. He frowned and looked back to his horse. Something was different than the last time he'd come here, but he couldn't figure out what. Then he knew. The dead weeds in the gravel edging the drive had been cleared, but only in front of the house. He went down to take a closer look, and found lugged tire tracks. Glancing around first, he followed them down the slope to the end of the abandoned stables.

Booted foot prints in the dust led to the hay doors, and he followed them along the side of the stables to the doors to the stalls. A new lock glistened in the sun. Jack stared at it then spun around and broke into a run, heading across the dry weeds and packed earth and up the shallow hill to the drive. He took the stone step in one stride and stopped in front of the door to the house.

A new key lock with a dead bolt above it had been installed there. Going to the nearest window, he cupped his hands around his eyes and peered through the streaked glass into the great room. Nothing had changed. Dust covers were in place, and as far he could tell, nothing had been moved. He went back to the door and pounded on it. "Hello! Hello? Anyone here?"

When there was no response, he stopped, suddenly feeling like the trespasser he was on the land he loved. He stood at the top of the step, unsure what to do. Someone had been here to make sure the property was secured. Possibly Charles Michaels. Or had he hired someone to come out and check on things, then change the locks?

At least something was happening. Jack headed for his horse, then rode off down the driveway and turned back to the family ranch. He needed wheels. "This could be very good," he thought as he pulled out his cell phone and put in a call to John Longbow at the police station.

As soon as Santa Fe was in the rearview mirror, Grace felt the gnaw of hunger, but didn't want to take the time to have a sit-down meal. She couldn't remember when she'd eaten last, not even peanuts on the flight, but right then the hunger was starting to be tinged with nausea. She needed food. Not sure how long it would take to get to Wolf Lake, she started looking for signs for take-out food. One proclaimed Willic G's, The Best Food Around, Eat-in/Take-out, just two exits ahead.

A few minutes later she found the off ramp, drove onto it and down a narrow road. She could see a grouping of buildings back under the highway overpass and headed toward them. The cluster comprised little more than a gas station, a teepee-shaped souvenir shop with a heavy emphasis on Indian and Western collectibles, and a group of trailers beside a broad parking lot that serviced an old adobe building with a huge sign proclaiming Willie G's Diner.

She pulled into a space in front of the dark wooden entry doors, shadowed by a heavy beamed overhang. A flat roof, trimmed in overlapping half pipe tiles, and plastered pink walls that were chipped to show spots of adobe brick gave the place an old Southwestern style. Only a few vehicles were parked in front—an old blue pickup truck and a very big motorcycle, painted patriotically in red, white and blue with an eagle decoration on one side. An eighteen-wheeler was parked off to the side.

Grace slid out into the blanketing warmth of the afternoon, thankful she'd worn a short-sleeved white shirt and denim shorts with sandals. As soon as she stepped inside she was greeted with cool air. The space was larger than it had looked from the exterior, with low-beamed ceilings and worn Salito tiles underfoot. Western music hummed in the background.

"Help you?" someone asked, and she looked toward a set of swinging doors to the kitchen. An older man, dressed in stained cook's whites, smiled at her as he stepped into the room. He came to the counter and wiped his hands on a white rag. Lines fanned the edges of his eyes, and his gray hair was pulled back from a center part in a long braid.

"I need some food to go," she said, crossing to the counter and slipping onto the nearest stool.

"Just name your poison," he said as he passed her a single sheet menu protected by plastic.

She realized it was about the same as the menus in most of the diners she'd worked in—sandwiches, burgers and fries, chili, even some pizza. "I'll take a turkey sandwich on wheat, not toasted, with steak fries and the largest cola you have with lots of icc, please."

He nodded and crossed to a soda machine, packing ice in a large take-out cup before filling it with soda. He brought it back and set it down in front of her. "Thought you could use this first," he said, and reached for a straw from under the counter.

"Thanks."

He didn't move to put in her food order. "Where you heading to?"

"Wolf Lake."

"You're too early if you're looking for the casino or hotels that way," he said. "Not even up yet, but they will be." He shook his head. "So, what you got left is picking up some native art, or souvenirs, or maybe taking in one of the tours near the Rez."

She undid the straw and pushed it through the lid. "None of that," she said, then took a sip of the chilled drink.

Thankfully, he turned, saying, "Gonna get your food," before heading through the swinging doors. Next thing she knew, he was pulling on a cook's cap over his gray hair. He winked, then got busy with her order.

She took another drink and glanced around. No waitress was in sight, and only five customers were at the tables near the front windows. The cook looked as if he was doing everything by himself, moving quickly around the kitchen. He came out with two plates of food for one of the tables, then hurried back into the kitchen, reappearing almost immediately with a large white bag. "There you go, Ma'am. Napkins and ketchup in the bag."

She paid, then grabbed the bag.

"Drop by on your way out of town if you're going this way," he said. "I'll get you some real food when you've got the time to sit and enjoy."

"If I come this way again, I'll do that," she said, slipping off the stool. "You know Wolf Lake very well?"

He chuckled. "Heck, yeah, born and bred on the Rez, then slipped on down into town when I was, oh, around twelve. Been there ever since, except when I'm down here running this place. If you need a place to stay, my niece runs a bed-and-breakfast in town. Nice place, too, and reasonable."

"Thanks, but I have a place," she said, hoping the house was livable.

"Where's that?" he asked, reaching for the white rag and starting to clean the counter.

"On a ranch on the other side of town, from what I was told."

"What ranch?"

"Wolf Ranch."

His hand stilled and his dark eyes looked right at her. "Wolf Ranch," he echoed. "You sure you have that right?"

"Yes, sir, I do," she said.

"You're a friend or something with the new owner?"

She had a feeling the man was upset for some reason, but his voice stayed even. "I am the new owner," she said, and loved the words as they came out of her. The new owner. That sounded so great, but the cook didn't look pleased at all.

"I knew that whole mess with the Carsons was crazy, but sure never expected old Jackson Wolf's property to be bought by a tiny thing like you."

She'd been called a lot of sexist things by

men over the years, and she hated it, but she barely reacted anymore. Now this man was calling her a "tiny thing," and she knew it wasn't a sexist thing to him. He just couldn't believe she had the land—a woman, on her own, coming in to take it over. "I didn't buy it," she said by way of clarification. "But it's mine."

"Yeah, I heard," he said in a low voice, "I guess you didn't buy it."

"Sir, I need to get going," she said.

He came around the counter toward her. "First of all, I'm Willie G., not 'sir' to anyone, and secondly, I was a friend of Jackson Wolf, the original owner. Old man used to head the council for years on the Rez. Town's named after his people. Great man," he said. "And that was his place, a Wolf place."

She had decided from the start that she liked the idea of the land having a history, but obviously this man didn't think she had any right to be there. She tried to divert the conversation. "What's it like there?"

"Fallow. Empty," Willie G. said, "for maybe four or so years, since the old man passed. Age ninety-two, I think, and still on that land until the day he died."

"I'm here to check it out," she said, sticking to the bare facts and not letting his attitude make her defensive. She had nothing to be defensive about."

He shook his head. "So, it's come to this?" he asked softly, as if talking to himself. "Stupid man," he muttered, then must have realized he'd been speaking out loud. "Sorry, Ma'am, but life gets crazy sometimes around here."

"It does everywhere," Grace said and started for the door.

"Miss?" he called after her.

She turned just before reaching for the handle. "Yes?"

"Who have I been talking to?"

"Grace, my name's Grace."

"Okay, Grace. I know this will sound strange, but if you decide by any chance that that hunk of land isn't for you, would you let me know? I've been looking for a bit of land around that area."

She was as shocked by his question as he'd seemed to be when she'd told him she owned the land. "I won't be selling it, I don't think."

"Just let me know, one way or the other, okay?" He reached for the order pad lying on the counter and quickly wrote something on it before tearing the page off. "Just let Willie G. know, okay?"

"Okay," she said, and started to shift her load so she could take it from him, but he simply reached over and dropped it in her bag.

He opened the door for her, calling after her, "Safe trip, Grace."

His interest in the property had taken her back, but once she saw what condition it was in, she might hunt the man down and see how much she could get out of it. She slipped inside the sweltering interior of her car, put her purse and the food bag on the seat, then started the engine and flipped the air conditioner on. She put her drink in the holder in the console, then reached into the white bag to get a French fry.

Cool air flowed into the space and she put the car in gear. Glancing up at the restaurant, she was a bit surprised to see Willie G. still standing there in the doorway watching her. He lifted a hand in her direction, that smile back in place, before ducking inside. She felt odd for a moment, then pushed the feeling away and drove back toward the highway.

# CHAPTER THREE

GRACE REMEMBERED THE crumpled paper Willie G. had pushed in the food bag. She took it out, saw a phone number with his name under it, then folded the note and dropped it into her purse. She glanced at the directions the attorney had given her, then kept her eyes open for the turnoff to Wolf Creek.

After just a few more miles, she finally saw two signs. One was a billboard, announcing the way to the reservation, and the other, much smaller, informed travelers that they had twenty miles to go to arrive at Wolf Lake, population 3,201, altitude 5,106 feet.

She'd been surprised at the altitude and the heat, but one seemed to go with the other. The off-ramp curled back under the overpass, and Grace found herself driving north on a two lane, paved county road that cut through hauntingly beautiful land. Not much green, and the few trees seemed twisted and stunted by the heat. But the colors were stunning.

The sky was starting to be invaded by the suggestion of purple, gold and orange from the west. The shadows of majestic buttes and mesas that rose from the high desert floor were lengthening. Small dust devils skipped over the packed earth, leaving puffs of cloud in their wake. The land made her feel very small and insignificant.

A few cars passed her in the opposite lane, but she hadn't seen anyone in her rearview mirror since she turned onto the highway. Gradually, she started to notice patches of green off to the west, along with trees here and there that looked tall and ancient. Over the next few miles, the green patches grew in proportion to the parched earth. Finally, a sign for Wolf Lake appeared, overshadowed by a more elaborate one for the Reservation ten miles beyond the town. At a rise in the road, she could see Wolf Creek, maybe three miles to the northwest. It was a simple layout, a long main street, with streets branching out from it. The first buildings were clustered together, as others then fanned out in the colors and shadows of the low sun. Beyond those were large chunks of land, with greenness and distinguishable pastures.

When she finally drove onto the main street after passing through a section of construction, she realized the place had been fine-tuned for tourists. The buildings that lined the street were separated from the road by an old-fashioned raised wooden walkway that used to protect people from snakes and mud. Now they added a quaint charm.

Some of the businesses had been determinedly fashioned after frontier structures, with a mix of aged wood and stone and brick. Others were designed like Willie G's, with adobe and chipped stucco shouting "Southwest." When she had time, she'd come back and walk the wooden sidewalks, but for now the elaborate window displays in the businesses were a blur of color and glitter. The only thing she noticed was the bed-and-breakfast Willie G. had told her about, then she was heading out of the town.

She looked at her odometer, made a note of the miles, and was about to reach for another French fry when the roar of an engine sounded behind her. A bright red Jeep gunned past, then cut back into the lane with very little distance to spare.

She caught a glimpse of the driver, a man with a cap pulled low over an angular face. He was staring at her instead of the road as he raced ahead, rounded a curve, and disappeared from sight.

"Jerk," she muttered, realizing that even though there were no traffic jams out here, the area still had its share of crazy drivers.

She popped the almost forgotten French fry into her mouth, aware now of the ranches that seemed to spread all the way to the horizon, checkerboarded with green and brown sections. The houses and ranch buildings were far off the road, barely visible, but the entrances were fancy, with intricate gates of wrought iron, wood, stone and brick.

She rounded a curve and saw a new sign for the Reservation in the direction of the foothills. Then her attention was caught by the entry to yet another ranch, but this one was different. It was a simple entrance, almost plain, with worn stone pillars on either side of a dirt drive. The wooden gate stood open. On the pillar to the left, chiseled into a flat stone halfway up from the dead weeds and dirt at the base, were two weather-eroded words. Wolf Ranch.

Grace slowed and made the turn into the entrance, but then she stopped, unable to drive between the pillars. Excitement, apprehension, curiosity and that bit of fear kept her foot on the brake. So much was at stake that she could barely breathe. She fingered the steering wheel, then touched the gas pedal and slowly drove through the pillars and onto the dirt drive that cut up a gentle hill between neglected wooden fencing.

Some of the crosspieces had fallen into dead weeds and grass, while others sat at crazy angles. The ranch looked as if it had been neglected for more than a few years. It felt deserted, no, abandoned, waiting for someone to come along and make things right again.

"Well, here I am," she said over the low hum of the engine and air conditioner. She imagined the weeds gone, the fences up and painted white, surrounding green fields, the front pillars hung with iron gates. A huge tumbleweed bounced over the drive in front of her, curiously lifting at the last moment to sail over the broken fence and into the pasture.

Stacks of piping were arranged on either side of the broken fence, tangled with weeds. She had water rights. Her papers stated that, and if there was water, green grass would follow. Her heart was starting to beat faster, excitement pushing out other conflicting emotions.

She was near the top of the hill when she spotted a building off to the right. It was long and low, tumbleweeds piled randomly along its foundation. A stable, she thought, some of its many doors boarded shut. Then as the car crested the hill, she saw her house.

Without realizing what she was doing, she again stopped dead on the drive. As the air conditioning blew a cool breeze over her skin, she just sat there trying to take everything in. The backdrop of the clear sky above, streaked with pale colors from the west, trees to both sides, maybe thirty feet from the house that was much larger than she'd even dared to hope for. Low and sprawling, it was built of adobe and heavy dark wood, making it seem part of the surrounding land. A porch ran end to end along the front, shading windows that reflected back the view to the south. A massive rock chimney rose through the central ridge of the deep red and brown tiled roof.

She could see how much work the place needed, from the dried wood of the porch posts to the faded trim and weeds, but to her it looked incredible. The colors from the sinking sun were deepening gradually, the rays bathing the house in an almost ethereal light. Long shadows were gradually creeping toward a stand of huge cottonwoods nearby.

She rolled down her window to stillness, the air carrying a gentler heat now, and from out of nowhere, a sense of peace touched her. Until a voice by her open window set her heart hammering.

"Hello, there."

She turned to see a tall man staring down at her. He had to be over six feet, darkly tanned, with high cheekbones set in a face that seemed all angles and shadows under a baseball cap. She tensed as he gripped the window frame with a strong hand and leaned down toward her. The glint of a gold wedding band flashed as it caught a glimmer of sun.

"What…what are you doing?" she gasped.

He immediately drew back, his large hand

held up, palm toward her. "Hey, I'm sorry. I thought you saw me."

She hadn't even sensed movement before he had suddenly appeared. Gripping the steering wheel tightly, she looked away from him. "Well, I didn't," she muttered.

If a man had approached her car like that in L.A., she would have felt threatened, but she figured this man must be working here in some capacity. The attorney had said he'd made sure the place would be ready for her when she arrived.

He didn't come closer, but didn't leave, either. "Are you parking the car?" he asked.

Without a verbal response, she did just that, going slowly to the front of the house and parking beside a small stone pillar by the pathway to the porch. She wasn't sure if she should get out of the car or stay put.

She watched the stranger in the rearview mirror slowly coming toward her. Dusty jeans on long legs, equally dusty cowboy boots and a chambray shirt open at the neck made him look all cowboy, except for the dark baseball cap. Jet-black hair was straight and long enough to touch the collar of the shirt. The shadow of a new beard darkened a strong jaw.

Before she could make a move, he was at the window again, bending down. This time she got a better look at him. Midnight dark eyes were deep set, studying her intently. Rough features and high cheekbones gave him a handsome look in her opinion. Then he smiled at her, flashing a single deep dimple to the right of his mouth. Something in her relaxed.

"I didn't mean to scare you," he said in a deep, slightly roughened voice. "I was just waiting for you to get here."

He had to be a worker, waiting for her arrival. She reached for the door handle and the man stepped back to let her get out. "I was told you would be here," she started to say, then glanced toward the barn, stunned to silence. A red Jeep was parked by the big doors. The same Jeep that had sped past her on the highway.

"That was you on the road, wasn't it?" she managed to get out, spinning around to confront him. "You could have killed us both!"

JACK WAS STUNNED as he faced the tiny blonde in beige shorts that revealed remarkably long legs for someone who barely topped five feet.

*"You could have killed us both!"*

She was right. He could have killed them. He'd been acting crazy. But the accusation tore at him, and he felt cold in his soul. Robyn's accident had made no sense, and the only explanation had been that she was going too fast. He crossed his arms over his chest and tried to get control. The shaking was there, deep inside, but he held it at bay and concentrated on the woman in front of him.

Willie G. had called him maybe fifteen minutes ago at the office. "Heads up, boy, there's a lady coming your way, name's Grace, a little, cute blonde, and she claims she owns your Grandpa's ranch. She just left here."

Jack had run out of the office, calling to his assistant, Maureen, "Check on the records for the land as quickly as you can!" She would understand immediately that "the land" was the Wolf Ranch.

Jack really didn't remember most of the drive to the old ranch, except for the car that he'd impatiently gunned past. Just before he'd driven through the gate, Maureen had called to tell him the property had changed hands in August, deeded from Charles Michaels to a Grace Anne Evans. She couldn't find any money trail.

Now he was looking at Grace Anne Evans, and when he could finally speak around the tightness in his throat, he said, "I was in a hurry." And he'd been stupid and totally taken off balance, he should have added. All these weeks he'd planned to deal with a man, someone he'd researched and knew very well on paper. Now he was facing a stranger, maybe midtwenties, with a few freckles dusted across her small, straight nose. And those eyes. He actually wondered if that violet color came from her DNA or tinted contacts.

She lifted a hand to shade her eyes from the slowly sinking sun behind him. "How long have you been here?" she asked."

"Just a few minutes before you drove up."

"No, I mean, here, on the ranch?"

He shook his head. "When?"

Now she was looking confused. "You're the one who's supposed to be getting everything ready for me, aren't you?"

"Sorry, no." Why did he keep telling her he was sorry?

"Then why are you here?" she asked, trying to stand taller, but failing.

"I told you, waiting for you, as long as you're Grace Evans."

She shook her head, as if nothing was making sense to her at that moment. "I don't have a clue who you are, if you're not a handyman or a caretaker."

"Sorry," he said, inwardly cringing at that word again. "Neither. I'm Jack."

"Okay, *Jack*. I need to know what this is about, or I'm going inside and I hope, for your sake and the other drivers on the road, that you'll drive slower on your way back to wherever you came from."

He was a bit surprised at how such a tiny woman had no problem standing her ground. She'd had an edge from that first moment he'd approached her. He understood being careful with strangers, but she seemed to have an added toughness, despite her delicate appearance.

"I was told that someone named Grace Evans was coming here." He paused a moment. "And I'm pretty sure you're Grace Evans."

"You spoke to Mr. Vaughn?" she asked.

In this whole mess he'd never come across anyone named Vaughn. "No, I didn't."

"I don't get it, then," she said, cocking her head to one side. He'd run out of time. He was an attorney who could figure out a million ways around a legal case, and yet he was losing this woman. She was ready to kick him off the ranch, so he gave up any sort of attempt at finesse and simply spoke the blunt truth.

"I came to meet you and find out how you got this land and what you intend to do with it." That was simple enough, he thought, and actually felt a bit relieved to get it out there.

GRACE DIDN'T ANSWER his question. She stared up at him, then took a step back. "I don't know who you are, or why you think I'd share my personal business with you, but one thing I learned growing up was not to talk to strangers."

She knew she was bordering on rudeness, but she didn't even know his last name. And she was edgy, and tired from sleepless nights, then the flight out and the drive to the ranch. And she still hadn't eaten much more than a few French fries. And she felt a bit light-headed.

"I'm Jack Carson," he said without preamble and held out his hand to her.

Carson. He had to be a relative of the man who had owned this land before her father got it. Okay, she could deal with this. She met his grip, which was warm and firm. "Grace Evans. Not that you don't already know that." She drew her hand back. "And this is my land. I own it."

"You purchased it from Charles Michaels?" he asked, tucking the tips of his fingers in the pockets of his Levis.

"He's my father." She saw a flash of something like surprise cross his face, then it was gone. "And I didn't buy it from him."

"You're not the legal owner?"

"Yes, I am. He signed it over to me."

"Why?"

"He's my father, I told you that. He gave it to me. He said he didn't have any use for it, so I should have it."

"Where is he now?"

That seemed an odd question, but she didn't mind answering it truthfully. "I don't know. All of the land business was done through an attorney in Los Angeles, Mr. Vaughn." And that was all she was going to say. She would never tell anyone that her father hadn't even wanted to see her or Lilly.

"And he has no legal interest in this land anymore?"

*He has no interest in anything, period, except what he wants to do,* she thought. Bitterness didn't sit well with her, but she couldn't seem to get beyond it. And she sure wasn't going to tell this man about her father. "No, no interest at all."

"That's it? He just gave it you?"

"Yes," she said.

SHOCKED WAS THE only way to describe how Jack felt. Michaels hadn't wanted this ranch, so he gave it to his daughter? Just like that. Still, there had been something in her expression when she spoke about her father. Maybe sadness. Jack wished he understood her just a bit. He had to make her see it his way about the land. He had to know Grace Evans and what made her tick.

All he really understood was that Grace Anne Evans was the one with the prize. Charles Michaels was out of the picture. His daughter stood between Jack and what Jack wanted. And if he'd thought to recheck the deeding of the land before he came, he wouldn't be standing here figuring out things on the fly.

"I've got a question for you," Grace said, crossing her arms and shifting slightly to use his shadow to block the sun from her eyes.

"What's that?"

"You said you were told I was coming here. So, who told you?"

That was a simple question and he didn't hesitate. "Willie G. at the diner let me know."

"You're kidding me!" she said. "He told you about me?"

"Absolutely. He's an old friend, and he thought I'd like to know someone was claiming to own this place. He's very protective of this land and his people. Just ask him about the new entertainment center."

She brushed at her hair, the tendrils that had escaped the high ponytail lifting in the gentle breeze. "I should tell you that he asked me if I was going to sell this place, and if I decided to, to let him know so he could make an offer on it."

That didn't surprise him. Willie G. saw the land as the peoples' land, not possessed by individuals. They were just the caretakers.

Since he'd found out about the ranch being lost, he hadn't spoken to Jack's dad. But finding a woman who claimed to own it, a stranger, must have set off all sorts of warnings in Willie's head. "And what did you tell him?"

"That I wasn't considering selling." He saw her look around, her gaze taking in the house and outbuildings, then skimming the distant hills. "I don't think I would ever sell it," she said in a near whisper.

And it was legally hers. When Maureen had confirmed that Grace Anne Evans was indeed the owner of record, Jack had known right then that his quest had changed course dramatically. She was his target. She was the one he'd have to deal with.

"So, you're keeping the land?" he finally asked.

"So far, yes, I am," she said without hesitation.

"But if you find you don't want to, that this place is too isolated or too hard to handle or not your taste, you'd be selling it, wouldn't you?"

She turned away from him again to look

at the house. "I don't see any reason for me to sell."

It couldn't be sentimentality over her father that was stopping her. The man had never been here as far as Jack knew, and Michaels had only owned it for a month or so. He was surprised she wasn't put off by the parched earth and obvious neglect. But she seemed pretty determined to stay, and he didn't know what cards to play to make sure she didn't.

He'd have a background check run on Grace Evans first thing, to figure out where she stood in life, then go from there. "Where are you from?" he asked.

She didn't turn back to him, but kept staring at the old adobe house. "L.A."

He'd been in Los Angeles for college and law school, so he knew most of the areas. "What part?"

When she told him, he frowned. The area she'd named was rough, on the edge of a high crime district. Maybe the ranch looked like Shangri-La to her.

She finally turned when he didn't speak again. Her eyes narrowed on him. "Is Herbert Carson your father or uncle or something like that?"

"Father," he said.

"I saw his name on the deed." She bit her lip. "What I can't imagine is why your father let this all go."

"Me, too," he said in a low voice. "But he did. And your father got the benefit of his stupidity."

That brought a look of incomprehension to her face. "What stupidity?"

"You don't think it's stupid to gamble away a place that's been in your family for over a century in a poker game?"

She knew all about it. It was there on her face, along with a slight blush. His father had bet the land on a single hand of poker, and her father had won it on a single hand. "You know," she said, a statement, not a question.

"Yes, and my father was a drunk who fell off the wagon and lost any semblance of control." He heard the disgust in his voice and didn't bother trying to pretend it wasn't there. "Just like that, it's a done deal."

She nibbled on her bottom lip. "I'm so sorry," she breathed with a slight lift of her slender shoulders. "I'm sorry."

He didn't want her sympathy. "Is your father a professional gambler?"

"Professional? I don't know, but it's a huge part of who he is."

"He never wanted the land, did he?"

Her color deepened again. "He never wanted anything that held him down."

"You wanted it, though?"

"I never knew about it until the attorney contacted me and told me he'd signed it over to me." Her voice was not quite steady. "So, he gave it to me." Her eyes lifted to meet his and he was taken aback by the intensity in them. "Actually, he owed it to me," she said. "We have quite a pair of fathers, don't we?"

He just stood there. This had gone off in a direction he'd never seen coming, and he knew that he'd hit the end right then. Until he could figure out what to do next. "I guess we do," he admitted.

Grace motioned to the house. "I have to get my things inside."

"Do you need help?" he offered.

"No, I don't," she said, then headed for the car.

"If you need to know anything about this place, just call me. I'm in the book."

She had the trunk of the car open but stuck

her head around it to look back at him. "I'll be fine," she said.

Jack waited a moment while she grabbed a small bag out of the trunk, then closed it. Without a glance at him, she headed for the steps and up onto the porch.

By the time he was back in the Jeep, ready to head down the driveway, he turned and saw Grace in the doorway watching him. She raised a hand in a vague wave, then disappeared inside.

In that moment, a memory flooded over him. His grandfather at that door watching three boys on their horses leaving at the end of a long summer's day. The lift of one hand in a wave, the call out to them, "Straight home!" before he went inside and shut the door behind him.

Jack's breath caught in his chest, and he turned from the sight of the empty doorway. His grandfather was gone, but he wouldn't let his land be gone too. He'd find a way to get it back. He wished he hadn't spoken to her about the poker game. That look of sadness in her eyes lingered in his mind, but he wouldn't let that stop him. He couldn't let that stop him from doing what he had to do. And if things worked out, soon Grace could go back to L.A. with enough money to move to a better area of the city, and he'd get a huge chunk of his life back.

# CHAPTER FOUR

GRACE STOOD ALONE in the great room of the house, and felt close to tears. She was tired. She hadn't slept well since Mr. Vaughn's visit, and now she was here. She'd just never expected someone like Jack Carson to show up. He was upset about the loss of his family's land. She understood that. Even worse that his father had been drunk and lost it in a poker game.

When she'd first arrived and seen the house, she'd felt like jumping up and down and yelling, "It's mine, all mine!" Now all she wanted to do was cry. She hugged herself, trying to shake off this sudden depression, and quietly examined the room in front of her, taking in every detail. Heavy beams zigzagging overhead, tile floors well worn with age, rough plaster walls, and a fireplace surrounded by comfortable leather furniture. Everything fit perfectly together. Five minutes later, she'd discovered three decent size bedrooms, one empty, one used as storage for furniture and boxes, and the last containing an old iron double bed along with a sturdy dresser. White sheets and a deep turquoise blanket were folded on the bare mattress, and two pillows were stacked by the linens. The main bathroom had a pedestal sink and a claw-foot tub with a shower over it. The second bathroom was tiny, with just a small shower, sink and toilet.

Heading back to the great room, she crossed instead to the low archway that led to the kitchen. The square room was small but held an old refrigerator and stove. Counters ran along the side wall with a large sink under one of the two windows. A table with four chairs sat beneath a third window on the back wall beside a door to the outside.

She opened the first cupboard and found plates and cups and some well used pots and pans. When she tugged on the back door, her breath caught at the view, a wide swath of bare land between two stands of towering pines. Far in the distance majestic mountains rose, their sheer sides streaked with angular shadows. There were no sounds of traffic, no smell of fumes, and although dusk was close, the sky was overwhelmingly beautiful, without a single cloud in sight. The air had cooled, and she could make out the low hum of insects and the rustle of distant leaves.

This was incredible, like a dream that had somehow become real. The land, the house, the sky, the air—she felt that peace again, just as she had before Jack showed up, along with a sense of belonging. As she stood there staring at the beauty of the land, a huge weight slipped off her shoulders. She felt as if she could breathe easily for the first time in a very long while. She was sorry for the way her father had obtained this ranch, but she was going to make it something special.

She went back through the house to the front porch and sank down on the stone step. Taking out her cell phone, she tapped out her mother's number, got her voice mail, and almost blurted, "Get out here as soon as you can. We've got a home and I need you and Lilly here with me!" But she stopped herself.

No, she'd wait until she could talk to her mother directly. And until then, she'd absorb as much as she could of this place. She looked up and was surprised to see someone by the stables. The man turned, and with a wave, came up the drive toward her. Raw-boned, gray-haired, with narrowed eyes in a deeply tanned face, he stopped a couple of feet away from her. Pale amber eyes remained narrowed on her, but he held out his hand.

"I'm assuming you'd be Grace Evans. The name's Parrish. I was hired on as cleaner and caretaker, at least for now, and I apologize for not being here when you arrived."

When she shook his hand, she could feel the calluses and the sureness in his grip. "That's okay," she said as she drew back.

She spotted an old pickup truck parked right where Jack's Jeep had been sitting before. It was oxidized, maybe a green or blue, she couldn't tell, but it almost blended in with the barn. "You got any luggage you need inside?" he asked.

"There's one more bag in the trunk," she said, and before she finished speaking, he was heading for the car. He popped the trunk and took out her last suitcase while she hurried to collect her purse from the car seat. "So, where are you from?" she asked as they got to the door.

With the toe of his lug-soled work boots,

Parrish pushed the door open and went in before her, setting her luggage inside to the left of the door. "All over, but right now I'm bunking down in the stables," he said, turning toward her. "If you need anything, come on down and get me."

"I thought you might be from the town or close by."

"No, Ma'am, just lucky enough to get paying work for a while."

"Mr. Vaughn hired you?"

He looked confused. "No, Ma'am, a property management company over in Santa Fe. I came out yesterday early to check things out and put new locks on the doors, although, from what I've heard, around here locks are pretty much optional."

She liked hearing that. "It's safe?"

"Like I said, from what I heard." He turned to leave, then stopped and looked back at her. "I'm heading back to town to get the rest of my supplies. Anything you need me to get for you?"

She had the sandwich from Willie G.s' till in the car, and she couldn't even begin to think what she might need beyond that. She'd wait until tomorrow and go into town herself.

"Not right now," she said, "but thanks for asking." Her last words were spoken to his back as he ambled off toward the stables.

Grace watched him slide back one of the doors and disappear inside. Right then, her cell phone rang in her pocket. She took it out, looked at the LCD screen and smiled. She hit the green button and put the phone to her ear as she walked back into the house. "Hello, Mom," she said, excitement returning in a rush. "You won't believe what's here."

JACK WAS UP late that night, his mind going over and over his unplanned meeting with Grace Evans. He had a feeling he'd only get one good chance to get her to agree to sell, and he didn't want to blow it. But he needed information, and he hadn't gotten the call with it yet.

He glanced at his bedside clock. Midnight. He reached for his cell phone and lay back in the big poster bed. After punching in a number, he stared up at the shadowy ceiling as he listened to the rings. On the fourth one, the Chief of Police answered. Jack knew John had the night shift, but he thought he'd be out driving around or sleeping in the back room. "Hey, John, it's Jack."

"Hey, bro, what can I do for you?"

"Did you get the information I asked for about Grace Evans?"

"I actually just got through running it. We had another demonstration out by the site of the new casino and I didn't get back until a half hour ago. People are just crazy when they get in a group like that."

Gage's construction contract to build an entertainment center halfway between the main highway and town still had people upset, although they were gradually coming around. "What did you find out?" he asked, sitting up and moving to push back against the headboard.

"I've got it right here." Jack heard rustling. "Okay, here goes. Grace Anne Michaels Evans is twenty-six, no college although she applied to an art school in the area, but didn't finish the enrollment process. She got married to a Jerald Evans, had a daughter, Lilly Joy, six months after the marriage dissolved. Jerald Evans is now in Maine, remarried and some sort of big rig operator. Grace works at a diner in L.A., not a good place, and seems to have taken a temporary leave while she comes out here.

"She lives in a small rental apartment with her mother, Gabriella Michaels, and her daughter, and two weeks ago, her bank account went up to almost fifty thousand dollars thanks to one deposit. Most of it is still there.

"Never been arrested, has just a couple of traffic tickets, and, oh, I forgot, she was born in L.A., and seems to have stuck pretty close to that area most of her life." He exhaled. "A real city girl, it looks like. Not one you'd think would be coming out here to set up camp."

Fifty thousand dollars. Another gift from her father? A born and bred SoCal girl, and she was going to live out here.

"Hey, you still there?" John asked.

"Yeah, just thinking about what you said, about the city girl thing." A germ of an idea was forming. "Why would she want the hard work of ranch life? No malls, no drive-thru on every corner."

"Maybe she thinks it'll be good for the child?"

"Yes, that could be what she's thinking about."

"So, what are you going to do now Michaels is out of the picture?"

"I figure Grace Evans might need a guide to show her around the land, so she can see how large it is, how much work and money it would take to keep it up, and maybe, if she's offered enough to go back to L.A., she just might accept and leave."

He heard John's low chuckle over the line. "I'm thinking that your thinking might be spot on."

"It's all I've got right now," he admitted.

"Okay, count me in if I can help."

"Thanks," he said and hung up.

He looked around the shadowy loft, thinking again how convenient it was to live above his law offices, then got up and crossed to the window. The town was "rolling up its streets" for the night, few people in sight, only the odd car making its way slowly down Main Street. In his opinion, there was no better place to grow up and live out your life than in Wolf Lake. He'd have to make sure he didn't give voice to that opinion when he was around Grace Evans.

GRACE BARELY SLEPT. It was due, in part, to all the excitement after her long conversation with her mother, and in part, concern, since Parrish was sleeping in the stables. He seemed nice, but she'd locked the doors, anyway, just to be safe. After finally eating the turkey sandwich from Willie G's, she'd soaked in the claw-foot tub, staying in the comforting water for so long, she almost fell asleep. But when she actually got to bed, she was wide awake. Her mind played and re-played the day's events. The part with Jack Carson made her uncomfortable, so she thought instead of the first glimpse she'd had of the house. The fresh air. The clear skies and sprawling land.

By the time she felt the tug of sleep it was midnight, and she gave in to it willingly. Dreams wove in and out of her mind. So many memories. Her father, a giant in her three-year-old eyes, hugging her, rolling a ball back and forth with her, his smiles, and then he was gone. Her mother tired from working two jobs, yet having time for her, always.

The day an envelope had come with her name on it, then opening it to find it was just a flier from a kid's store, not a letter from her father. Then high school, meeting Jerry, knowing almost from the first weeks of their marriage that she'd made a mistake, trying to make it work until he found out she was pregnant and walked out. Her first glimpse of Lilly as the nurse laid the baby in her arms, and the instant love she had felt.

So many things, both good and bad, mingling, then coming here, seeing the house, feeling that peace for a few seconds, that sense of home, and meeting Jack. Sadness touched the dream. He wanted the land. She knew that, but he couldn't have it. She wanted it. She had to have it. He'd never realize how desperate she was. She would make a home here, a place Lilly could always come back to, always.

A noise sounded, a strange cry, and Grace woke instantly, bolting upright in the dark room. The iron bed creaked and groaned as she shifted to listen. Then she heard it again. A coyote howling. It made her shiver and she lay back down, pulling the covers up high to her chin. She stayed like that until dawn, then knew she wouldn't sleep again. She got up, padded barefoot to the kitchen and looked through the rest of the cupboards.

Apparently Parrish had stocked some staples, even a small jar of instant coffee. She got out a mug, heated water in a saucepan and made herself a cup, then headed back to get dressed. Between sips of coffee, she dressed in khaki shorts, a loose blue shirt and her sandals, then headed for the front porch.

The air had a coolness to it, despite the heat from the day before, and she could hear the sound of birds off in the distance. The sun was inching up from the east, washing the land in cool light, and she stayed where she was for a long time, just looking and listening and making plans.

Finally she stood, took her mug into the kitchen and grabbed her camera. She needed photos to show her mother and Lilly. Going back down the step to the drive, she took several shots of the stables. Then she headed down the drive to photograph the stone pillars at the entry with the ranch name. The ground was rough, and she felt it through her sandals. Next time she'd wear running shoes.

At the road, she touched the rough letters of the sign with her fingertips. Would they keep the same name? Or would they think up one all of their own. She kind of liked that idea. A sound caught her attention, a cry, no, it wasn't a cry. It was the soft whinny of a horse. She turned but didn't see anything at first. Then around a curve in the road, a rider appeared on a huge, butterscotch horse. The rider, a big man with a dark Stetson on, nudged the horse into a brisk pace when he saw her.

She thought of heading back up the driveway until she realized she knew the man. Jack. He waved to her and called out, "Good morning!"

She watched him dismount and take the reins in one easy motion. The horse was massive, all muscles, and towered over her. Nervously, she kept her distance. "Good morning," she said to Jack.

He took off the Stetson, and hooked it on the saddle horn before turning to her, raking his fingers through his dark hair. "You're up early."

She raised the camera. "Taking pictures of the place."

"I'm actually glad to meet up like this. I wanted to talk to you about something."

"Please, not the land," she thought, but just nodded. "About what?"

"Do you ride?" he asked.

"Some."

"I was wondering if anyone was going to show you around the land, the boundaries, that sort of thing?"

She hadn't thought about doing anything other than walking. "Not yet."

He shrugged, the shoulders of his white shirt straining under the action. "I understand that this is your place now, and since I've lived on this land all my life, I thought I could take you around and answer the questions you must have."

His offer made a great deal of sense. She knew she'd never see it all if she went on foot. "I don't want to take you away from your work," she said.

"No problem. It's slow for me now, so I have time on my hands."

"Then, I would appreciate it, but I don't have a horse."

"Okay, but do you have time now to take a short hike, just enough to get your bearings?"

"Sure, that sounds fine."

He looked down at her feet. "Do you have anything more substantial than sandals?"

"Of course," she said. "Let me go and get changed."

They walked together up the driveway, the

horse following docilely. As Parrish came out of the stables, Grace ran up to the house. She dug out her barely used white and purple running shoes and went back outside.

Jack had tied his horse to the stone pillar, which was apparently a hitching post, and put a bucket of water in front of the animal. Parrish was nowhere in sight. Jack looked up as she came toward him, the Stetson back in place, shadowing his face. She motioned to her shoes. "How are these?"

He eyed them. "They'll do." He looked toward the house. "Let's go 'round back and head out that way? It's not too rough."

She got his meaning. "I'm used to walking," she said, "so don't worry about it being too rough."

"Good to know," he said, but she didn't miss his slight suggestion of a smile.

She fell in step with him, skipping a bit to keep up as they went around the house. "Is your horse okay back there?"

"Gizmo? Sure, he's a patient sort," he said, giving her a look with his dark eyes.

Grace almost missed her step, but managed to keep up with Jack as they headed toward the massive pines. As they got closer, she noticed a worn path that cut through the stand.

Jack motioned to it. "This way," he said.

She hurried after him into the dim light of the woods, the silence broken only by the muffled sound of their feet stepping on the spongy layers of fallen pine needles. The scent of earth and pine was pleasant as they made their way without speaking. Then the light began to get brighter through the lacing branches, and they headed up a rise that Jack took easily. At the highest point, she realized they'd changed direction somewhere along the line. They were facing directly west, she thought, the sun behind them, and she got a good idea of the way the mountains almost circled the lowlands.

She motioned to the rolling brown land slightly below them, the trees much more sparse here. "What is this?"

"A small part of the…of your ranch and some of the best grazing land this area ever saw."

There was no trace of anything in the brown earth an animal could graze on. "But, it's dead."

He exhaled harshly. "Looks that way." She

thought for a moment the cryptic comment was all he was going to say. "This was the way my grandfather found it when he came down from the Rez to make a home here," Jack said at last. "Dead. Nothing growing. But he worked all this land, building it from nothing, until it was able to support sheep and cattle and his family, all seven kids. He was known for his breeding stock, and this grazing land was the best in the area."

His eyes never met hers, but stayed on the land sprawling out ahead of them. "What happened?" she asked.

His sigh was heavy. "My grandfather turned ninety and hated having to be helped to do anything. As strong as he was all his life, he couldn't keep this place going, and he wouldn't accept help. So, he gradually worked less and less land, and concentrated on the breeding part. But that died off, too. He didn't want anyone to work the land without him there, and we honored his wishes until he was gone. He passed away at ninety-two and the heart just went out of this place."

She squinted at the brown expanse, trying to imagine the land lush and green, with livestock grazing on it. The challenge seemed staggering, but she could figure it out.

"Why didn't your family get it going again?"

He closed his eyes for a long moment. "Things happened," he said in a flat voice. "Life happened." Then he turned and looked straight at her. "But it has to be brought back."

"Of course," she said, his dark gaze fathomless.

"Of course," he echoed.

"He built the house, didn't he?"

"Yes, everything on the land. He did it all with local materials, hauling rocks and stones, cutting the wood, making the adobe blocks." He pointed off to his right. "That cut in the pine trees was deliberately cleared by him. If you sit at the table in the kitchen, or on the back stoop, or look out the window of the main bedroom, you can see the Rez through that clearing."

She followed the direction he pointed but all she saw were the mountains and the foothills at their base. "Can you see it from here?" she asked.

"Right there. See the top of the foothills, that large green area and the smaller ones running out from it. Those rocks that look like a circle—they're near the entrance of the Rez."

She squinted again in the direction he'd indicated. Although she couldn't make out buildings, she could see the rock pattern and the greenness beyond it. If there were structures, they fitted seamlessly into the landscape and looked as if they had been there forever.

"Yes, I see what you're talking about. That's where your grandfather came from?"

"That's where he was born and generations before him were born. My mother was the only child not born on the Rez. She's the seventh and only daughter after six sons. Two are still up there, two are in distant places, and the other two are close enough. My mother never left this area. She and my dad built a ranch to the west, three times as big as this. But bigger isn't always better."

The more he talked, the more she felt his undying connection to this place. And it made her uneasy on some level, but as she looked around her, she also knew with certainty that she was supposed to be here. "So, their place is to the west?"

"Yeah. Come on, and I'll show you." He started down into the dead pastures. They walked in silence across the barren ground, the sun starting to heat up. "Watch your step."

"I'm okay," she said. "These shoes are comfortable."

"I was talking about snakes, not comfort."

She stopped in her tracks, not moving, and Jack had to walk back to where she stood. "Snakes?"

"They won't be around too much out here, but you always have to keep your eyes open."

Snakes. She'd never even thought about them.

Jack touched her shoulder and she jerked. "Stay behind me, and I'll do the checking, okay?"

All she could do was nod.

"You might think about getting some boots to wear outside if you plan on doing much walking."

Grace nodded again, and motioned vaguely for Jack to lead the way.

Boots. She'd get some first thing.

# CHAPTER FIVE

JACK WALKED, ADJUSTING his stride so Grace could keep up. He felt a tinge of guilt for the snake remarks. If there were any out, they'd be more afraid of humans than the reverse. He had impulsively offered this hike to implement the plan he'd come up with in the middle of the night. After talking to John, finding out what a "city" person Grace Evans was, he'd reasoned that she didn't have an iota of an idea what it would take to restore and run the ranch.

He'd known he was right when he'd watched her pick her way through the trees, ducking to avoid branches she would have cleared even if she'd stood straight. Her body language said, "The less contact the better." And he'd felt encouraged when they'd talked, when he'd shown her the dead land, hoping the work ahead of her would put her off And then she'd asked that question about why the ranch had sat untended for so long.

The past had intruded without warning, making him face things he never wanted to face squarely again. How could he have told her, "Because my wife was killed and my dad is a drunk." He couldn't even say those words out loud. Besides, she already knew too much about his family's bad side. Instead, he'd mentioned the snakes.

A city girl? Absolutely. Her eyes had widened, and darted back and forth in search for something moving in the weeds. He'd almost felt badly for her, seeing her revulsion and fear. He'd told her to follow him, and she did, so close he could hear her breathing from time to time.

He kept going, uneasy. It hadn't been like that when he was a kid, running over here every chance he'd had. He finally spoke, intent on skirting the painful memories, but putting this place in perspective. "When my brothers and I were kids, we used to come and stay with Grandpa. He'd put us to work with him, feeding the animals, helping with a produce garden from early summer to the fall. We'd follow him in the pastures, him on the tractor and us behind, breaking clods. We ate a lot of dust."

"He worked you like that?" she asked, and he knew he'd been way off base thinking she'd be horrified at all the work it took to keep the place going. Instead, she was reacting to what she thought of as child labor.

He found himself explaining himself. He owed that much to his Grandpa. "We wanted to work with him. He was our hero." Narrowing his eyes, he kept going. "He loved this place."

Then another question took him off guard. "Why wouldn't he let you work the land later, when he needed help?"

He stopped and turned to look down at her. "Well, because…we worked *with* him when we were kids. When he couldn't work any longer, he didn't want anyone else taking over. That sense of being able to do for himself was important to him. And for most his life, he could do anything."

He cut off any more words, shocked that he'd disregarded his own plan not to tell her anything too personal. He headed off toward a long line of low-growing brush and weeds and stunted trees about three hundred feet away. He wanted her to see what lay beyond that barrier.

GRACE WISHED JACK would keep talking. She was fascinated by the change that came into his voice when he spoke about his grandfather and brothers and it kept her mind off snakes. She loved her mother, but longed for a larger, close family. She'd never had grandparents. Her father had told her mother his folks were "no longer" in the picture, and her mother's parents had passed away when she was a teenager.

They had some family on the East Coast—on her mother's side, but her mom rarely heard from them. No cousins, distant or otherwise. That was why she was so thankful Lilly had her grandma.

They walked, coming to a kind of barrier of low trees, vines and bramble. Jack turned to the left, striding ahead of her for about twenty feet. "We can get through here," he said, motioning.

She caught up to him and was surprised to see a parting in the crazy tangle of vegetation. The opening was narrow, held back by old pieces of wood stuck in the ground. With an easy motion, Jack ducked through the passageway and disappeared from sight. She was shocked he'd fit through and even more shocked when he called out, "Come on down."

She couldn't move. "What about snakes?"

"Can't see any, and if there are some, they're here for the shade. They'll be angry if we disturb them, so we won't." His disembodied voice held just a touch of something she thought might be amusement. "Come on— I'll keep my eyes open for anything."

She hesitantly went closer to the opening until she saw Jack standing in a shallow creek bed that looked bone-dry. He held out a strong hand to her, and now she could see the humor lifting the corners of his lips. Taking a breath, she gripped his fingers for support as she navigated the fairly steep decline. Once at the bottom, she let go of him and looked in both directions along the partially shaded trench. Rocks, sand, weeds, hardy plants that looked like bushes laced with vines, but no snakes.

It was quiet down here, the now towering

growth on either side shutting out almost every noise except a soft chirping.

"This way," Jack said, striding down the eroded path.

She followed, staring at his broad back. There was no question of walking side by side in the narrow cut. "So, does this ever have water in it?" she asked.

"At certain times of the year. There can be flash floods, and you'd be hard put to get out of here before the wall of water got to you."

Without thinking, she looked behind her, then back at Jack. "When does that happen?"

"During the monsoon season."

"Monsoon?" She stopped dead in her tracks. "You're kidding, aren't you?"

He slowed and turned. There was no smile on his face now. "No, I'm not. Monsoons hit this area anywhere from July to the early fall. We're almost at the end of the season, and this year it's been pretty clear. Actually, they help with the land, greening it up a bit, making it softer, better pasture and easier to plow."

"I thought monsoons were tropical storms, way south of here...like very south of here."

He shrugged. "I've seen heavy rain, wind, lower temperatures, large hail and the lightning…." He gave a "believe it or not" shrug. "The lightning is spectacular."

"Hail?"

"Huge balls of hail. I've seen them break windows, beat cars down, a lot of damage."

She hugged her arms around herself. Snakes and monsoons. She'd never given either a thought. "Okay, so are we in danger being down here if a monsoon hits?"

He did laugh then, that dimple appearing at the side of his mouth. "No, not today," he said. "So, relax."

She could tell he wanted to keep going, but she held back. "Before we go any farther, what else goes on around here that I need to know about?"

"Such as?"

"Anything that can drown us, or bite us, or—" She held out her hands, palms upward. "Anything. Just tell me now."

He considered her with those dark eyes, then cocked his head slightly to one side. "Okay. Small stuff. Spiders, scorpions, lizards, that sort of thing. Larger animals. Wolves, coyotes, even had a bear once, but that's usual. Mountain lions—"

"Stop," she said, her skin starting to crawl.

"Enough. I understand. But I need to know how you survived living here all these years?" That smile, darn it, it was there again.

"I'll tell you, this is our home, and it's their home, and we live in some sort of peaceful coexistence when we respect the fact that they were here first."

"That's baloney. Do you have some philosophical discussion with a mountain lion when it attacks you?"

The smile stayed. "Not usually. That's when I use the shooting skills I was taught as a kid by my grandpa." The smile changed just a bit, his expression wistful. "He knew everything there was to know about coexistence and taught me and my brothers what we needed to know to survive in one piece."

"Good, good," she muttered, about to ask if they could go back right then.

"Now, come on. We're safe, and if anything comes up that isn't expected, believe me, it won't surprise me and I'll deal with it." When she didn't move, he said, "We only have a short distance to go."

She had made it this far, she thought. Might as well go a bit farther. Then she'd get back to the house, go into town and get the boots.

A gun was out of the question. She hated guns, but maybe a heavy stick to carry when she was out walking. "Okay," she said, and he took off.

"Used to come this way to go hunting with my brothers. This was a shortcut. We discovered it one day, and we made up stories about the Indians going this way, that they dug it just so they could move unseen. Of course, Grandpa explained about erosion and water eating at the earth."

"But your idea was more fun, wasn't it?" she asked.

"It sure was." He sounded a bit wistful again as he walked ahead of her.

"What did you hunt?"

"Everything," he said over his shoulder. "Rabbits, squirrels, some birds. Bigger game depending on the season. The only rule was we had to eat what we killed."

The idea of killing anything was hard for her to deal with, but to clean it and cook it afterward—that made her queasy. "That's coexistence?"

"Yes, you only take what you need to sustain yourself or your family," he said. "My grandpa was firm on that. Willie G., he's the same. He's a huge protector of the land. We're just caretakers, and both men always said, 'They aren't making any more of it. What's here is all there is ever going to be' and they were right."

His words made her feel this place was even more special. It had been cared for and nurtured for years by the Wolf family, and maybe now it was her family's turn to look after it.

He rounded a corner, and the path climbed slightly upward. A few moments later, she and Jack stepped into brilliant sunshine at the mouth of a gully. The trees were farther back now, mostly to their rear, and the sight in front of her was nothing short of spectacular.

They had come out on a rise, overlooking a ranch so beautiful it was hard to believe it was real. Pasture after green pasture, white rail fencing crisscrossing the landscape. Cattle roamed in the distance, horses beyond them, and past that, she could make out a sprawling two-story ranch house that looked as if it was molded to the land it sat on, the turquoise sky a dazzling backdrop.

"Wow," she whispered.

"That's my parents' ranch, Carson Acres.

They built on the land Grandpa passed on to them when they got married."

Grace shaded her eyes from the bright sunlight, drinking in the vision. "How far does it go?"

"You're on the boundary between the two places, and their land reaches the foothills to the north and west." He motioned to the mountains where he'd pointed out the Reservation before. "Just below the Rez, butted up against it." She could feel him watching her. "So, what do you think about all of this?"

Grace looked up at Jack, knowing a smile was curving her lips. "It's incredible, so vast and overwhelming."

"Yes, it is. And it's a lot of work and expense to keep it going, too. I'd hate to tell you what it costs per month to keep that place working. And that wouldn't include new livestock for replacements or the payroll that fluctuates depending on the season. We have five wells going all the time, and it's a full time job to regulate them."

"Do I have wells?" she asked, remembering the water rights.

"Two for irrigation. They'll probably need work before they'll be up and running."

"There's water in the house," she said.

"That's from a small well near the house. The other two are straight irrigation wells."

She felt her smile falter a bit. "When I need them, I'll get them fixed. As long as I have water in the house."

"I guess that will work."

"With a well, does that mean there aren't any water bills?"

She could tell her question wasn't the smartest when she saw the flicker of amusement in his eyes come and go. "Yes, there are no water bills, just electric bills. Although, if your windmills are still working properly, that should help, unless you're going to irrigate all the feeding pastures."

Her mind spun. Feeding pastures. Windmills. There was so much she didn't know. "I've seen windmills, or wind turbines, whatever they're called near L.A. out by Palm Springs. They look simple enough, so there can't be too much that can go wrong." Another flicker of emotion crossed his face, but she couldn't read it, and was pretty much glad about that. She couldn't feel any dumber if she tried.

"There's lots, unfortunately." As if he read

her mind, he said, "The blades can turn, but if they aren't serviced properly, well…." He shrugged as if it was patently apparent. "No electricity."

Obviously, that made sense, but she did have electricity at the house. "Good to know," she murmured, and hoped the warmth she felt on her face came from the sun and not from her blushing.

JACK SAW THE uncertainty shadow her face, and the color rise in her cheeks. Another score for his side. He'd thought the "dangerous life" discussion in the river bottom had been very effective. The disgust and unease in her expression were hard to miss. But now, she definitely looked worried, and he felt like a bully. He didn't like it, so he pulled back a bit. No need to hammer her over the head with the truth of her situation. "Life's a bit different in Los Angeles, I guess?"

"I sure don't have a well or snakes where I live," she said.

"Yes, but you have malls, the beach, entertainment, glamour, gourmet coffee shops selling five dollar lattés. Out here we've only got one coffee shop, no movie theater is closer than fifty miles, and just the beginnings of a casino complex. That's in the future, and what we'll get from that is a lot of gambling." As soon as he said the words, he realized he never should have mentioned gambling. The color on her cheeks deepened, and Grace turned from him.

"You know, I need to get back. I've got some things to do before I leave."

Any apology was left unsaid. "You're going back to L.A. already?"

"Yes, in the morning." She turned and made her way carefully back to the sandy bed of the dry creek.

Could it all be this simple? She came, she saw, she left, despite what she'd said about not selling? Now that he'd shown her what lay ahead, could he name a figure to buy the ranch and that would be that? He followed her down the path, his turn to focus on her slender hips and the way her hair in its high ponytail swung in time with her strides. Her running shoes were no longer purple and white, but filmed with dirt and silt. Not a country girl by a long shot.

Silence hung between them until they reached the opening in the vegetation. He watched as she looked up at the wooden supports, trying to figure out how she'd get out. He came up behind her. "Here, let me help," he said as he spanned her waist with his hands and lifted her up to get her footing so she could grab the wooden frame and pull herself out.

When she was through the opening, she turned to look down at him, and he was thankful he was never one to blush. For a moment that feeling of her, light as feather, him lifting her, had startled him. He wasn't sure why, and with a sharp shake of his head, he didn't try to understand his reaction. He pulled himself up, and the minute he straightened, Grace strode off across the dry pasture.

She was going back to L.A. tomorrow, so he would have no further chance to build his case for her sale of the land to him. They were halfway back to the house when he finally broke the silence. "Life out here can be tough," he said. "My grandpa was just tougher."

"I guess so. You said that ranch was your parents' land. Where's yours?" she asked, not breaking stride.

"I help them out sometimes, but I wouldn't qualify as a rancher right now."

That caught her attention, and she cast him a long sideways glance. "Right now? That means you will be or want to be in the future?"

Here it was. His chance to tell her he wanted this place, to bring it back to life, and him along with it. But the words stuck in his throat. "The possibility is always there for me," he generalized.

She kept walking, and by the time they broke out of the trees near the house, he felt the nerves at the back of his neck tightening. She stopped and turned to him. "Thank you so much for the tour and the information," she said. "I appreciate it all."

He knew that his last chance to broach the question of selling was right then. Taking a breath, he asked, "If you were to sell this place, how much would you take for it?"

She didn't move and he knew he'd done it all wrong, but he couldn't take the question back. In a court room, he could get any information out of a witness. But this woman totally baffled him. "I don't understand something," she said, narrowing her lavender eyes.

He didn't understand anything right then himself, except the fact that he was bumbling around like some first year law student, instead of focusing and getting to the point. "What's that?"

"I hadn't even made it out here before Willie G. offered to buy this place. Now you're asking about buying it. I understand that it used to be in your family, but am I missing something else?" She smiled faintly. "Is there gold here, or oil, or some hidden treasures?"

*"Just my life,"* he thought, but shook his head. "I'd like to keep it in our family." That was true enough, but barely the full truth.

She nodded. "I understand that."

"There are strong emotional connections for people. With Willie G. it's the land connection, land he's been on all his life. With me, it's the family connection, the history of the Wolf people." She nodded again. Then he realized something. "You must have some emotional connection because your father gave it to you, no matter how he got it."

Jack saw her eyes narrow even more before Grace turned from him. "He never came here, did he?" she asked as she started toward the house.

He fell in step with her. "I think he only had it for a few weeks, maybe a month, before he moved it on to you. No one ever saw him around here."

"He should have seen the place," he thought he heard her mutter, but couldn't be sure.

They walked around to the front of the house and Grace went up the porch step, turned and looked down at him. "Thanks again."

The morning sun was haloing her face, turning her hair the color of pale spun gold. "You never answered me about considering selling."

She cocked her head slightly to the right, and studied him openly for a long, almost uncomfortable moment. "No, I didn't, did I?"

He waited, not saying anything else, just waiting for the tiny woman on the step above him to give him some sort of answer.

"I'm not sure," she finally said. "There are things I need to do first, people to talk to. This isn't just about me."

"You're coming back?" he asked.

"Yes, I'll be back, but I'm not sure when."

Jack felt a slight easing in him. She hadn't made a final decision. That made sense. So, he'd just have to be patient for a bit longer. "Okay," he said. "Just one thing more?"

"Sure."

"When you get back, if you've decided to sell, will you give me first right of refusal before you go to anyone else, even Willie G.?"

She started to shake her head, and Jack tensed again. "I don't think I—"

He cut her off before she could say any more. "Whatever you decide, sell or stay, please contact me first. That's all I'm asking."

"Okay," she finally said.

Jack headed for his horse, mounted, then looked back to find Grace in the open doorway of the house, as she had been yesterday when he'd left. Their eyes met, and she lifted a hand in a wave. He answered with a nod, the same way he'd left his grandpa so many times. But this time a slender woman who had the only thing that meant anything to him was there in the doorway. Memories overlapped with reality and he turned his horse and rode off.

## CHAPTER SIX

GRACE WENT INTO the house, crossing the great room to her bedroom to change into shorts and sandals before she went into town. Boots, that's what she needed. Kitchen supplies, food and maybe some jeans, real jeans, heavy, protective jeans.

Even before Jack had asked her if she'd be back, there was no question that she'd be returning. She hadn't left yet and she was already anxious about coming back. She'd wanted to just tell him that she and her family would be staying. She wasn't about to sell this place.

But she'd stopped herself. She'd been here less than two days, not nearly time enough to figure this all out. The move was a huge change for her, and especially for Lilly. She wanted to make the right decisions. Their happiness depended on that. She brushed her hair, put it back in a ponytail, then grabbed her purse and headed for the door.

She saw Parrish by the stables as soon as she stepped onto the porch. When he spotted her, he held up a hand and jogged over to the house, stopping at the bottom step. "Mornin', ma'am," he said, touching his straw hat.

"Please, call me Grace," she said as she put the house key back in her bag. She'd leave the door unlocked. That decision felt so good after living behind three locks for so long.

"Grace, okay, just wondered how it went with Mr. Carson?"

"He showed me a bit of the land, and gave me some information I needed." She frowned. "I was wondering. What do you know about the windmills on the property?"

He motioned to the west. "One on the west side, one on the southeast section, both used to pump water and run electric fencing."

"They're working?"

"They're off, but they look okay. Just have to get them primed to go, would be my guess."

She was relieved. "What about the house well?"

"Nice little well, right by the stables. Pumps maybe sixty gallons an hour and has a holding tank on higher land. Lots of water for the house use, and around here."

Another big relief. "Thank you. I didn't have any idea about any of that."

"Why would you? I hear you're from L.A., and I doubt you had any private wells to worry about there."

She smiled. "Sure didn't." Scanning the area, she asked one last question. "What would you guess this whole place would be worth?"

That brought a slight frown, but when he spoke, Parrish was amiable enough. "Good question. Told you I'm not from around here, so I couldn't make an educated guess."

"How would I find out?"

"You planning on selling it?"

"I don't think so, but...." Jack's words made her wonder if she would be able to do much more than just live in the house. The land seemed a huge undertaking. Irrigation, planting, livestock. "It's a huge place."

"Nah. By ranch standards, it's just a nice, comfortable piece of ground. Now that place next door, Carson's, it's huge. I wouldn't want to take on that. Just don't let this place scare you."

*A nice, comfortable piece of ground.* Somehow those words pushed away some of her doubts. "I saw the ranch from a distance and it goes on forever. Jack told me the land goes right up into the foothills to the reservation."

"Like I said, huge." He glanced at her bag. "You goin' somewhere?"

"Into town. I want to find out about a few things, and I need boots, tall boots."

"Check with Oscar in the General Store. He's got everything, from food to the boots."

"Thanks, I'll do that. Then I want to see if there's any work I might be able to find in town."

He studied her. "What do you do now?"

She wished she could say she was an artist, but that wouldn't be true. "Waitressing."

"There's a few places in town, nice restaurants, a few diners. They might need help."

"Thanks." She headed down the steps and Parrish moved to one side.

"Have you got your camera?" he called after her.

That stopped her. Turning, she said, "Thanks," and hurried back up the step and into the house. "Thought you might like some shots to show people when you get back to L.A." he said as she came out again.

"Absolutely."

It took all of ten minutes to get to town, not a long trip at all, and not one red Jeep in sight on the way. She parked in front of the General Store, which stood right beside the "one coffee shop" Jack had mentioned. The bed-and-breakfast run by Willie G's niece was on the other side with a few cars parked in front.

She walked into the coffee shop and ordered a coffee and a breakfast sandwich, then took a table by the front windows that overlooked the main street. There was a rhythm to Wolf Lake, a slow pace that seemed pleasant. A few people were walking the raised sidewalks, and shops were starting to open. A bright red van passed by, Wolf Lake Family Center written on its side and the shadows of kids bouncing on their seats in the windows.

When she'd finished her breakfast, she paid and headed back outside. The town was just getting going for the day.

The General Store had a bit of everything, just as Parrish had said. Quickly she found a pair of dark brown boots with low heels and tooling on the sides in her size. She left them at the counter with the teenager working there, then went to get peanut butter, bread and bottled water. When she got back to the counter, a bald man was waiting for her behind the register.

"Morning," he said, smiling at her. He motioned to the box with her new boots in it. "These yours?"

She set her supplies on the counter. "Yes, they are."

"Visiting our little town?" he asked as he rang up her order.

"Yes," she said.

As he began to bag her things, he asked, "Where you from?"

"California."

He glanced at her. "Big state. North or South?"

"South, Los Angeles area," she said.

"Oh, yeah," he murmured as he totaled her order.

She wasn't sure if that was a simple, "Oh," or an "Oh, no, not a crazy Californian." He told her what the total was, and while she dug in her bag for the money, she asked, "Would you know where the elementary school is?"

"Rez or town?"

"Town."

"It's west, one street past Manno's Garage on the left. You can't miss the school. It's right at the end of the block. The new part looks like something out of a carnival and the original school is the same as it has been for fifty years, all bricks and plain. Kindergarten through eighth grade. All my kids and my grandkids have gone there."

She was used to schools being subdivided into pre-kindergarten, kindergarten, grades one through five, then grades six through eight, up into high school. "Is it a good school?"

"Best around here," he said as he handed her the change with a chuckle.

She smiled at him. "And the only one, I take it?"

He nodded his bald head. "You got it. Except for the one on the Rez. It's real small, but good, too. Good setup."

"How many kids go to the one in town?"

"There's maybe a hundred and fifty, tops."

"Thank you." She picked up the single brown bag with her purchases in it and put it on the box, then lifted both into her arms.

"I'm Oscar—I own the place."

"Good to meet you. I'm Grace and I appreciate the information about the school."

"If you're looking at the school, are you planning on sticking around here?"

"I think I might be, so I wanted to check it out."

He looked really interested now. "Is that so? Where are you gonna be living?"

"On a ranch farther west," she said.

"Which one?"

"Wolf Ranch."

He stared at her, motionless for a moment. "Wolf Ranch?"

"Yes." She would have headed for the door, but Oscar spoke again.

"I wondered when someone would show up."

She hesitated. "Excuse me?"

"The way that all happened with the Carsons, losing that place because of the husband. Never did have any respect for the land. He's a retired banker. You'd think he'd at least have respect for the money that land's worth. Old Jackson Wolf must be turning in his grave." He looked stricken. "Years and years it was Wolf land, and now...." He motioned to her. "No offense, Grace, not that you don't have every right to claim it from what I've heard, but Herbert Carson is an idiot. And what he's done to poor Jack." He shook his head. "Oh, man, what a real shame that is. Didn't deserve that kind of low blow."

She didn't want to hear this. She really didn't. The deal was done. She understood that Jack wanted to keep the land in the family, but she didn't understand why this man looked so bothered that he'd lost it. The store owner was acting as if he was part of the Carson family.

"I'm sorry," she said quickly, not sure why she was apologizing to him.

"A lot of people are," he said ruefully, then smiled at her. "Not your doing, we all know that, it's just hard to take."

"I understand," she said, but really didn't. She hurried outside, grateful for the fresh air. She had begun to have trouble breathing. Willie G. didn't want her to have the land, Oscar was upset about it, Jack wanted it and a lot of people in town thought he should.

"Great," she muttered as she stashed her purchases in the car and drove off. It didn't matter what people thought. The land was legitimately hers. Once she saw the garage, she turned left at the next street. It was lined with old houses, some restored, some not, a scattering of mobile homes, and a few vacant lots. The street dead-ended right into the parking lot for Wolf Lake Elementary School.

It was just the way Oscar had described it. To the left, a bright red, domed building stood in the center of multiple wings spreading out from it. Each wing looked like a string of giant toy blocks, each in a bright color. The original school building was a fraction of the size of the newer one, and looked as if it was being used for the administration.

She parked and found her way to the central hub and a long walkway bordered by signs with pictures of children on them and words like, "Honor, Trust, Kindness, Integrity, Pride." By the time she found the main office, she didn't know what to expect. The interior space was huge, the wings leading off from the hub and a round desk in the middle.

A large woman behind the desk with very short dark hair and a huge smile asked, "May I help you?"

When Grace explained why she was there, the woman excused herself and then came back with a colored brochure.

"All the information you need is in there," she said. "Our teachers' profiles, the layout, our budget, our funding, our scores on state testing, and if there's something you don't find, please just ask." She motioned to some nearby couches. "Have a seat and read through it, if you have the time, then we can talk further."

She'd make the time. Crossing to the closest couch, she dropped down on the soft suede and opened the brochure. Five minutes later she heard a voice she recognized. "Hi, Naomi, just dropping off papers for Rodney."

She looked up to see Jack Carson at the desk, smiling at the woman she'd spoken to. The hat was gone, and his jeans had been exchanged for dark slacks and an open-necked white shirt. His hair was combed back and looked damp, as if he'd recently taken a shower. She didn't move, wondering if he'd even glance her way, half wishing he wouldn't.

The next moment he turned in her direction, dark eyes on her, and smiled.

THE LAST THING Jack had expected was to find Grace Evans in the main office of the elementary school, curled up in the corner of one of the sofas. The morning had been good and bad, and he'd thought the situation would have stayed that way until she came back from L.A. and told him what she'd decided. Now she was there in front of him, slowly standing, a bright brochure in her hands.

He dropped a file on the desk and patted it. "Make sure Rodney gets those, okay, Naomi?" he asked without looking away from Grace.

"Right away, Jack," the woman said.

He crossed to Grace, and as his eyes skimmed over her, he had to smile. The sandals were back. He wondered, if she stayed here any length of time, how soon those sandals would be relegated to the back of the closet in favor of some decent boots. "I didn't expect to see you here."

"I don't know why you would have," she said in that soft voice, her lavender eyes holding his gaze.

"So, you're checking out the school?" he asked, the answer obvious.

"Yes, I am."

"What do you think?"

"So far, it seems pretty remarkable. The new structures are incredible."

"My brother Gage designed the addition. The locals worked with him and his crew, the same way the entertainment center is being built. It's been four years since this was finished, but it still looks great."

There was an awkward silence, which Grace finally broke. "The windmills are fine and so is the house well."

He blinked, his mind blank for a moment, then he remembered their talk about the water situation. "How do you know?"

"Parrish, the man helping me—he checked them and said they're in good working order. The house well is the same, pumping just fine."

"Good to hear," he said. She hadn't wasted any time checking after he'd told her. "So, you're heading out tomorrow morning?"

"That's the plan. I need to get back, but Oscar at the store told me that this school is the best ever. I wanted to check it out for my daughter, in case we stay."

"Of course." He knew there was a child, but didn't know she had a girl. And the school was nothing like the older, smaller one he and his brothers had gone to years ago. The old building had only four classrooms. Naomi was back, looking at the two of them, and Grace nodded to her. "I do need to ask you a few things."

"No problem."

"I'll talk to you when you get back?" Jack asked.

"Yes, of course," she said, standing and passing him to go to the desk.

He headed for the door, glanced back as he left, and saw Grace going around to meet Naomi near the back opening of the circular desk. She moved quickly, determinedly, the way she seemed to do most everything. Then both women went into the corridor that he knew led to the lower grades.

Once in the Jeep, Jack took a minute to think. She had a child. John had told him as part of his background check of Grace. It didn't seem real though, not until now.

He never thought about children anymore. He and Robyn had both wanted them badly, but since then, he'd wondered if he only wanted them because Robyn had.

He abruptly started the engine. That was a moot point. There never would be any children with Robyn. He backed out, drove away from the school and over to his office. The reception area was totally empty when he walked in but a moment later, Maureen, his assistant, rushed through the door. A buxom, fifty-something woman with unnaturally bright red hair and an efficiency that would put anyone to shame, she was breathing hard when she got to him. "I've been…looking for you."

He put both hands out at his sides. "You found me. Now, breathe."

She was flushed, and held up a hand, then finally shook her head. "Okay, okay. I went to Oscar's store and he said that Grace Evans was in there earlier and she was asking about the school. I thought you should know right away."

"I already know."

She ran a hand over her face. "Great, Oscar could have told me he had told you. It would have saved me from racing over here when I saw you!"

"Oscar didn't tell me." He saw the question in her eyes. "I saw Ms. Evans at the school when I took Rodney the insurance readout."

"Oh, okay." She swiped at her face. "So

much for good gossip." Going around the large front desk in the wood paneled room, she dropped down in her chair. "So, what did Ms. Evans say?"

"Nothing much."

"You talked, and you, the great attorney, didn't get any information out of her?" she quizzed him.

Jack started toward his office in the rear, then stopped and came back.

Giving Maureen an evasive answer to a question never worked. She was all about details, and over the ten years she'd been sitting in that chair, he'd never gotten away with it. "I found out that she really is leaving tomorrow morning, and that she's coming back soon, probably within a week or so, I'd guess."

"See, did that hurt telling me that?" she asked with smile.

"It always does. But, you know what? I'd love to know if she's just coming back to see about selling, or if that means she's planning on making a move to the ranch."

"Ask John, he's the one with all the databases to get answers for you."

"I'd rather you figured this one out. No need to call him in again, unless we have to.

"It's your call, boss."

"Wait a few days. Then try and find out if she's releasing her rental in L.A., and whether her daughter's registered at the school here."

"You're not asking much, are you?"

"Not for you. You could do that in your sleep."

"What are you going to do when I leave?"

He frowned, thinking about her resignation sitting on his desk. In a month, she was quitting to open a business with her husband, a turquoise jewelry exchange in town. She'd promised to come back off and on to help him out, but having her full-time would be a thing of the past at the end of September. "I wish I could talk you into staying until the end of the year."

She shook her head. "Can't. Would if I could, but can't. Bruce needs me full time to get the business ready for the busy season when skiing starts up."

"I know. Just remember, if or when you decide you need to get away from Bruce, I'm here."

She grinned. "Of course." Then she turned to her computer. "I'll find out what I can about your Ms. Evans."

AN HOUR LATER, Grace was headed back to the ranch. The visit to the school had been great. She'd had a tour of the campus, the recreational facility in the back, the computer center, art center; and she'd had a chance to meet the first grade teacher. The school seemed like heaven compared with the one Lilly was going to.

She wondered what Jack had been doing at the school. Maybe he had kids there and was taking in some paperwork? She knew he was married—from the gold band he wore, but she hadn't thought about children. There could be a few "little Jacks" running around playing cowboy. The thought made her smile as she put away her few groceries. She just bet he was a terrific father.

Her smile faded. She wished Lilly had a terrific father. She so didn't want her daughter following in her footsteps.

Grace put on her new boots, not sure if she was supposed to wear socks with them or bare feet. Since she had no socks with her, the decision was made. She quickly made a peanut butter sandwich, grabbed a bottle of water and went out on the front step.

An engine sounded in the distance, then

came closer as the old, oxidized pickup truck appeared on the rise. Parrish waved to her as he swung toward the stables and brought the truck to a stop by the double doors. When he got out, he turned and headed toward her. "I see you got to town, huh?" he asked, smiling at her boots.

She lifted the half-eaten sandwich. "The boots and this are a dead giveaway, I guess."

"Not that. I was just there, too, and I heard all about you."

The sandwich stopped halfway to her mouth. "You what?"

"Yeah, the town's buzzing about the new lady out here on the Wolf land. How the father double-dealt his son right out of this place."

"Oh, my gosh," she said softly. "They're upset about me being here."

He shook his head. "Nah, they're upset with the old man, the dad, losing it like he did. They take land around here seriously. And Wolf land, apparently, is right up there with the most important in the area." He grinned at her. "Small towns have some of the best grapevines."

She couldn't smile at what she knew was supposed to be a joke. "So it seems."

"Hey, don't let it get you down. Everyone seems to think you're darn nice, despite the situation."

Now she could smile a bit. "Well, that's a plus. Nice. It's nice to be nice."

He chuckled, "It sure don't hurt."

"I'm going to get things set up in the house, then leave early in the morning to catch my flight back to L.A."

"How soon you coming back?"

She took another bite from her sandwich, chewed, then said, "Probably in a week. Although if I decide to move here, it might take longer to get things tied up."

"You got a lot to settle?"

She chuckled. "Not really. But with a six-year-old, things can get complicated."

He cocked his head to one side. "So, you've got kids."

"One, a daughter, Lilly Joy."

"Dang, she'll love it around here. What little girl doesn't want to ride a horse and pretend to be a cowgirl?"

Grace liked Parrish. He seemed to always say the right thing to help her get focused. Yes, Lilly would love this place, she'd embrace it. "You're right. Do you have kids?"

"I've got a son in Tennessee, but he's still trying to figure out how to give me grand-kids."

"Kind of slow in that area?" she asked, smiling.

"Seems to be," he said. "When you've got time, come on down to the stables and I'll show you what's what."

She stood, putting the last of her sandwich in her mouth, then took a drink of cool water. "How about now?"

He nodded and led the way. Recently cleaned stalls lined half of the long building on one side. At the end was a tack room, with precious little tack in it, and a kind of stor-age room that doubled as a place for a ranch hand to sleep. A small cot had been neatly made, and a pair of work boots sat beside it, along with a stack of books, most of them mysteries.

"I live in here for now," Parrish said.

"It's pretty small." She motioned around the tight space.

"Nice and cozy, and it's got everything I need."

"Good, I'm glad it works for you," she said as she started back down the aisle. "How much do you think a horse would cost? A nice, gentle horse that a child could ride, if we move in?"

"Don't know, but I can ask around, if you want."

"Yes, please, if you would. Lilly's always loved toy horses."

"Big jump from toy to real."

"Yes, it is. I'd have to get her riding lessons, so she could do it right."

"And boots," he said, thinking the same way as Jack.

"Absolutely," she agreed.

They stepped out into the warmth of the sun, both just looking around. "I can see it's getting to you," Parrish said in a low voice.

She glanced at him. It had already gotten to her. She just wanted to make very sure that this would work for everyone. "I do like it here," she said, a great understatement.

Parrish nodded. "Good, good. I'll check about the horse for you. No pony, right?"

She thought about it. "No, just a horse. A calm one."

He tugged at his cap, and with a, "See ya," went to his truck and rumbled down the driveway.

Grace spent the rest of the day going through the storage room. She found two more bed frames, a small chest for Lilly and a plain white dresser for her mother. Putting furniture in each of the bedrooms gave a semblance of order to the house. After another peanut butter sandwich for dinner, she sat in the great room facing an empty hearth.

She probably should have told Jack that she wouldn't sell. But she'd had too many disappointments in her life to count her chickens before they hatched. Her plans to become a great artist, her marriage. Maybe when she got everyone on the ranch, things wouldn't work out the way she thought. What then?

One thing she'd learned from her mother through the years was that you always had to have a backup plan. Things very seldom turned out the way you thought they would, and you had to be prepared. Jack's offer to buy the land would be her backup plan. The thought made her feel a whole lot better.

# CHAPTER SEVEN

GRACE STARED INTO the empty hearth and wondered what Jack's wife thought of him wanting to buy the place. Did she plan on them moving here? Or was his desire for the land all about getting it back in the family? She shrugged those thoughts off and was heading to bed when her cell phone rang.

"Hi, Mom," she said, glad to hear her voice.

"Just wanted to know how things have gone?"

"I went to the school and it's remarkable. I think Lilly would love it there."

"That's so good to hear." She paused, then asked, "What do you think? What do you really think about us all moving there to live?"

She bit her lip hard, wanting to say, "Let's just do it." Instead, she said, "I like it, really like it, but it's very different here. It's well water and huge skies and no neighbors within spitting distance."

Her mother laughed softly. "Actually, that sounds wonderful. Especially the neighbor part. And the school…I love that, too."

"I asked the caretaker to look for a horse for Lilly, a nice gentle horse."

"Oh, my, that's…I don't know. Isn't she awfully young to be on a horse?"

"No, not really, but I'd get her lessons. I'm not sure we can even afford a horse in the first place, though."

"I have to ask you something, and it's crazy, but it's bothering me."

"About Lilly?" she asked immediately.

"No, no. Just something that happened a few minutes ago. The landlord came by and wanted to see if we were moving."

"How could he know about that?"

"My thoughts exactly. Not even Lilly knows we're considering it. He said that he wanted to know if the apartment was going to be available by the end of this month."

"I don't understand." She sank down on the edge of the bed. "Why would he ask that?"

"He said there'd been an inquiry about this apartment to find out if it would be available anytime soon."

That almost made Grace laugh. "Why

would anyone be interested in it? It was empty for four months before we moved in."

"That's what didn't add up, but I guess it's just some strange coincidence."

"What did you tell him?"

"I said I'd be in contact with him if we ever decided to move."

"That's fine." Grace fell back on the soft bed she'd made up earlier with the linens and pillows she'd found in a wardrobe. The beams crisscrossed overhead, shadows gathered in the corners of the room. "I wish I knew that we could do this, but there's so much to running a ranch. Just the water supply gets complicated, and then there's windmills and drainage and livestock."

"Who have you been talking to that's put all of that in your head?"

She closed her eyes. "Jack Carson, the son of the man who owned this land. He wants it back, and asked how much I would take for it."

"What did you tell him?"

"That I hadn't made up my mind, but I promised to give him first dibs if I decide to sell."

"Is Mr. Carson pressuring you? I don't like that idea at all."

"No, no. He walked me around part of the property, told me some things I needed to know, and said if I was going to sell it, to give him first chance at it."

"Don't let him sway you one way or the other," her mother said seriously.

"I won't." But his words had made an impact for sure. Jack had lived here all his life, and knew the land like the back of his hand. What did she know about a ranch? She shook off her doubts, realizing her mother had given the phone to Lilly.

She promised her daughter she'd be home by lunch tomorrow, and almost ended the call. But she found herself telling Lilly they would be taking a trip for a bit. Hearing how excited Lilly was, she acted impulsively. "Let me speak to Grandma again, sweetie?"

Her mother took the phone. "Yes?"

"Get things ready and we'll figure out what we have to do to make this move work for us. If it doesn't, I can sell the property later and with the money we can move wherever we want. Tell the landlord we'll be out in two weeks."

A soft sigh came down the line. "Good thinking. Let's do it."

"Yes," Grace said, opening her eyes and peering at the ceiling above her. "Let's do it."

JACK WAITED AS long as he could, almost a week, before heading over to the old ranch to see if Grace was there, or if Parrish knew what was going on. He found the older man on the roof of the house. He parked his Jeep by the porch and looked up as Parrish walked to the edge.

"Can I help you?" he asked.

"I just wanted to know if Grace is back yet?"

"Nope."

"Do you have any idea when she'll be coming?"

He shrugged, his eyes narrowed in the late afternoon sun. "Nope."

Single answers drove him crazy, both in everyday life and in court. This man seemed to be a master of them. "She didn't give you any indication?"

He started to say, "Nope," again, Jack was sure of it, then seemed to reconsider. "She said she'd be back, maybe a week or two, and that I should look around for a safe horse for her little girl."

Jack tried to keep his face neutral, but he felt his heart catch a bit. Getting a horse sounded permanent. "Any luck?" he asked.

"Yeah, there's a little bay that's up for sale, real nice, calm. But, then, I don't know much about horses, so I could be wrong."

"Is it Bingo Sage's horse?"

"How'd you know?"

"He's been trying to unload that horse for about a year. She's a biter. Nice and calm and sweet, then she swings her head and tries to bite anyone she can, most likely whoever is on her back."

Parrish rubbed his chin. "Good information."

"I'll tell you who to talk to if you want a good child's horse. You know the owner of the General Store, Oscar?"

"We met a few times."

"He's got grandkids and they're getting too big for their horses. In fact, he's got a really nice little Paint mare. Tell him I sent you, and he might let you take it for a trial, to make sure the child and the horse match temperaments."

Parrish walked to the side of the roof, beyond the porch and turned to lower himself down. He jumped the last six feet, landing solidly on the dried earth. Coming toward Jack, he said, "I'll contact Oscar and go take a look."

"Do you have tack here?"

"There's a few pieces in the stables."

"What about the hay barn?"

"It's too unsteady, needs to be redone to secure it. I don't go in there. Sure don't want a kid to."

Jack had forgotten about that. "I've got extra tack if you find you need some."

"Thanks for that," Parrish said.

"Let me know when Grace is coming back?"

Parrish shook his head. "Tell you what, I'm thinking maybe you'd do better asking Grace about her plans, rather than getting them secondhand. Just wait here." Parrish took off for the stables at a jog, and when he came back, he was carrying a piece of paper. "Here you go."

Jack saw a phone number printed on it. "Thank you," he said. "It's appreciated."

"The info on the horse is appreciated. Not

that she said she was for sure buying, but she's interested."

"Either way," he said, holding up the paper, "this helps a lot."

"Good luck," Parrish said, turning to leave.

"Parrish?"

"Yeah?"

"What's wrong with the roof?"

"Nothing. For its age, it's darn near perfect."

"What were you up there for?"

"Checking the chimney to make sure no critters made nests in it while the house has been empty."

"Any problems?"

"Let's put it this way, there's going to be a few ticked-off bats if they ever try to get back in there to nest. I put wire over the opening and a spark suppressor, too.

"Grandpa had a huge barn owl get down there, and come out in the great room. He just opened the door and let the thing go out."

Parrish smiled. "He sounds like he was a cool old guy."

"He was, very cool," Jack murmured and headed for his truck, paper in hand.

Grace sank down on the drab sofa in the living room of the apartment and slowly rotated her neck to ease the soreness there. Her last shift at work had been two days ago, and ever since, she'd been packing. Finally the boxes were all in order for the moving company to pick up tomorrow. Once they were gone, all she had to do was get the suitcases in the car, along with Lilly and her mother, and they'd drive away from this place forever.

That thought made her feel so good. Being away from the land for almost two weeks had been too long for her.

Her phone vibrated in the pocket of her slacks and she pulled it out. The screen showed a number she didn't recognize. Nine o'clock at night. She cautiously hit the answer button. "Yes?"

"Grace?" The voice shocked her. Jack.

"Yes," she said a bit cautiously.

"Sorry to call out of the blue, but Parrish gave me your number." She recognized Jack's voice. "I hope that's okay."

"Why did he give it to you?" She hadn't meant to be so blunt, and she immediately regretted her words.

"He thought firsthand beat secondhand."

Before she could ask what he meant, he said, "Have you figured out when you're coming back this way?"

"Actually, yes. We're leaving here the day after tomorrow."

"Flying?"

"No, driving."

"It's a nice drive coming in from the west."

"I bet it is," she said, but thought of all the desert area in Arizona her maps had shown. She wanted to just ask, *"What's the real reason you're calling?"*

Then he told her. "Have you made any decision about the ranch?"

She felt like saying, "I'm staying," but didn't want to make that commitment yet. Just in case. "I'm still considering everything," she finally said.

"When you get back, we can do boundary rides."

"What's that?"

"We'll ride and follow the boundary of the ranch so you can see everything, get a grasp of the size and how it has to be handled."

"Thank you," she said, "But I told you there are no horses at the ranch, and I—"

"I'll bring one for you."

That surprised her. "Oh, no, you don't have to—"

"No, I don't, but I will. I wouldn't mind riding the boundaries myself. It's been a long time since I did."

"We'll talk when I get back," she said, but thought she'd rather not get on a horse again in this life. Her two experiences as a kid had been less than fun. She didn't want to repeat them. She should have told him that when he'd asked if she rode or not. "Okay, then, you have a good trip," he said, and the line went dead.

She slowly closed her phone, and sank back on the sofa. Her mother came out of the bathroom and crossed to sit down beside her. "Making a call?"

"No, I just got a call from Jack Carson."

"What did he want?"

"To find out if I'd decided about the ranch or not."

"How did that go?"

She shook her head. "It didn't, because I didn't tell him. I said I still needed to figure some things out."

Her mother turned toward her. "Why?"

"I just don't want to put him off if it turns

out we have to sell. Maybe he's the kind who gives up easily. I need to know that, if this venture fails, we still have an out."

Her mother shook her head. "I'm afraid I taught you too well about covering your back."

"No, you taught me to be smart and careful, to not go off on some tangent and to ignore the future." She didn't add, *"Like my father always did."* Both women already knew that.

WHEN GRACE, LILLY and Gabriella finally drove between the stone entry posts at Wolf Ranch, Grace felt as if she'd come home. Just two days at the place, and it felt right to be there. Her mother quietly took everything in and Lilly, in her navy overalls and yellow T-shirt, her hair up in twin ponytails, didn't stop talking.

"Look, Mama, it's smoking behind us!"

Grace glanced in the rearview mirror. "No, sweetie, that's dust, dirt going up in the air."

The child had already turned to something else that amazed her. "Oh, look, a bird!"

A covey of small birds burst out of the tangle of dead weeds, rocks and dried grass.

They flew with squawks up into the air and out of sight. Lilly laughed. Then she spotted the stable. "Is that the house?"

"No, it's the stables. That's the place where the horses and chickens can stay."

"Oh!" she gasped, and Grace watched her eyes widen with wonder. "Horses?" she whispered.

"No, maybe a horse," Grace corrected, slowing the car to a crawl so her mother could see the house as they approached it.

"Oh, Gracie, it's nice." Gabriella's voice held almost as much wonder as Lilly's. "Really nice and big."

"Yes, it is," Grace agreed and pulled to a stop by the porch steps. "We're here," she said, and Lilly quickly undid her seatbelt and pulled her door open. She was out in a flash, running across the dusty ground, heading for the porch. She took the single stone step at a run, then turned to Grace, who was just getting out of the car.

"Hurry! Hurry, Mama," she called, motioning with her tiny hands for Grace to catch up.

The air was warm, but not oppressive, and the house did look welcoming. Parrish had tamed the dead weeds in the front and had come up with a few chairs to put on the porch. "I'm coming," Grace said, leaving everything in the car to go to her daughter. She took out the key and handed it to Lilly. "Open the door," she said. Lilly managed to get the key in the slot and Grace helped her turn it until the lock clicked open.

The door swung back and the little girl suddenly became very still. Her large bright eyes peered into the great room, then finally she looked up at her mother. "Can I?" she asked hesitantly.

"Of course," Grace said, then added, "It's all yours."

With that, Lilly was off, darting here and there in the great room, all smiles and squeals. She disappeared into the hallway, doors opened and closed, then she was back, grinning ear to ear. "Can I go outside?" she asked, almost skidding to a stop by Grace.

Gabriella came up behind Grace and touched her on the shoulder. "I'll watch her while I get things out of the car."

"Okay, but please, watch out for snakes, or…things."

"Come on, pumpkin," she said, offering her granddaughter her hand. "Let's go explore."

Grace watched Lilly jump from the porch to the ground, bypassing the stone step completely. Putting both hands high above her head, she began to twirl and laugh.

The stable doors moved back and Parrish stepped out into the sun. He looked up at the house, then smiled and waved to Grace. "Welcome back," he called.

She returned his smile, then saw Lilly shrink back a bit toward her grandmother. Grace had drilled into Lilly never to talk to strangers or go with them. And Parrish was a stranger.

The older man strode up toward them, and as Grace reached her mother and Lilly, he took off his straw Stetson. "Mom, Lilly," Grace said. "This is Parrish, the caretaker. Parrish, my mother, Gabriella Michaels, and my daughter, Lilly."

"Right glad to meet you both," he said, then turned his attention to Lilly. "Ever been on a ranch before?"

Lilly was still a bit hesitant, pressing against her grandmother's leg. Shaking her head to make her ponytails dance, she said, "Never. But I was at the zoo once and they had lions and tigers and a really weird alligator."

"Sounds great, but a ranch is more about horses and cows and chickens."

That did it for Lilly. Grace could see her ease a bit. "Horses?" she asked in that young awestruck voice again. "Really?"

He glanced at Grace, as if to say, "What do I tell her?"

"Yes, most ranches have horses," Grace said, "and maybe we'll get one someday. Who knows?"

Parrish nodded. "We've got the perfect stall for a horse, maybe a Paint, really pretty, with brown spots. We can get it all fixed up so it would be ready if you ever get one." Parrish looked at Grace. "You all want to come down and look at the stables?"

Grace shook her head. "I've seen them, but I know Lilly and Mom would love to take a tour."

"Great," he said, motioning them to follow him. Lilly took off at a dead sprint and was waiting by the open doors by the time the other two got there. Grace watched all three disappear into the darkened interior, then she turned to the house

She stepped inside, feeling good about her daughter's total happiness. So far, so good, she thought with real relief. So far. Slowly, she walked around, just touching the walls and fireplace, inspecting things she'd missed on her first visit, and ended up in the kitchen. When she opened the refrigerator she was surprised to see replenished staples…milk, eggs, bacon and butter. Parrish must have done that and she appreciated it.

She went back to the front door and out onto the porch. But instead of going to the car to start unpacking, she sank down on the stone step and just sat there. The peace was almost tangible, the same way it had been the first day before Jack had broken it. Complete and so very welcome. With her arms around her knees, she looked off into the distance, and the only sounds she heard were coming from the stables, laughter and a high-pitched squeal, then more laughter.

No matter what his motives, her father had done a good thing for all of them. "Thank you," she whispered into the air, and felt an almost childish wish overcome her that her father could see all of this.

At that moment, a sharp cry came from the

stables and Grace was on her feet running before she even began to figure out what she'd heard. Almost out of breath, she raced into the semidarkness of the stable and headed down the aisle to her left. "Lilly? Lilly!" she called.

Rounding the corner near the tack room, she came to a stop to find her mother sitting on a hay bale, holding Lilly to her, while Parrish hunkered down in front of the two. "What happened?" she asked breathlessly, grabbing Parrish by the shoulder.

"It's okay, Grace," her mother said in an even voice. "She's okay, just a bump."

Parrish was putting down a towel and picking up a bandage . "She's fine," he said as he eased the bandage onto a small scrape on Lilly's elbow. The child whimpered, but the tears were gone. "She tripped over a rake I should have put away and scraped her arm on the side of the stall." He slowly stood and looked at Grace. "Nothing at all."

Lilly was already squirming off her grandmother's lap. "Nothing at all," she echoed, and showed her bandaged arm.

"Okay," Grace said. "If you're sure?"

Lilly nodded. "I'm sure."

"Ready for some lunch?" she asked.

Lilly hesitated. "But Mr. Parrish said he'd show us where the rabbits run."

"It's a pasture to the east, a nice little nook that is sort of a rabbit haven at the moment, since the land isn't being worked." He looked down at Lilly and held his hands about a foot apart. "Some of them rabbits have ears this long!"

She started to bounce in place. "Please, Mama, can't we go see?"

Grace looked at her mother. "Why don't I get the things out of the car and you go on a rabbit hunt." When her mother nodded agreement, she looked at Parrish. "Just, please, be careful of the snakes. I need to get Lilly boots as soon as I can."

He shrugged, "Of course." He looked down at Lilly's sandals. "Thing is, you gotta have on good shoes to do this, not necessarily boots, but not sandals."

Lilly's face fell. "I don't have any boots."

Grace broke in. "She has high-topped tennis shoes, and Mom has some too. Would that be okay?"

He nodded. "Sure would be better than sandals."

Five minutes later, the three of them set off with bottled water to see the rabbits' run.

Grace managed to make some sense out of Lilly's bedroom and her own, and by that time the rabbit hunters were back. Lilly was glowing. But as Parrish headed back to the stables and the others went into the house, the little girl yawned, then rubbed her eyes.

"How about you take a nap, and when you wake up, we'll have a late lunch?" Grace suggested.

Remarkably, there were no cries of, "naps are for babies," or "I'm too big for a nap." Lilly just nodded and took her mother's hand. Within a few minutes, she was fast asleep on Grace's bed.

She went back out to find her mother in the kitchen. "Did she really go down that fast?" Gabriella asked. "She's exhausted." Grace sank down in a chair at the table. "Just worn out."

"No wonder." Gabriella came to sit across from Grace. "She never stopped running the whole way there, and when she spotted the rabbits, it was off to the races! Even if she caught up to one of them, she wouldn't have known what to do with it."

They both laughed, then her mother said softly, "It's lovely in here. It's so much more than I expected."

"Me, too." Grace laid her hands flat on the table top. "You know, no matter why or how Dad did this, it's perfect. He'll never know how perfect."

Gabriella sat silently for a long moment. "Just because he couldn't use it for himself doesn't mean he didn't know it would be good for us."

She was right, not defending the man, just seeing the way it all came about. "Yes, absolutely. I just wish that there wasn't baggage with it."

"Baggage?" Gabriella frowned.

"Just Jack Carson, the man who wants it back. I wish he wasn't in the picture."

"I thought we agreed that his wanting it makes it more secure for us if things don't work out. He's our backup plan."

Again, she was right, but it didn't feel as comforting to Grace as it had before.

## CHAPTER EIGHT

GRACE MOTIONED TOWARD the hall that led to the bedrooms. "I put your bags in your room, the first door you come to, and Lilly's room is next. She's sleeping in my room at the end of the hallway, in the back, for now. There are two bathrooms, and the bigger one has an old claw-foot tub."

"Better and better," her mother said, leaning back in her chair. "What was Parrish saying about a horse? I thought you hadn't decided yet."

"I asked him to look around for me, for a smaller horse, safe for kids, and for someone to give her riding lessons. I don't even know what a horse costs, but I'm sure it won't be cheap."

"You might be surprised."

She looked at her mother and narrowed her eyes. "What do you know that I don't?"

"Parrish wants to talk to you about it, but

Jack Carson told him about a nice horse that the man in the General Store owns. Used to be his granddaughter's and she's getting too big for it. She wants a horse she can use for 'barrel riding,' whatever that is."

"How does that make it cheap?"

"Parrish spoke to Oscar and Oscar said that he'd let you take the horse for one month, as a trial, and if you like it and Lilly likes it, he'll take three hundred for it."

Grace was surprised. "I'd heard a good horse was more like three thousand."

"He said that she's a good horse, but not a purebred. Her name is Mosi—it means cats or something like that."

"Wow, you two worked in a good conversation on your rabbit hunt."

"He seems to be a really nice man, very good with Lilly."

"I'm glad he's here," Grace admitted. She shifted in her chair, then brushed at the hair that was coming loose from her ponytail. "That horse sounds perfect. I mean, there is a trial period and all. I just wish I knew more about horses."

"Jack Carson recommended it, so that seems like a seal of approval."

"Lilly's going to want it, I know. And once it's here, it won't go back, not unless it's mean or bites."

"That's all good," her mother said.

A rap on the door caught their attention and Grace went across to answer it. Parrish was standing there. "Ma'am," he said. "I was wondering if you want me to start doing anything with the irrigation. I got the wells primed and they look good. Next step is trying them out."

"Oh, I guess we should. Sure, if you can."

"No problem."

She felt her mom come up behind her, and Parrish flashed her a smile. "So, where's the little one?"

"Sleeping," Gabriella said. "We wore her out."

"Parrish," Grace said. "That horse of Oscar's, it sounds good, but I don't know."

"If you'd like, why don't you go ask him about it, then go see it. He lives on land south of town, not too far."

"I don't know."

Her mother spoke up. "Go now. Then you can figure this out for yourself."

"But Lilly needs to eat and—"

"Since when are you the only cook around here?" her mother teased her.

"Okay, but I won't be long." She looked back at Parrish. "Thanks for finding out about the horse."

"No problem." He looked past her. "Finger okay?"

Grace turned and noticed a bandage on her mother's right forefinger. "What did you do?"

"Nothing, just got a sliver in my finger from the fence, but it's fine. Mr. Parrish gave me the same treatment as he did Lilly." She held up the finger. "See?"

"And she didn't cry," the man said, deadpan, then turned and ambled off.

"I need to go into town to find mattresses for you and Lilly," Grace said, "and I could check on the horse while I'm there."

"Good idea, the mattresses, I mean. What's a bed without one?"

"Uncomfortable," Grace said and they both laughed before Grace hurried to get her bag, and with one last look at a sleeping Lilly, she headed into town. As she drove onto the main street, she resisted the urge to stop at a couple of the shops, but kept going. The day was clear and warm, no clouds in sight, and the town seemed to gleam in the sunshine. She spotted the General Store, then glanced across the street and one down to see a faux wood-fronted, two-story building with a shingle, Law Offices, hanging from the front fascia. The building sat between a real estate office and a rug shop.

On impulse, she swung left to park by the law offices instead of the general store. Her mother needed a job and she'd been a part-time paralegal on and off. Maybe she could find out if there was any work like that in the area.

She pushed open the door and stepped into the reception area as a bell sounded above her. She stopped by a large desk in the wood paneled space that fronted three doors in the back wall. There was no sign of anyone, and the only sound was soft music coming from hidden speakers. "Is anyone here?" she called out.

Footsteps sounded on wooden floors, then the middle of the three doors opened and Jack Carson stepped into the room. He wore an open-necked white shirt, dark slacks and boots and his face was stamped with the same surprise as she knew hers must be.

JACK HAD SPENT most of the day in the office trying to concentrate on a case of disputed water rights and going over one of two applications for a replacement for Maureen. But his ability to concentrate had been close to none, the way it had been since Grace Evans had showed up at the old ranch two weeks ago. He'd been fighting the urge to call her again and now she'd materialized out of nowhere right in his office.

His breath hitched in his chest as he crossed to the desk. "Welcome back."

"Thanks," she said, glancing at the application he still had in his hand. "I'm sorry if I'm interrupting a meeting with your attorney."

She was as small and blonde as he remembered, the blue shirt she wore with jeans and those sandals only emphasizing her delicateness. She looked up him, waiting, and he finally got himself on track.

"I'm the only attorney in the place, and my assistant has obviously gone on some errand."

She looked flustered and shook her head. "Oh, I didn't know you're an attorney."

"You were looking for one?" he asked, part of him thinking she wanted to get paperwork ready to sell and the other part thinking she wanted to have someone check the papers so she could keep the ranch.

"No, well, yes. I was just going to ask if there are any openings for a paralegal position here."

He knew she was a waitress, so why would she be asking about a paralegal position? "You're looking for work?" His heart sank at the logical conclusion. She was staying. When he found out from Maureen that she'd given up her lease on her apartment in Los Angeles, he'd thought that was that. She was going to come back and stay. Then he'd decided that she could be giving up the lease and moving to a better place.

He knew he wasn't going to stop hoping he could get back his family's land until she told him for sure that she wasn't selling. "Just seeing what's available," she said.

He wasn't a liar, but he wasn't about to tell her about the position for an assistant in his office that would be open at the end of the month. Instead, he hedged with a partial truth, "The office isn't running up to speed right now. Maybe in the future."

She turned away with a quiet, "Thank you."

He didn't mean to cut her off, to have her leave, but before he had a chance to stop her, she turned back to him.

"You know, I'm glad I ran into you," she said. "I really wanted to thank you for telling Parrish about the horse that the man at the General Store wants to sell."

Jack was blank for a minute, then remembered his talk with Parrish. "Oh, sure, are you going to try her out?"

She grimaced. "I'm on my way there, but I don't know anything about horses."

"I grew up with them, had one since I was old enough to walk." He hesitated a moment. "If you're on your way there now, I can go with you. I can tell you if she's good or not."

He could almost see her thinking, should she or shouldn't she, then she nodded. "That would be a huge help."

He went around the desk, tossed the application he still held onto the file cabinet by Maureen's chair, then crossed to where Grace stood. He wanted time with her, ways to make her see how challenging ranch life could be, and that a large chunk of money was much better than a chunk of dusty New Mexico land that meant nothing to her.

They went out together and crossed the road to the General Store. Once inside, Jack spotted Aaron, Oscar's nephew, a tall, gangly boy of seventeen. "Is your uncle around?"

"No, he's back at the place, got problems with the irrigation, so I get to hold down the fort. You need something I can help you with?"

"We just wanted to talk to him about Ashee's horse, the Paint. He said he wanted to sell it and get his granddaughter a cutter for barrels."

"He's out there, if you want to go and see the horse."

Jack turned to Grace. "What do you say? Like to drive out there with me, and we can both check out the Paint?"

"I guess so," she said without a lot of conviction. She turned to the teenager. "Do you by any chance have mattresses for sale?"

"No, don't have any, but I'm sure someone around here could get you one."

"I need two, actually."

Jack watched the exchange. "None at the house?"

She looked at him. "Just one, but I need two more."

He nodded, then without saying anything else, the two of them headed to his parking spot behind the law office and got in his Jeep. As they drove through town, they passed a huge glass and iron building, the sign announcing Wolf Lake Hospital. The building was as modern as the rest of the town was determinedly quaint.

On the other side of a huge parking area stood a massive brick building with Wolf Lake Family Center chiseled over the entry portico. Grace had been silent until then, but she finally spoke.

"For a small town, Wolf Lake has the best amenities I've seen in a long time, even in Los Angeles. The school, that Family Center, and the hospital. Are they all flash and show or are they well run, too?"

"They're every bit as good as they look," he said and told her about the Family Center's work with local kids who were challenged or needy. He found himself telling her about Gage and Merry. "My brother helped design both places, and he and his fiancée are going to adopt a little girl whom Merry's been helping at the center."

As the hospital fell away behind them, he

kept talking. "The hospital is really good, too. Exceptional, actually. One of my oldest friends, Moses Blackstar, is the chief of staff, and a terrific doctor. He oversees the twenty-four hour emergency care and a clinic on the Rez as well."

Jack stopped himself, wondering how that was going to discourage her from living here permanently. He'd forgotten for a bit that his job wasn't to sell Wolf Lake to her. He glanced at Grace, but she was staring out the side window. He found himself reaching out to touch her arm and he could tell he startled her. "I'm sorry," he said. "I just wondered if you had any more questions."

She finally turned and met his gaze before he looked back to the road that was now cutting through pastureland on both sides. "No, just thinking," she said softly.

"I was wondering what you're thinking about this place, about your ranch and this town? Is it too isolated? Too rough? Too bleak?" He stopped himself. He was being too obvious. He had to keep quiet and let her ask questions, then go from there.

"Actually, I like both the town and the ranch, I think. I know the ranch needs a lot of work, and it's a whole different way of life for me, that's for sure."

"Yes, I'd expect it is."

He heard her take a deep breath, then let it out softly. Finally, she said, "There is something I need to tell you."

Jack flashed her a look, but she was staring at her hands clenched together in her lap. "What is it?" he asked, hoping against hope she'd already figured out that this place wasn't for her.

"I need to be honest with you. I should have said something earlier, but was worried if I did that you would withdraw your offer on the ranch permanently."

He slowed the truck as the entrance to Oscar's ranch came into view. "What are you talking about?"

"I want to give living here, running the ranch a try. I need to, but if I fail, if it all goes wrong, I don't want to just lose everything." He stopped by the closed gates and turned to her. The knuckles of her clenched hands were white. "My mother always taught me to have a backup plan." Those violet eyes met his. "You're my backup plan."

He stared at her, then realized what she was

saying. She'd try, and if she failed, she wanted him to bail her out by buying the ranch. "If you mess up, you'll sell the land to me?"

"Basically," she murmured.

It wasn't the clean break he'd hoped for, and it wasn't going to happen tomorrow, but soon, it would happen soon. He knew it. She'd cave sooner or later. A sense of relief seeped into him. Up to now he'd been afraid she would shut the door forever, but she hadn't. She hadn't even locked the door, let alone shut it for good.

She stared at him, then finally said, "Well?"

"Well, what?"

"What do you think?"

"I don't believe I've ever been anyone's backup plan before."

She blinked twice, then managed a slight smile. "You're not angry?"

"No, I'm not angry," he admitted truthfully. As high color tinged her cheeks, he wondered when the last time was that he'd seen a woman blush.

GRACE FELT FOOLISH, unable to keep eye contact with Jack. She'd thought he'd be offended by the truth—that he'd walk away, but he appeared to be fine. She felt her tension ease, and was grateful. The minute she'd seen Jack come into the reception area at the law firm, she'd known she couldn't lie to him anymore. And she'd expected him to ask her about her decision right then and there. When he hadn't, she'd decided she had to be honest with him. Just to get it over with. And now she had.

He wasn't angry, he wasn't pouting, and he was actually taking her to see the horse for Lilly. It was amazing. "I'm sorry," she said softly, just to make very sure he understood she really was.

"Forget it." He put down his window and pressed a button in a raised key pad by the Jeep. She heard a squawk of static, then a voice.

"Who's there?"

"Jack Carson for Oscar."

"Come on in," the crackly voice said. "Down at the pump house."

Jack drove through the gates as they swung open. The ranch was called *Nava Heaven*. Three separate drives led from the gates, and Jack took the one to the left. They drove under towering cottonwoods that almost formed an arch overhead. Rounding a curve, the trees thinned, revealing a panorama of grasslands beyond. He kept driving, heading for a corrugated metal building where a tractor sat by open double doors.

They had barely pulled to a stop by the tractor, when Oscar came out of the building's shadows. He squinted, rubbed his face with a red kerchief, then headed over to them. Jack got out and Grace followed.

"Hey, boy," he said to Jack, then nodded to Grace. "Ma'am. What're you all doing out this way?"

"Looking for you," Jack said. The two men shook hands. "We came out to see that Paint you said you were thinking of selling."

Oscar looked back into the metal building. The whining and thudding of a piece of machinery filled the air. "This'll wait," he muttered. "Can't get the darn thing to the bottom thirty." He tossed the kerchief onto the seat of the tractor, then motioned Grace and Jack to follow him. "I need a break, come on."

They made their way back toward the trees, then cut through a passageway made for large vehicles. When they stepped out they were in front of a huge barn with stables on one side.

"Here she is," Oscar said, going to one of

the corrals where a small white horse with two-toned brown markings calmly nuzzled a hay holder.

"This is her. Pretty and even-tempered. A good combination, but my granddaughter's wanting to get into barrels and she's a rider, period. I thought we should find a new home for Mosi. Not being rode much can break a horse's heart."

The Paint lifted her head, her soft brown eyes on the people coming toward her.

"She's got a nice form," Jack said.

"Been here since she was a yearling, trained up fine, good ride for a six- or seven-year-old, but not for a pre-teen. No problems. No bad habits."

Grace tentatively reached out and touched the silky side of the horse's muzzle. The animal stood quietly, letting Grace stroke her. "She seems so calm."

"She is, Ma'am," Oscar said. "I told Jack, if you're interested, she's yours for a month. A trial, because some horses and kids don't mix. That's a fact. Got to make sure things are right between the horse and rider, before you make a commitment."

Grace looked at the horse and braced herself. "I heard you'd want about three hundred for her."

Oscar came closer, touched the horse on the muzzle and she snuffled softly. "That'll be fine, or whatever you think she's worth to you and your kid. I'll throw in her saddle too. She's real used to it and it's comfortable for a little person."

"That sounds fine to me."

Oscar smiled at her. "Then it's a deal."

Jack stood close behind her. "You're going to do it?" he asked. "The feed store in town delivers hay and grain, and Parrish has the stable pretty much ready to accommodate her."

Grace looked into the soft brown eyes of the horse and nodded. "Okay, you've got a deal. A month's trial." Then she had a thought. "I don't have a trailer or anything, and I'm not sure—"

Oscar cut her off. "No worry. Jack's got a trailer, a double. That should do it." He looked past her at Jack. "That work for you?"

"Sure," he said.

"Then it's settled."

Jack surprised her when he asked, "Any idea where she can get two mattresses.

I'm guessing they need to be doubles?" He glanced at Grace and she nodded.

"Actually, I have a couple in storage, almost new, real clean." Oscar looked at her. "I'll throw them in with the horse."

"Thank you," she said quickly. "Thank you very much."

Five minutes later, Grace and Jack were in the Jeep again, pulling away from Oscar's ranch and back toward town. Grace glanced at Jack. The man was silent, watching the road ahead, and gave no indication what he was thinking.

"I appreciate all of this," she said.

He cast a sidelong look at her, his dark eyes as unreadable as his expression. "It's a good deal. Oscar won't do you wrong."

"That's a relief," she said. "Can I ask you something?"

"Sure."

"What is the busiest and best restaurant in town?"

"The Place fills both criteria," he said as they got closer to the hospital. "Upscale, good food and it's a busy place most weekends, with both locals and tourists."

It sounded interesting, especially if she did

evenings and her mother could find something for the daytime. "What sort of food?"

"Steaks, and everything that goes with them," he said.

"Sounds good."

"How about going by there now?" he asked out of the blue.

She looked at him again. "Excuse me?"

"I'm hungry and I'd like some company for a very late lunch." He looked at her as they stopped at the main street. "What do you think? Do you have time for it?"

Grace didn't know what to say. For a fleeting moment, she actually thought she'd love to sit in a nice restaurant and talk, but that thought fled as soon as it materialized. Not a good idea, partly because she was refusing to sell Jack the property, but mostly because he was a married man. She glanced at the simple gold band. That wasn't cool. And she didn't want to blurt out, "Wouldn't your wife mind?"

Instead, she settled for, "You must have places to be, people to see, judges to talk to."

He grinned at her, letting the Jeep idle. "No, I don't. I was ready to leave for the day when you showed up."

Then she said it. "Wouldn't your wife mind?"

For a moment, he just stared at her, then turned abruptly and focused on the cars passing in front of them. "I was just asking you to lunch," he said.

She was thankful he wasn't looking at her when she felt the fire in her face. She hadn't meant to imply anything else, but obviously he'd taken it that way. Before she could say she was sorry, he spoke. "Do you want to come or not?"

His expression was grim. She didn't miss the way his hands gripped the top of the steering wheel, and she suddenly realized she didn't want to be responsible for this tension. "Yes, I am, if you still want me to."

He didn't say a thing as he eased the Jeep onto Main Street, heading back the way they'd come. Neither spoke as they headed west, then Jack pulled the Jeep into a parking area to the right of a stylized, two-story, Victorian house. Pretty plants lined the front of the property, and there was gingerbread trim and slate-blue clapboard siding.

They got out and walked up to the entry. Inside the home, the foyer was huge, decorated with cabbage rose wallpaper, thick oriental carpets and dark mahogany chairs and small tables. A dark-haired woman dressed in a simple white blouse and midcalf slim black skirt came out to greet them.

"Jack!" She smiled warmly. "Hello there. I haven't seen you in a week of Sundays." Without hesitation, she hugged him. "Darn good to see you." She turned to Grace. "Hello, and welcome to The Place."

Jack finally spoke up. "Grace, this is Clare Money, owner of the restaurant."

"And wife of Terry Money, the other owner," she grinned and held out a hand to Grace, her grip firm. "So, you're new to town?"

Grace nodded, and wondered what Clare knew about her and the ranch. "Yes, I am. Jack recommended your establishment."

"Good, I'm glad he did. Doing late lunch or dinner?"

Jack glanced at Grace. "Either," she said.

"Okay, both." Clare grabbed some menus, motioning them to follow her.

They stepped through a wide doorway trimmed with heavy burgundy curtains and down into a large circular dining area with tall, narrow windows lining it on two sides. Clare led the way to the back area, and put them at a table with two high-backed velvet chairs and a stunning view of a lush garden and the low lands that rose up to meet the mountains.

AFTER THEY WERE SEATED, and Clare left to get them coffee, Jack turned to look out the windows. He had an overwhelming urge to ask for another table. This one had privacy and that great view. He didn't really want either right now, not with this woman. But he didn't move. He watched Grace staring out the window, and wished everything didn't look so incredible. Her eyes were almost shining with appreciation.

Slowly, Grace turned to him. "This country is incredible, just incredible." Before he had to think of something to say, she shrugged. "But I guess you're totally used to it."

He sat back in the chair. "I guess I am."

"And you know everyone in town?"

He took in the slight smile on her pale lips. "Most."

"Well, you know Clare."

"Sure, I went to school with her and Terry

way back in the dark ages. Terry's from the Rez and Clare came here when she was maybe four or five, from Seattle, I think."

The dining room was only a third full, if that, and he watched her glance around, then back to him. "Do you know everyone in here now?"

He followed the direction of her gaze, scanning the other diners, then turned back to Grace and nodded. "Guilty. All but one, and I think he's probably a college friend of those two women he's sitting with. They said he'd be visiting them around now. So, maybe technically, I do know them all."

She smiled, her forearms on the white tablecloth, slender hands lightly clasped. "You know, that makes me a little jealous."

# CHAPTER NINE

BEFORE JACK COULD ask why she was jealous of him in any way, a waitress came to the table. "Welcome," she said, a smile on her round face. "Nice to see you again, Jack. It's been too long."

Jack knew Jacquie, too. She was from the Rez, maybe late-twenties, and going to night school to get her teaching credentials to work at the school where she lived. "You're ready to order?"

Jack knew what he wanted, but Grace hadn't made a move to look at her menu. "Maybe a few more minutes," he started to say, but Grace shook her head.

"It's okay, I'm ready if you are?"

"Sure," he said.

"I'd just like a plain cheese omelet with cheddar cheese, and mild salsa, if you have it. Also, a side of fresh fruit and whole wheat toast."

"Absolutely," the waitress said with a smile, then turned to Jack. "The usual," he said and she left with nod.

"See, that's what I mean. You know everyone in here, and all you had to say was 'the usual.' The waitress knew exactly what you wanted. And I bet you aren't in here every day, either, maybe once a week or every two weeks."

She'd nailed him. "And that makes you jealous, because?"

"I've worked in restaurants for years, and every once in a while I've had a customer who would come in for a few days in a row, but none ever stuck around. I could walk into any restaurant myself in my neighborhood and they wouldn't know me and I wouldn't know anyone either. That's par for the course."

He could see where this was going. And he couldn't deny any of it. "L.A.'s a huge city. Wolf Lake could be dropped down in the center of it and no one would notice."

"You're right. Because no one notices, period."

Jacqui brought their coffees, then headed back to check on their food. Jack knew what Grace meant. He'd been in L.A. for his college and law school, and when he'd come home he'd made maybe two good friends he still kept in touch with. "That might seem nice and comforting to you, but it can backfire. Everyone knows everything about you." He smiled at her. "That can get a bit uncomfortable."

"Tell me about it," she said.

He studied her. "You say that as if you've had firsthand experience."

"No, just everywhere I've gone here, people know about the ranch and that...." She shrugged. "You know, the details, and they aren't happy. Not with me, they've been nothing but friendly, but in general they seem to be offended by the whole deal."

"Wow, I'm sorry, I didn't realize that more than a handful of friends knew what my dad had done."

"If the whole town is considered 'handful of friends,' then you're right."

Her eyes held a glint of humor in them, and he was glad she didn't feel offended by whatever the townspeople had said to her. He didn't want her run out of town on a rail, just discouraged enough to realize that Wolf Lake wasn't right for her or her family.

"They mean well," he said as he reached for his coffee mug. Inadvertently his wedding ring clinked on the heavy ceramic.

He almost drew back, but made himself pick up the coffee and take a sip. Grace had asked him what his wife would think about her having lunch with him. Jack knew if Robyn was still alive, none of this would be happening. "Just tell her you're a widower," he ordered himself, but he knew he wouldn't do that.

"You get used to it," he said instead, setting the mug back on the table with a dull thud.

Right then, the waitress appeared with their food. Jack's "usual" was eggs and steak, and he'd been more hungry than he thought. Grace finished everything as well except a half slice of toast before she nudged her plate away from her.

Their eyes met and he found himself smiling easily at her. "You've got a good appetite," he said.

"I always do." She laid her knife and fork on the almost empty plate. "My mother's the same way. She can eat a horse and be ready to eat again if you offer her a good dessert."

His smile grew. "And she's as tiny as you are?"

"Two inches taller, but I think she's the same weight as when she was a teenager." She sipped the last of her coffee.

"Is your dad the same?" he asked, and the smile tightened on her face, then faded away.

"I really don't know. I haven't seen him since I was three, and my memory of him is pretty sketchy."

"Why did he give you the ranch?" The question was out before he realized he was going to verbalize it.

Her face stayed tight, but she answered simply, "I have no idea. He didn't tell the attorney anything either. The closest I can figure is, maybe he had an attack of conscience about abandoning us like he did, and since he can't stand to be anywhere for too long, the idea of a ranch didn't appeal to him, so he got rid of it and eased his guilt in the process. Then again, maybe he doesn't have a conscience."

She spoke the words without emotion, but Jack knew there must be a ton of pain behind them. Charles Michaels tossed away his whole family. In a way his own father had done the same thing, not by leaving, but by drinking.

Swallowing his anger at both men, he shrugged. "He doesn't know what he's missing," he said, and didn't mean the ranch. How could a father walk away from a three-year-old daughter and never look back? That was unthinkable to him.

"Why did your father let the ranch go?" she asked abruptly.

Tossing his napkin on his plate, he said bluntly, "He was drunk, so drunk he didn't know he'd even lost the land until he saw it in writing." Jack forced himself not to flinch when an unconnected memory hit him hard. His father, passed out with an empty bottle of whisky, almost two years ago, when Jack had needed him the most. When Robyn had died.

The fight had been explosive on both sides, culminating with Jack walking out of the main ranch house and not speaking to his father for almost six months. By then his dad was sober, and a truce had been formed. Now that truce was shattered.

Before she could probe any further, he asked her, "Was your father addicted to gambling?"

He regretted the question when that familiar blush rose in her cheeks, but it was her eyes that made his breath catch. The pain in their lavender depths was raw as she spoke in a slightly breathless rush.

"No, he was addicted to having no ties, no demands, nobody telling him what to do or where to go. He just happened to support that lifestyle by gambling and, obviously, still does."

He was surprised at how her words affected him. Abruptly, she stood, and tugged a wallet out of her pants pocket. Before she could take out any money, he tossed some bills on the table to cover their tab. "I've got it," he said, and she didn't argue.

They drove back to his office, and she was out of the Jeep almost before he'd stopped. "Thanks for taking me out to Oscar's, and for lunch," she said.

"I'll send a man over to Oscar's with the trailer and get the horse out to the ranch and hopefully the mattresses," he said before she could rush off. "What time's good for you?"

She hesitated. "Anytime. Parrish should be there if I'm not." With a "Thanks for everything," she swung the door to the Jeep shut.

Jack got out and went around the back of his vehicle to her compact sedan. When she started to pull the door shut, he grabbed it by the frame. He didn't know what else to say, but felt he had to say something for both their sakes. Then it came to him. "You know, the less we talk about our fathers, the easier things might be for us."

Grace looked up at him for a moment, her eyes touched by that sadness again. "Yes. I agree." Her tongue lightly touched her lips. "Thank you for everything."

This whole situation had gotten so confusing, and Jack knew he needed to refocus. Her decision to try to make the ranch work could be a good compromise for him. The best, of course, would have been a quick turnover in his favor, but at least she hadn't cut him out as a potential buyer if she decided ranching wasn't for her. She was staying for the moment and his best bet was to remain as close to her as he could. He'd be patient, until she realized she was in over her head and the best way out was to sell the ranch to him.

GRACE DIDN'T UNDERSTAND this man who looked down at her so intently.

"How about the perimeter ride I mentioned before?" Jack said. "We can follow the property line all around the spread, and you'll have a much better idea of what's ahead than just trying to walk it."

His eyes held hers expectantly, as if he really wanted to do this. She couldn't figure out why. What was in it for him? "I'm sure you have other things to do."

"To be honest with you, I'm working as little as I possibly can right now. I've got time on my hands."

"But I still don't have a horse, and probably won't get one, other than Lilly's." Even if she had a horse to ride, she wasn't totally convinced she'd be able to stay on its back.

He waved that concern aside. "No problem. I've got a horse you can use, a nice and easy Bay. I'll come over around dawn tomorrow before there's any heat, and we can start the tour then?"

She wanted desperately to see as much of the ranch as possible, but it seemed awkward to have the man who wanted her land to show her around. An unsettling thought flashed in her mind. She was actually beginning to enjoy spending time with Jack, even though she didn't know much more about the man himself than when they'd first met.

"I guess we could give it a try," she said. "But not tomorrow. I have some important things to do."

"Okay, the day after, then, early as possible." He didn't give her a chance to refuse, just stood back and swung her door shut for her.

Quickly, Grace started the car and pulled out onto the street. Stupid. What if she got on the horse and fell right off, or worse yet, the animal took off with her on it? She cringed at the idea of trying to stay on the beast and carry on a conversation with Jack at the same time.

She was almost halfway back to the ranch before she realized how totally preoccupied she'd been just thinking about riding with Jack. She'd totally forgotten she wanted to get some supplies at the store. Debating whether to turn around or go tomorrow, she decided that going back was better. She didn't know what would be entailed getting Lilly registered and probably into school the next day.

Making a U-turn, she headed back and in minutes was parking in front of the General

Store again. Getting out, she quickly took the two steps up onto the walkway, and would have gone right inside if a tall woman, with black hair falling down her back, hadn't stepped right in front of her. The two almost collided, but both managed to step in the opposite direction. "Nice move," the woman said, her loose sweatshirt and jeans as casual as her makeup-free face, but not nearly as relaxed as the fuzzy pink bedroom slippers she was wearing.

Grace chuckled. "You, too, especially with those slippers on."

The woman glanced down. "That's what comes from living right next door. I've been known to run over here in my bathrobe early in the morning when I run out of food for my guests."

Grace glanced behind her, then back to the woman. "You work at the bed-and-breakfast?"

"I own it." She held out a slender hand. "I'm Mallory Sanchez."

Grace took her hand. "I'm Grace Evans."

"Oh," Mallory said, and Grace braced herself for the now familiar response. "I've heard about you and the Wolf Ranch."

"You're Willie G.'s niece, aren't you?" Grace said, remembering.

"Please, don't blame me for that. No one asked me who I wanted for an uncle." Mallory laughed. "He's great, actually, just very determined and a bit crotchety at times. I, personally, think it's terrific that you're out there. That place has been empty for so long, way too long."

Grace felt relief and a bit of gratitude that someone had finally said it was good for her to be there. "Thanks for that."

Mallory read her right. "Oh, you're getting some flack, aren't you?"

"No, just, well, under the circumstances and all, this hadn't been a very welcome change for the people around here."

"Oh, sure, I understand about the Carsons and the Wolfs. That ranch has been theirs forever, I guess. But they all have their own lives, and more land than you could shake a stick at." She frowned slightly. "Now, Jack, I do feel for him. After everything, maybe he just can't lose any more."

Jack lose? "What about Jack?"

Mallory hesitated. "I meant, after all he's gone through."

Grace didn't understand. "He seems to be doing okay. He's got his work and his family. I mean, his father gambling away the land was a terrible thing to do, but it's not life and death."

There was a look of sadness in Mallory's dark eyes. "No, it's not. But it's important, maybe too important for him."

"I understand he wants it. He's even offered to buy it if I decide to sell."

"I mean, it's just another loss in his life," she said softly.

"What other loss has he had?"

"His wife, Robyn, died in an accident about two years ago and we haven't been sure since then that he'd make it. This land business is the first thing he's had any interest in since her death."

Grace stared at the woman. In a town with a penchant for knowing and talking about everyone else's business, not one person she'd met, including Jack, had even hinted at him losing his wife. With a sickening realization, Grace finally came close to understanding what was behind Jack's need to get the family land back. "It was going to be a home for his wife and kids?"

Mallory looked around. "Do you have a few minutes?"

"I suppose so."

"Come on into Oscar's and we can get some coffee. I know I need it. That's why I'm over here. I ran out because of all the guests."

Grace wasn't sure she wanted to know much more, but she did need an answer to her last question. "Okay," she said, and followed Mallory into Oscar's and a handful of tiny tables by the front windows.

"Sit and I'll get the coffee," Mallory said, heading toward the kid at the counter who had been in the store earlier.

Grace glanced out the window, watched the traffic, or what passed for traffic in Wolf Creek in the late afternoon. A single car crawled past in the three minutes Mallory was gone.

"Here you go," Mallory said, handing Grace a steaming mug and motioning to a small pail on the table. "Cream and sugar." Then she sat back. "So, you're from L.A.?"

"Yes, I am, or I was."

"So, you're staying?"

"I…yes, I am. At least, I need to see if I can do this or not. I'm not sure."

Mallory nodded. "I know the feeling. My husband passed away a few years back, about six months before Robyn's accident. Henry and I had the B&B, and I didn't know if I should keep it or sell it. I finally decided that I'd try to keep it going, and if I couldn't, I'd let it go."

"How did that work for you?"

"I'm still taking it a day at a time." She took a sip of coffee, then put down her mug with a shrug. "It's simpler that way. Day by day. So far, it's worked out."

To hear Mallory put it so simply and so clearly resonated with Grace. "That's it exactly. I want to make this work, I need to, but I'm not sure I can."

"If you can't, then what?"

Grace shrugged. "I don't know. I guess sell, then move on, but I don't want to do that. I've done that all my life, from rental to rental with my mom, then with my mom and my daughter."

"You've got a child? No one told me that."

"Lilly is six years old. She's the most important person in my life. I'm doing this to make a home for her. For all of us."

"Henry and I wanted to have kids, but we

were so busy we didn't really have the time, then there was no time left." She segued without a blink of an eye. "Robyn was a teacher at the Rez school, loved kids so much, and Jack loved her more. They wanted kids, they always did, but it never happened. Then she was gone."

Grace felt her throat tighten, and asked her question again. "They were going to live on the ranch?"

"I don't know. I never heard Robyn talk about that. All the time I knew them, they lived in the loft over his law offices. With Robyn's work on the Rez, their place in town made it easier for her to do extra tutoring with the kids."

Jack had lost everything, she realized, by losing his wife. "I thought…Jack seems to love the ranch."

"That ranch was always special to the Carson boys growing up. Their grandpa was the center of their universe. He died a year before Robyn passed. Maybe if they'd had kids…." She shrugged. "As I said, it's been hard for Jack."

"You know the family well?"

"Oh, sure, and Moses Blackstar, a good

friend of mine, well, he's been close to all three of the Carson brothers since they were really young. He's probably Jack's best friend, or maybe it's a tie between Moses and John, the local chief of police. People around here tend to stay friends for life." She chuckled. "Mostly because they don't leave here for very long before they head back."

"Jack mentioned Moses. Isn't he the doctor at the hospital?"

Mallory nodded, then looked past Grace and smiled brilliantly. "Oh, hello," she called out, waving someone over to the table.

Grace turned to see a man approaching them. He was medium height, with short black hair, a sturdy build and dressed in gray slacks, a checked cotton shirt and the ever-present cowboy boots.

"Speaking of Moses," Mallory said, "here he is."

He looked down at Mallory with as much pleasure to find her there as she'd shown at seeing him. He touched her shoulder. "Glad I found you," he said in a deep voice.

"Grace was just saying that Jack's been talking about you."

The man looked at her with eyes so dark

they seemed black. "Grace? Not *the* Grace Evans?"

"Exactly," Mallory said.

Grace wasn't surprised that he knew about her. It seemed anyone who had contact with the Carsons knew about her. She took the hand he extended. "Nice to meet you. Jack told me a bit about your work at the hospital."

Moses grinned. "Don't believe anything he said."

Mallory went to get another mug and Moses pulled a chair over from another table.

"It was all good," Grace assured him.

"Oh, then he's absolutely right about everything," the doctor said. He looked at Mallory, seated beside him. "So, how did you get to know Ms. Evans?"

"I literally ran into her just a bit ago," Mallory admitted before she took a sip of her coffee. "I thought, since she's on the old Wolf Ranch, and she'll be dealing with Jack and the Carsons, she ought to know a bit about them."

"Such as?"

"About Jack."

Moses's face sobered, and Grace could see

concern or pain in his midnight eyes. He exhaled, but all he said was, "Oh."

"I appreciate it." Grace fingered the warmth of the ceramic mug in front of her. "I had no idea why Jack wanted the ranch so much."

"It's not the ranch he really wants," Moses said, his voice low.

"Then what is it?"

"Maybe a reason to be here, I don't know. I don't do psychiatry or that sort of thing. I almost wish I did." He looked at Mallory and seemed to shake himself slightly, as if he didn't like the direction his thoughts were going. "I really just came in on the way back from seeing…." His voice trailed off. "A patient," he said finally. "That elderly lady that's your guest, she told me you were coming over here. So, I wanted to double check to see if we're on for tonight?"

"Oh, yes," Mallory said quickly, and Grace didn't miss the slight flush in her cheeks, or the lowered lashes.

"Great," he said, then stood, taking another sip of coffee. "Unfortunately, I don't have time to finish this." He smiled at Grace.

"Welcome to Wolf Lake. I really do wish you all the luck with that ranch."

"Thank you," she said, and meant it.

He looked as if he was going to lean toward Mallory and kiss her, but he just reached over and touched her chin with the tips of his fingers. "See you later," he said, then left.

Grace looked at Mallory. "So, you're dating?"

Mallory made a face. "Is it that obvious?"

Grace smiled. "A bit. He seems very nice."

"He's terrific. I never thought I'd ever…." She shrugged. "How about you, you're married?"

"Was," Grace said, surprised that the old bitterness didn't find its way into her tone. "He left, and it's just me and my daughter, and my mother." She stood. "I need to get some supplies and get back to the ranch. I've been gone too long."

Mallory stood up, too, and waved away Grace's attempt to pay for their coffees. "I'll take care of it," she said, and called over to the teenager. "Aaron, tell Oscar I need coffee, regular grind?"

"Sure, Mallory," he called back. "I'll bring it on over in an hour or so, if that's okay?"

"Just fine," she said, then turned to Grace. "I enjoyed meeting you like this. Come on by when you're in town again, and we can visit some more?"

"I'll do that," Grace said.

"What is it they say in L.A.? Oh, yes, 'We'll do lunch.'"

"I've never said that, but I'm sure someone has." Grace smiled at Mallory as the woman left the store.

She made her way over to the meat counter. Jack's wife had died. Jack had loved her. Jack wanted the ranch. Maybe he needed it. She felt an ache in her middle thinking about his loss, not sure how she could survive if a husband she loved were to die. Maybe she wouldn't. She didn't know, because she had never loved a man like that. Never.

It shocked her that for a single moment, she felt the same twinge of jealousy she'd experienced in the restaurant earlier. It made no sense, but it was very real and almost brought tears to her eyes.

# CHAPTER TEN

AS GRACE GOT back to the ranch and pulled off the highway onto the dirt drive, she experienced that feeling of homecoming again. She relished it. Slowly, she drove by the stables and stopped her car. But this time it wasn't to look at the house. Instead she watched Lilly running around, blowing bubbles and laughing as they floated up into the sky.

Her mother sat on the porch step with Parrish, smiling at the little girl. Grace had always hated the way people overused the word awesome, but right then, her world looked awesome. She drove up to the house, and Lilly was at her car door before she could make a move to get out.

"Mama, Mama, hurry!" she cried, grabbing the handle and swinging the door open.

"What is it?" Grace asked, sliding out into the warmth of the day.

"We got a cat!" Lilly jumped up and down

and clapped her hands together. "A real, real cat!"

They hadn't even been on the ranch for a full day, and they already had a horse coming and now a cat. She looked over at Gabriella and Parrish. They both smiled and shrugged.

"It will be a good mouser," Parrish said. "It's been hanging around the stables for a week or so, and I haven't seen one mouse in all that time."

"Come on," Lilly said, grabbing Grace's hand. "Come see Sunny!"

Gabriella nodded. "She's a ginger cat, really friendly."

Parrish stood and came toward Grace. "You need a few more at the stables to keep down the vermin population. She's a mouser, but she'll be outnumbered sooner or later."

"We'll see," Grace said, then Lilly had her by the hand, tugging her toward the stables.

JACK GOT TO his parents' ranch later in the day and made arrangements for one of the stable hands to go to Oscar's to pick up the horse and mattresses for Grace and drive them over to the ranch the next morning. When he saw his father's truck parked by the house, he headed back to town without seeing his mother.

Maureen was at the office, sorting through a large filing cabinet by her desk. She swiveled her chair around as he came in.

"I have a proposition for you," she said as he was about to walk past her to his office. "Are you interested?"

Maureen's eyes looked quizzical behind her rimless glasses. "If it's about investing in your new business, I told you, I might. I'm thinking about it." He leaned his hips against the desk. "I'll be sure to let you know soon."

She shook his comment off with a wave of her hand. "No, nothing like that. It's about your Mrs. Evans."

That got his attention. "What are you thinking?"

"She seems to be in love with the idea of having her own ranch, is that about right?"

"I'd say so."

"She's in over her head with it, you believe that?"

"Absolutely."

"Then help the poor girl."

That made him frown. "What are you talking about?"

"Look around, find another piece of land that's set up for a ranch, but a hobby ranch, in a good location, green and well cared for, then push her toward it."

Her suggestion surprised him, mostly because he'd been thinking the same thing. A smaller, manageable place that he could offer her in trade for the old ranch with some added money to sweeten the pot. But he'd let that idea go. He'd realized in the time he'd spent with her that it wasn't just any ranch she longed for, it was the one she owned. Despite the pain her father had obviously caused her, the ranch was a gift he'd given her, a tenuous connection that might be all she had from him in this life.

"I thought of that, actually," he admitted to his assistant.

"And?"

"I doubt it will work, at least, not yet."

He stood to go into his office, but Maureen wasn't through. "What, are you giving up on getting the land back?"

"Oh, no," he said. "That'll never happen. I'm doing what I can do, for now, and hopefully things will turn around."

"Now, that's cryptic," Maureen said with

a growing smile. "Oh, P.S., I saw you with her just after noon, driving west out of town. What's that all about?"

"Went to Oscar's to look at a horse he has for sale."

She shook her head. "So, you're helping her settle in?"

"No, I'm not. But she didn't know anything about buying a horse, and I offered to take her out there to look at it."

She held up her hands. "Okay, okay, that sounds logical, being a Boy Scout." She frowned up at him. "You *were* a Boy Scout when you were a kid, weren't you?"

"Not even close," he muttered and walked to his office.

Before he shut the door behind him, he heard her say, "I should have figured."

He'd barely settled behind his desk when the door opened and Adam strode in. His uniform was gone, replaced by jeans and a T-shirt. With no preamble, he came to the desk, pressed both hands flat on the polished wood to lean forward and demanded, "Tell me, what in the heck do women want from men?"

Jack tipped his chair back, and clasped his hands behind his head. "Beats me."

"Great! Just great!" Adam turned and started pacing. "I thought you'd have some ideas."

"What's going on?"

Adam was silent as he paced back and forth, then he turned on his heels to approach the desk again. This time he dropped down in one of two chairs used for clients. "I never expected to love someone, I mean, really love someone, in this life. I thought that was all some greeting card sentiment, then Faith came to Wolf Lake, and it was a done deal the first time I saw her." He ran a hand over his face roughly, then raked at his hair, spiking it. "I love her. Just plain love her."

Jack braced himself. "You broke up with her?"

Adam's head shot up. "Oh, no, no, not even close."

"Then what's wrong?"

"Everything. She's in Chicago and I'm here. This isn't the way it's supposed to be. Especially not now."

"Why now? Is it this mess with Dad? Or her dad's problems?"

He looked blank for a moment, then his dark eyes widened slightly. "No, no, no. It's just I have to tell you something, but you can't tell anyone else, and I mean, no one! Not John, not Gage, especially not Maureen. I'm telling you because you never spill anything, even by accident. You'd laugh off torture to keep national secrets."

"Okay, okay, just tell me."

"Okay, I—"

Jack stopped him. "First, give me a dollar."

"What?"

"Give me a dollar," he said, holding out his hand.

Adam frowned, but dug in his jeans' pocket and found four quarters. "How's that?"

Jack reached across the desk to scoop the coins out of his brother's hand, then sat back. "Okay, now whatever you tell me, I can't tell anyone else, because you're now my client."

Adam barked a laugh at that. "Good old Jack, you always had a way to make things work out."

For some reason, Grace Evans came to mind. No, he couldn't always make things work the way they should. He was flying by the seat of his pants with that woman, making it up as he went along, intent on keeping her from reaching that final decision to never sell the old ranch. "No flattery, just tell me what's wrong?"

Adam hesitated. "Nothing's wrong, not *wrong*, but…."

"Come on, spit it out," Jack said.

Adam sat back, resting one booted foot on the opposite knee, and nodded. "Okay. We're married."

That brought Jack straight up in the chair. "You're married?"

"I wasn't about to leave Faith in Chicago to deal with that mess with her father, it just wasn't doable." He sighed. "So, we went to a justice of the peace, got married, and I stayed with her."

Jack looked at his "baby brother," and finally grinned from ear to ear. "Wow!"

"Yes, wow!" Adam was grinning too, but sobered quickly. "Now, she's there and I'm here, and no one can know."

"Why not? Everyone would be thrilled." He paused, the memories of his marriage to Robyn as fresh as if it had happened yesterday. The joy, that feeling of completeness. A pain settled in his middle, but it eased when he thought of what Adam had found with Faith. "Mom would absolutely love to have Faith as a daughter-in-law."

"I know, I know, but she'd also want to be there for the wedding."

"How are you going to manage that?" he asked. "Time travel back to the past?"

"Another ceremony, one here, at the ranch, small, just family. Her father might be able to get permission to leave the state in another three months, right around Christmas. Faith thought we could pull it off and no one would need to know we're already married."

"Devious, but probably not a bad plan," Jack admitted. "I agree, but I didn't know how hard it would be for Faith to be in Chicago and me to be here. And when she finally comes out here, how's that going to work?"

"That's your problem, bucko," Jack said with another grin. "You can figure it out."

"I was hoping Gage would take the heat off of me, now that he and Merry are engaged."

"I wouldn't worry. Mom's preoccupied with other things these days. Lately, I don't even go to the ranch unless I have to."

"I know," Adam said. "I just needed you to listen, I guess. It's been eating me up inside, not being with Faith every day." He stood with a shrug.

Jack came around from behind the desk. "Congratulations," he said and hugged Adam. For a second, he thought about Grace and her saying how jealous she was of him fitting so well into this town, having friends, people who knew him. But right then, he was the one who felt jealous. Adam was married. Adam was totally in love. And Jack was happy for him, but he still couldn't suppress that twinge of envy.

"Anything I can do for you about the property?" Adam asked.

Jack remembered he hadn't told anyone about Grace's response to his offer to purchase the old ranch. He sat back on the edge of the desk and folded his arms on his chest. "She's not selling…."

"Oh, man," Adam said. "I am really sorry."

"Don't be, it's not final. She wants to try and see if she can make a go of it on the land. If she can't, I told her my offer's waiting, and if she can…." He shrugged. "That won't happen. She won't be able to do it."

"How so?"

"You know she's from L.A., and, as far as

I can tell, she's never even been near a farm or a ranch."

"So, you're okay with just sitting back and waiting?"

"No," he said honestly. "I can't do that. I'm going to keep close enough to make sure she realizes she's in over her head sooner rather than later."

"That's your plan, to be negative about everything?"

"No, realistic. There's a huge difference."

"If you say so. If I can do anything to help, let me know, okay?"

"Sure, but one question?"

"Shoot."

"Why didn't you tell Gage about you and Faith being married?"

"Because I figured you'd understand, having been there." He stopped, heaving a huge sigh. "Boy, I'm sorry," he said. "I wasn't thinking."

"Hey, no problem." Jack meant it. People watched what they said around him too much. Life was what it was, and they shouldn't have to censor themselves for fear of offending him. "Maybe you'll get lucky and Gage will hurry up and make a big splash of a wedding."

"Wishful thinking," Adam said.

Jack stared at the closed door long after his brother had gone. He found himself thinking about Grace again. If things had been different, he would have genuinely hoped she'd make a go of it on his grandpa's ranch. She was excited, her eyes bright whenever she looked out over the land. He slowly straightened and flexed his shoulders. Tomorrow morning, they'd do the perimeter ride, about a third of it. He'd make it last for at least three or four days, giving him plenty of time to be honest with Grace. He'd lay out the way ranches operated and all the work they required, especially one that needed a full overhaul. Day after tomorrow. He again sat down behind his desk.

He shook his head. When was the last time he'd actually looked forward to something? If he thought about the future, all he'd seen was a void, something he had to fill any way he could. But not now. He looked at the paperwork on the desk and ignored it. Instead, he left as soon as Maureen had closed up the office.

Standing on the walkway, letting people pass him by, he gazed out at the town. Adam was married, Gage was looking forward to his marriage and an instant family when he and Merry adopted Erin, meanwhile, Jack was going to take a ride with Grace Evans. A small step, he told himself. But an important one. And at the end, he'd have the ranch.

WHEN JACK RODE his horse up the drive toward the old adobe house, leading a gentle Bay behind him, dawn was just spreading in the east. He didn't see anyone around. Then the front door opened, and Grace slipped out onto the porch. She was dressed in jeans, a pink tank top and what looked like boots, actual boots on her feet. She waved to him, then headed down the steps. He could see her smile even from a distance.

He stopped by the porch, dismounted, and undid the Bay's reins from the loop on his saddle. As he turned to Grace, who was right behind him, he thought for a minute that another Grace was coming out of the house. The woman wore jeans, too, with the same slender frame, but her pale hair had as much gray as blonde, and was only long enough to brush her neck. She was about two inches taller than Grace, and he guessed this was most likely her mother.

The woman smiled at him, and Jack noticed her eyes were a silvery-blue, not violet. "Good morning," he said to the two of them.

"Hi," Grace said, and lifted her foot. "See, boots. Safe from snakes."

"Very nice boots."

Grace put her foot down. "Lilly's still asleep on the lovely mattress Oscar sent. She's worn out from never leaving that horse's side all day yesterday. She would have slept in the stable last night if I had let her."

"So, she likes Mosi?"

"Absolutely, and thank you so much for getting her over here for me."

He waved off her thanks. "Not a problem." He glanced at the other woman. "I take it you're Grace's mother?"

"Oh, I'm sorry," Grace said. "Yes, this is my mother, Gabriella Michaels. Mom, Jack Carson."

"Very nice to meet you," she said pleasantly, then she frowned. "I am very sorry for the way this turned out for you, but I can promise you that this property will be in good hands."

"That it is," Parrish said as he came out of the stable. "Very good hands."

Jack felt outnumbered and decided to forego a comment. "I brought a horse for you," he said to Grace. "Gentle, a good ride. My mother rides her occasionally, but she needs exercise."

He watched Grace eye her mount. "She looks fine."

Parrish spoke to Gabriella. "Can you come and help me gather up the toys the child left down here yesterday? Don't want that pretty horse to choke on a three-inch toy stallion."

Gabriella laughed, and with a wave to Grace and Jack, she took off with Parrish into the stables. Grace went to check on her daughter, then came back out with a small bottle of sun block. Jack watched as she started to rub it into her arms and shoulders. As if she felt him watching her, she held the tube out to him. "Want some?"

He shook his head. "No, thanks." He glanced at her bare head. "You'd do well to think about getting a hat, something light, maybe straw."

Her hand went to her pale hair, touched by streaks of gold from the rising sun. "Oh, yes, I found one." She ran back inside, reappearing with a floppy straw hat. She pulled it on, the wide brim all but hiding her face. "This will do."

"Let's get going," he said and turned to the horses. He watched Grace approach her mount, cautiously reaching out to touch the animal's muzzle. She jumped back when the horse shook its head and whinnied. "Just take it slow," he told her.

She nodded, her eyes never leaving the horse. "What...what's her name?"

"Lucy," he said, but Grace didn't make a move to get on her back. "Slowly go around to her left side, and get up in the saddle."

"Sure," she agreed, but without much conviction. Slowly, she made her way around the horse, grabbed the saddle horn and the back of the saddle, then tried to hoist herself up. She didn't go more than a few inches before her boots hit the packed earth again.

Jack moved behind her. "Let me give you a boost," he said, spanning her slender waist with both hands. "Now, pull," he instructed her, at the same time swinging her up. She felt light as air, and he could feel her breathing. Then she was mounted, and the connection was gone.

"Okay, okay," she said, a bit breathlessly. "Got it."

"Good." He stroked the horse's neck. "Now, hold the reins loosely. She'll follow my horse, just give her her head."

"How?" she asked, her hands gripping the saddle horn.

He almost laughed at her question, but instead, he picked up the loose reins and held them out to her. "Just hold them loosely, and she'll do what she needs to do."

GRACE TOOK A deep breath, accepted the reins and tried to relax. Jack went to get his horse, swung up into the saddle in one easy motion, then came up beside her. "Ready?"

She really wished she'd told him she was allergic to horses or something like that, or maybe that she'd never ridden at all. The truth was, her only rides had been a disaster, but then again, she'd been very young, and scared to death of the horse. Now she just felt awkward and a little afraid. She didn't know what she'd do if the horse suddenly took off. "Yes,

I'm ready," she lied, staring at her hands holding the reins.

"Grace," Jack said.

She made herself turn and look at him. He was smiling at her, that dimple showing up again. "What's so funny?"

"You. You look like you're going to your execution. Just relax. Let your hands relax with the reins, and breathe. Just breathe. Your horse will go wherever mine does. I promise."

She flushed, knowing her face had to be scarlet. She'd thought she could pull this off, but she'd been wrong. "Easy for you to say," she muttered.

Jack clicked his tongue and his horse started off. Without any prompting, her horse followed Jack's mount, even when Jack headed west. Maybe she would be okay, after all. She'd just act as if she knew what she was doing, but as they skirted the stand of trees and made their way into the open pastures, Grace felt every step the horse took. She tensed each time they came to a rise in the land and she began to wonder how long she could stand the pummeling against the saddle before she begged Jack to stop and let her walk.

"We'll head toward the west," Jack said over his shoulder. "Then north, toward that boundary near the mountains."

She made herself look ahead, instead of at the ground passing beneath her. The mountains were impressive. She thought she caught sight of the Rez, but wasn't sure. The distant shapes shimmered, almost floating into the turquoise sky. "How far is it to the boundary?" she asked, and could hear the breathlessness in her voice. Thank goodness Jack didn't seem to notice.

"Not far. Once we get there, we'll head along the boundary and see how far we can get before the heat gets too bad." He turned to meet her gaze. "How are you doing?"

"Fine, fine," she said, looking away from the man and his dark eyes before he could read the lies there.

"I have water if you need it," he called back.

"Good to know."

They rode in silence, Jack just a bit ahead as they kept to a narrow trail cutting through the weeds and scattered low shrubs. Grace watched Jack, the way his muscles rippled under his thin cotton shirt. He looked as assured and confident on his horse as she was uneasy. But he'd been riding most of his life. Maybe in a few years, Lilly would be a good rider, probably a lot better than Grace would ever be.

"We're going to cut northwest," Jack called back to her. "And there's a bit of climbing, but the horses know the way." He pointed into the distance. "That way."

Her horse slowed as the ground got rockier, and Jack seemed to be getting farther and farther ahead. "Come on, get going," she urged the Bay, but it didn't alter its pace.

Jack twisted in the saddle to look back at her, obviously sensing the problem. "Just gently nudge her with your knees. Light touch. Hold the reins loosely, resting your hands on your thighs. And find the horse's rhythm. Every horse has one, just find it and go with it."

If her horse had a rhythm, Grace couldn't find it, but after a bit, she felt herself give in to the jarring and rolling. Her misery was offset by the spectacular scenery, and as they got higher, she realized they were almost above the buttes and mesas, now far off in the distance behind them. "My property runs up this far?" she asked.

"No," Jack called over his shoulder and kept going, almost circling the last butte, but the horses took the incline easily. Amazingly, as the sweetness of pine touched the air, she realized that she hadn't worried about the horse, or staying on for a while. But when Jack slowed again and dismounted, she was more than a bit relieved.

He dropped his reins on the ground and his horse stayed put as he came back to her. "Let's get off for a bit so I can show you some things around here. He looked up at her and when she didn't move, mostly because she realized her legs were almost numb, he put up both hands. "Come on," he said, spanning her waist and lifting her up and over, then off the horse.

Her legs were weak enough that if Jack let her go right then, she would probably have fallen on her face. But he didn't let go, just shifted his hold on her to her shoulders, steadying her.

"You need your land legs," he said with a wry smile.

Boy, did she ever. She tried to take a step,

but found herself reaching to grab his forearms. "For Pete's sake," she muttered, "This is worse than the one and only time I was on a boat and got off on the dock." She'd save the explanation that she had fallen to her knees and couldn't get up.

"It happens to everyone when they haven't ridden for a while," he said. "We went a bit too long without stopping. I'm sorry."

She tipped her head to look up into his face. He was sorry. Well, she was embarrassed, especially when she realized that she liked the feel of his hands at her waist, his touch on her shoulders. That was crazy! She shook her head. Even with a hat, maybe she had sunstroke.

"Let me know when you're steady," he said.

She tested her legs, felt they were more stable. "I think I'm okay. You can let me go."

The instant Jack released her she felt an odd sense of loss. Immediately she pushed it aside. Her life was complicated enough right now.

# CHAPTER ELEVEN

"WHERE TO NOW?" she asked. She'd been so intent on the horse and riding, and Jack, that she had no idea where they were, other than closer to the mountains. They'd climbed quite high to get here, and massive rocks rose up out of the ground.

Jack secured the horses to a small tree near a boulder as big as a car, then came back over to Grace. "Okay, let's go," he said.

She fell in step with him, her back and calf muscles sore as they climbed a rough trail that looked as if it had been well used over the years. Just when she thought she couldn't go any further, Jack turned and held out a hand to her, pulling her gently up to a level lookout. When she turned back to see how far they'd come, the view almost overwhelmed her. She inhaled the sweetness of the air and gazed at the land below. The idea of it being hers was getting more and more real and she loved it.

Then she realized Jack had said they weren't on her property now. Turning to him, she found him studying her. "Spectacular, isn't it?" he said, his eyes narrowed to the glare of the sun.

"Yes, but you said we aren't on my land anymore."

"We cut off back a ways. I'll show you the surveying stake when we go back down."

"Then why are we up here?"

"Because we can see all of the ranch land from here."

Jack pointed to the west and a huge pine, knotted and distorted by wind, heat and storms. "That's the top northern edge of the ranch." He walked in the opposite direction and stopped almost at the end of the level lookout, waiting for her to catch up. No trees or rock formations blocked the view from here. "Now you can see where you are."

She looked down and she actually thought she could make out the old adobe far off in the distance. The tree stands, the dry pastures. "Is that the house?"

"Yes, it is." He turned and pointed up toward the mountain behind them. "The Rez is up there, and the Rez land goes down the mountain and ends at my parents' property line."

She was staggered by the amount of land she now owned. More than she'd ever dreamed of. Then again, she'd hardly even imagined having a house of her own. Jack motioned her to the edge of the lookout and dropped to the ground, letting his feet dangle over the side. He indicated the spot beside him on the rock. "Sit," he said.

Carefully, she inched forward, then slowly sat down. Lowering her legs to dangle over the side made her stomach lurch. She had no idea she was afraid of heights until she saw the sheer drop-off. Bracing herself, she sat very still, focusing her gaze up and away. No way could she look straight down.

"Over there," Jack was saying, pointing to a huge spread with sprawling green pastures that flowed from a central grouping of buildings. She didn't have to ask. It was his father's ranch. She'd only gotten a quick glimpse on their earlier walk. Now she was stunned at the size of the operation.

"That's incredible," she said and meant it. "It's like a piece of art, like *American Gothic* or something."

He chuckled softly. "I think you're right. It's been totally transformed from the land Grandpa came down to claim. It was raw territory back then. It took three years before he could bring his kids and my grandmother down to live there. All the irrigation, the plowing, everything was done from that point on. He dug the wells, fenced everything, raised stock and seven kids. All on his own."

JACK COULD FEEL Grace watching him and listening closely. But he didn't take his eyes off the ranch spread out below. "It was nothing but work for everyone. My mother used to follow the tractor and break up dirt clods along with my two uncles when she was about five years old. MawMaw, my grandmother, cleaned houses in the town before it was a town." He felt himself drifting back, the stories of his grandfather flitting through his mind.

"You must have been really proud of your grandparents."

That didn't begin to explain how he'd felt. And still did. Or how devastating it had been when his father's stupid actions had lost a huge chunk of that heritage. He pushed back and stood. "Are you up for a bit more climbing?" he asked.

Carefully she scuttled backward, away from the drop-off, then scrambled to her feet. "I guess."

He moved off, and Grace followed him up the rough steps cut into the granite bluff. It was just a short climb to an area rimmed on three sides with huge boulders and sheer rock facings. Two or three charred areas held the remnants of recent campfires, and a torn piece of red fabric had been mounted like a flag on a long stick and shoved in a cleft in one of the boulders.

"Kids still come here," Jack said as he kicked at some of the ashes.

He pointed to the far northwest, then moved his hand in a half circle in front of them. "If you stand right here, every acre of land you can see was once, or still is, Wolf land. Some of it went for the town, the rest was broken up into parcels for each of the seven Wolf kids. Three of them built on their land, my mother, and her two brothers, Aaron and Daniel. The other kids branched out, but kept the land. An uncle in Minnesota still has his and leases it out for grazing." He didn't add that the only piece that had been lost from the Wolf Grant was hers. Three hundred acres, the smallest spread, yet the most important to him.

He looked over at Grace. She had taken off her hat, and the light breeze lifted the stray tendrils of her pale hair, making them dance in the golden sun. "That's incredible," she breathed softly.

"Yes, it is." He'd wanted to point out the hardships, the struggle it had been to build the ranch, and still would be to restore it to working order. But all he'd done was bring back the past, making him feel the loss of his grandfather's land even more keenly.

He turned abruptly, his arm hitting Grace in the shoulder. He hadn't realized she was so close. She grasped his arm to steady herself, and on impulse, he reached out and brushed her cheek with his fingertips. Her warm skin felt silky to him, and it stirred something inside him that made him jerk back as if he'd been burned.

"Sorry," he said quickly. "You weren't going to fall."

"I know," she whispered, then her face twisted in a grimace. "My hat. I dropped it."

He looked around, but no hat was in sight,

then he went to the edge and looked down. Far below, caught in a clump of wild sage growing out of a split in the granite, was her hat. "There it is," he pointed out, but she didn't move. When he turned, Grace stood hugging herself, just staring at him. Then it hit him. "You're acrophobic, aren't you?"

She shook her head no but stopped. "Yes."

He walked over to her. "You should have told me."

Finally, she looked at him, her eyes wide. "I didn't know until now," she said. "I've never sat on a ledge like that before."

He should have felt that he'd scored a point. Her land included property with rocky cliffs at high altitudes, and she couldn't avoid them. But that didn't seem to matter right now. All he cared about was the fear he saw in her eyes.

"Let's go back," he said.

She turned almost before he'd finished speaking and headed down to the horses. He followed her and untied the animals, holding the reins out to Grace. She reached for them with an unsteady hand, and he was hit by a jolt of protectiveness that came out of nowhere. "No more rides up here," he said.

She bit her lip, like a child who was trying to control their emotions. And all he could think of was comforting her some way. But that wasn't up to him. Not even close. "It was just such a drop," she finally said in a barely audible voice.

"Now I know about you and heights, we'll rethink our rides, okay."

"Yes, thank you," she said, and turned to Lucy, trying again to get up in the saddle.

He was hesitant to help her the way he had before. But when she sighed with frustration, he went over to her and lifted her up. For a moment, her body was close to his and even when she was in the saddle and he moved away, her fresh scent lingered.

The day was over for him. He needed to get her back to the ranch, to get some distance from her. He looked down at his hand holding the reins and his gold wedding band glinted in the light. He really needed to rethink his plans.

He took the direct route back, not following the property lines, and by the time they got to the old ranch, he was edgy. Every sound from Grace ran riot with his nerves, and he was aware of her behind him every moment.

After what seemed forever, the old adobe came into sight.

"Thank you again for doing this for me," she said in a rush.

He didn't answer her, just shrugged and urged his horse in the direction of the house.

GRACE FROWNED AT Jack's back as he rode off. Part of being a good waitress was being able to read your customers accurately. But Jack Carson had her stumped. She thought he'd wanted the land more than anything, that he'd make an offer, then keep at her until she gave up and sold it to him.

But he hadn't even mentioned buying back the place. He'd made a joke about being a "backup plan" for her, but since then he hadn't brought up the subject. As they'd overlooked the panorama of his family's land, he'd spoken about his grandparents and their hard work with obvious pride. But he'd never once reminded her that she had what he wanted. Not once. And since she'd told him about her decision to try to make a go of it, she'd been waiting for the other shoe to drop.

Maybe that was why she felt so edgy now. Why she'd overreacted when he'd accidently bumped her. Why she'd let him steady her. She didn't know, and found she didn't want to spend time figuring it out. She had enough to worry about without wondering why Jack Carson acted the way he did.

They passed the house and rode down to the stables. Grace half expected Jack just to keep going.

She managed to get off the horse herself, lifting her right leg over the saddle, then sliding down until her boots hit the ground. Not graceful, but she'd done it.

Jack dismounted, too. "Let's leave Lucy here until we've finished the perimeter rides. Is that okay with you?"

"I guess so. Parrish has some stalls cleaned."

"Okay." He dropped his horse's reins and took Lucy's from Grace.

She followed him and the horse into the hushed stables. No one was around, not Lilly, or Grace's mother, or Parrish. She thought they were probably in the house. Jack led the horse back near the tack area, lightly looped her leads over a wooden rail and methodically unsaddled her. Quietly, he went about rubbing her down, talking to her in a low voice as he worked, then spoke without turning to Grace.

"The Paint's gone."

She looked around. He was right. Mosi's stall was empty. "I didn't see them outside anywhere, did you?"

"No," he said, putting the brushes back on their hooks.

"You don't suppose they'd let Lilly try to ride the horse, do you?"

"You got it for her to ride," he pointed out as he tossed the saddle blanket over the side of the nearest stall.

"Yes, but—" She backed up against the wall as Jack led the horse over to an empty stall. "Lilly needs lessons and—" All she could think of was her own first horseback ride, and how it had left her with bad memories.

His dark eyes met hers with an intensity that took her aback. "If you're going to live this life, sometimes you just have to let things happen," he said, then reached for the stall door and led Lucy inside.

He came out, secured the door, then Grace said, "So they just let kids do anything they want out here, even things that can hurt them." She hated the way her tone got louder and accusatory.

Jack shook his head. "Of course not, but ease up. She's with your mother, obviously, and probably Parrish, who seems to be very capable. So, things are good until you find out they aren't."

She actually heard herself say, "You have to have a child to understand what it feels like to be a parent."

She literally wanted to put a hand over her mouth, hating the way Jack's features tightened, his eyes narrowed. He hit the lock on the stall door, the sound of metal on metal clanging in the air. "Then I don't understand," he muttered.

Why had she said that, knowing what Mallory had told her about Jack and his wife. She couldn't believe how callous her comment was, how out of line. But just one look at Jack's face and she knew an apology wouldn't amount to anything. Instead, all she could think of was a vague generality that was better than nothing. "I'm just a bit overprotective."

"She's your responsibility," he said and walked out.

She hurried after him, and by the time she caught up, he was on his horse, starting toward the driveway. She didn't get a chance to say or do anything else before he said over his shoulder, "See you in the morning."

"Wait, I'm not sure about the morning."

That stopped him. He reined his horse around, looking back at her. "What?"

"I got Lilly registered at school yesterday," she called without going over to him. "She starts tomorrow. I can't leave until she's in school."

He was very still, then nodded. Okay, we'll wait until then." Without another word he turned, riding off down the driveway.

Grace stared after him, still feeling badly about what she'd said. Then she realized he didn't know what time Lilly started school. Maybe he wouldn't be back tomorrow. She almost couldn't blame him if he didn't show up.

Maybe that wouldn't be so bad, she thought as she headed to the house, hurting all over with each step. She needed a long, hot bath, but first she had to find her mother and Lilly. As she went inside, she took out her cell phone and called her mother.

Gabriella picked up on the third ring. "Hi, Grace," she said in a slightly breathless voice.

She stopped. "Mom, where are you and Lilly?"

The rush of wind sounded in the background, and she could hear Lilly laughing. "Out by the water station for the eastern grazing area."

She sounded as if she had been on the land all her life. Without asking what a "water station" was, Grace got to the most important question. "What's going on with the horse? It's not in its stall."

"Lilly got tired of talking to her through the stall door, and Parrish had an idea. Instead of Lilly hanging out at the stables until you got back from your ride, we all went on a walk, and Lilly is very, very happy and excited."

"And she's not riding Mosi?"

"No, no, we're leading her, walking her behind us. Parrish said it's a good way for Lilly and the horse to get to know each other. You know, bond." Grace could hear Parrish in the background. "Parrish says we'll be another hour or two, if that's okay? I need a breather before we start the trek back."

"That's fine," she said, relief leaving her weak in the legs. Then she had a thought. "What about snakes? Have you all got on good footwear?"

"Yes, we're properly shod," Gabriella said. "And we all have sticks with us."

She had no idea how sticks would help in a snake encounter, and maybe she didn't want to know. "See you in a while."

After hanging up, she started the tub and stripped out of her dusty clothes. But even after a hot bath, she couldn't get past the lingering guilt of her comment to Jack. After she'd dried and dressed in shorts and a blue tank top, she padded barefoot into the bedroom and started to put away some odds and ends. When she opened the bottom drawer in her dresser, she expected it to be empty.

Instead she found a cardboard box, maybe twelve inches square, an old shoe lace tied around it. She stared at her name, *Grace Anne,* printed on it in faded ink.

She didn't know how long she stood there just staring at the box in the drawer. Finally, she crouched down and touched it, then picked it up, and sat on the floor cross-legged. Shock had started to give way to something akin to sadness. Her dad must have put it there. That meant he'd come to the ranch at least once.

With shaking hands, she tugged on the shoe lace and opened the lid. An old photo album lay inside, innocuous enough, but almost paralyzing Grace. She had to force herself to take it out. But even when the album lay on her crossed legs, she couldn't make herself open it.

"Silly," she muttered to herself. If she hadn't been meant to find it, it wouldn't be here. It was that simple. But nothing was simple as she finally made herself lift the cover and open the book. She was startled to see that the pictures carefully secured to the first few pages were of her as a baby, some with her mother, two of her alone.

She'd seen the photos before. They were copies of pictures her mother had. But from the fourth page on, the photos were new to her. They were obviously taken from a distance, the first one a shot of her starting school, then a photo for each year until the fourth grade. The next one was of her junior high school graduation. Then a leap to her high school graduation. Two months later, a shot of her going into the restaurant where she got her first waitressing job near L.A.'s Civic Center.

She turned the page, almost thankful to find the rest of the book empty. She flipped through the photos again, then closed the book and reached for the box to put it away. But she knew the surprises weren't over when she spotted a couple of loose photos lying in the bottom of the box.

Her heart tightened to almost breaking when she picked them up. The first one was of her holding a year-old Lilly on her lap on a park bench while her mother offered the baby a rattle. When she looked at the second picture, she started to shake. She'd never seen the photo before. She was a toddler, maybe two or three years old, held high in her father's arms. As soon as she saw him in the picture, she remembered the wiry man who always wore jeans and T-shirts. A baseball cap was pulled low and shadowed his face, but the smile on his lips was clear.

The photo dropped from her fingers and fluttered to the floor. Tears overtook her so suddenly and fiercely that she couldn't get her breath. Her father had left, and turned his

back on everything he should have loved beyond reason, yet he hadn't lost track of her all
these years. He'd been watching her—or had
someone else watch her from a distance. Yet,
even now, he hadn't made a move to contact
her personally.

When she heard her mother's voice calling
Lilly to come inside, Grace moved quickly,
swiping at her eyes and fumbling to hide the
album and pictures. She barely had them in
the box when she heard the front door shut,
and a child's footsteps coming in her direction. She pushed the box under the bed, got to
her feet and grabbed a tissue from the night-
stand. Quickly, she blew her nose, then the
door to her bedroom burst open and Lilly
flew in.

"Mama, Mama, Mama," she cried, running to Grace and almost knocking her over
with a hug. "We went horse-walking and saw
a lizard!"

She drew back and grabbed Grace's hand.
"Come on. Come see Mosi. She's real happy."

Grace's mother was there, in the doorway,
frowning over Lilly's head as she studied
Grace. "Problems?" she asked, not coming
any closer.

"Just allergies," she said, blowing her nose again.

"Oh, sure," her mother said, but made it clear by her tone that she didn't believe her for one second.

Lilly was tugging hard on her hand, impatient to get back out to the horse. "Mama, please!"

"Okay," Grace said. "Just a peek, then we need to get some food on the table."

Gabriella moved back into the hallway. "I'll get that started, and you go and visit Mosi with Lilly."

"Okay," Grace said. She went back in her room and grabbed her camera, then headed down to the stables with Lilly.

Grace had never been one to take pictures of everyday life, but now she wanted shots of Lilly with the horse, with the cat, with Parrish. Maybe she could take pictures on her perimeter rides with Jack. She wanted to record these memories—for Lilly and herself, forever.

THAT EVENING, SLEEP didn't come easily for Grace, not after showing her mother the box of photos after Lilly was in bed. It had been hard on both women.

She'd put the box back in the dresser, and walked away from it. She'd look at it again, but not for some time. In bed, she couldn't relax, partly because her mind refused to stop racing, and partly because her bottom hurt.

She wasn't sure she could make it through another ride, but she wanted so much to see the rest of the ranch. She imagined Jack having to carry her into the house after a second day on the horse. And her last thought before she finally fell asleep was that being carried in Jack's arms wouldn't be so bad, not at all.

# CHAPTER TWELVE

WHEN GRACE WOKE at dawn, she tiptoed down the hallway, grabbed a bottle of water out of the fridge, and went back to the bathroom to get dressed. She closed the door, took off the oversize T-shirt she slept in, and then turned to the sink. In the mirror that fronted the medicine cabinet, she looked at herself. She could see the redness of sunburn on her nose, chin and forehead, her skin exposed after she'd lost the hat. She'd have to try and get another one soon.

She found the sunscreen and applied it liberally, changed into her jeans, a short-sleeved shirt and boots.

Two hours later, Lilly was on the small bus on her way to school. Grace stood on the front porch and saw Jack riding up the driveway. She had her camera hanging around her neck.

He lifted a hand in greeting, and Grace went down to the stables to meet him. She decided not to speak until she reached him. She wanted to gauge his mood, see if things were still a bit off between them because of her thoughtless words.

But Jack seemed relaxed as she approached. "I didn't know how to saddle Lucy or I would have tried," she explained.

"Wait a minute," he said, touching her shoulder as she turned into the stables.

The sun was at his back, and she had to squint to see him. "What's wrong?" she asked, certain he was going to beg off.

"Me," he said, and she noticed he looked tired. Fine lines that hadn't been there yesterday bracketed his eyes and mouth. "If you aren't feeling good, we don't have to go today," she said.

"It's not that." He gave a heavy sigh. "I want to apologize to you."

That stopped her dead. "What for?"

"I should never have said what I did about your child yesterday."

She didn't know what to say. He was apologizing to her when she knew it should be the other way around. "You beat me to it," she said.

"To what?"

"Apologizing. I sounded so...." She shrugged, not about to bring up the fact he didn't have kids again. "I'm just sorry I over-reacted. Everything was fine with Lilly. They were out walking the horse."

"That's good to hear," he said. "Can we just figure this is a wash between us?"

"Yes, please," she agreed.

He stared at her for a moment, then touched her shoulder again. "Let's get Lucy ready."

Grace watched Jack carefully as he dressed out Lucy, and thought she might be able to do it herself with a little instruction. Jack moved so easily, cinching and adjusting the saddle and finally throwing it onto Lucy's back. He did up the buckles, smoothed the saddle blanket, and checked the foot holders. Stirrups, that's what they were called.

He turned to her. "Done." He narrowed his eyes and studied her for a long moment. "How are you feeling today? Sore muscles?"

Was it that obvious? "Okay, and yes, I am sore." She didn't mention how much her bottom hurt when she sat down. "Don't they have softer saddles?"

He chuckled. "That is a soft saddle."

"Oh," was all she said before she took Lucy's reins from him and walked the horse out.

Before she could figure out how to ask Jack to give her a boost up again, he was behind her, his hands on her waist, then she was being lifted. She sank onto the saddle, got her feet positioned, and looked down at Jack. "I promise, I'll do that myself pretty soon."

A smile shadowed his lips, just enough to hint at his dimple. "When you grow a foot or so?"

"Low blow," she countered with her own smile. "And I do mean low."

He laughed, then after making sure she had her reins in hand, he nudged his horse. "Here we go," he said, and they set off toward the east.

A COUPLE OF DAYS HAD PASSED, and Jack and Grace were starting out for their last perimeter ride of the morning. Grace's horse matched Gizmo's pace, Jack looked so relaxed in the saddle she smiled to herself. It felt good to be out here with Jack. To have him tell her stories about the land, about the people. They'd gone past the entry to the Rez the day before, but hadn't crossed into that land. Then they'd headed down and met a rancher whose land was directly across from the old ranch.

They hadn't talked about Jack wanting to buy the ranch and Grace was grateful for that. She hoped it would be the same today.

JACK RODE IN SILENCE, fully aware of Grace behind him. He'd been awake a long time the last few nights, and when he finally slept, his rest was fitful and anything but refreshing. He'd finally given up trying to sleep in the loft last night, and had gone down to his office and stretched out on the couch there. But even when he got to sleep, he felt edgy. Images of Grace mingled painfully with fading images of Robyn.

He hated that. He never wanted to forget Robyn. But in the past few weeks, it had been harder and harder to remember things clearly. The impressions were there, but they were blurred, without their usual brilliance. Smiles floated just out of reach. The ache of losing her was less acute. Yet he desperately didn't want to feel as if she was gone completely from him. Ever.

He'd finally given up sleeping an hour before dawn. On impulse, he'd dressed quickly and driven to the cemetery set back on a hill on the north side of town. He found Robyn's marker easily. He'd been there so often in the past, but recently his visits had stretched out. The flowers he'd placed there were almost dead. He tossed them to one side, and hated the fact that he hadn't thought to bring any fresh ones.

He stood looking down at the headstone.

*Robyn Mays Carson*
*always in our hearts*

A sculpted image of a single daisy had been fashioned at the bottom of the monument. Her favorite flower. He sat near her grave for a long time, watching the sun spreading its colors on the eastern horizon. So many times he'd gone there to experience the connection they'd always had, but today it was harder to find. He felt a painful tug in his heart. No one had told him about the fading of memories.

"I will always love you," he'd whispered, then walked away, feeling as if he'd been leaving a part of himself in that silent place.

Now he was looking toward the east again, with Grace so close he could hear the soft release of air when her horse shifted or jerked.

"We won't climb today," he said over his shoulder.

"Good to know," she said.

He slowed, waited for her to get beside him. The new hat she'd bought protected her face and part of her shoulders with its broad straw brim. "How're the sore muscles?" he asked.

She shifted in the saddle a bit awkwardly and he knew she was still having a problem finding her rhythm. "Do you want to walk for a while? You've got your boots, and it's pretty level the way we're going."

She got herself down almost before the words were out of his mouth. "Yes, walking would be nice," she said.

He barely suppressed a smile. "Good. I'd like to walk." He looked around, spotted one of the windmills on the pasture land and led his horse toward it, Grace and Lucy following. "Let's tie them here, and we can come back in a while to get them."

"That sounds fine," she said.

He came to her, a foot of space separating them. "We'll take it easy."

"Thank you for being merciful," she said

with a smile that he found he looked forward
to when he was around her.

"You're doing better riding, you know," he said as they started off across the dried grasses.

"Thank you. I feel like I'm making progress. It's just I'm so out of my element around here, sometimes. I don't think I've ever been an animal person, but now I'm riding a horse, and there's Mosi and the cat in the stables. I'm just glad I haven't seen any other creatures… like snakes."

They stopped and he found himself laughing softly at her. "What?" she asked.

He impulsively touched her chin with the tip of his forefinger. "You and snakes. You got the boots and I saw Lilly and your mom both have boots. You're doing just fine." He felt a wobble in her chin, and drew back. "That sounded patronizing, didn't it?"

Her lavender eyes met his. "A bit."

"Sorry again," he said, taking off his cap to rake his fingers through his hair. He tugged his hat back on and exhaled. "It's my family's fault."

Her eyes widened. "What?"

"You know, two brothers, and a ton of

cousins all around this area, you get used to teasing and poking fun at each other, because they'll do it to you at the drop of a hat. And take your hat, too."

She laughed, thankfully, and so did he. Laughing felt so good for a change. "That's filed under acquired life knowledge."

"Oh, so that's the title they give it, not... surviving your crazy relatives?"

"It's probably a tossup," she said.

He looked ahead of them and changed plan midstream. "Tell you what, instead of going to the lower eastern pastures, would you mind if we headed higher again. I promise it won't be too far up and we won't go near any ledges."

"What for?" she asked, the smile gone.

"Do you want to know where the name Wolf Lake came from?"

She cocked her head, the rising sun shooting her hair with a halo of gold, and he literally felt his breath catch in his chest. "I wondered why it's called Wolf Lake and not Wolf Desert or Wolf Butte or Wolf whatever."

"We aren't exactly surrounded by water, are we?"

"I noticed," she said with a soft lift of her lips.

He looked away for a moment, then back at her again. "I'd like to take you to the lake, today, since it's our last ride and all."

"I'd love to see the lake," she said eagerly. Then a thought occurred to her. "Is this a joke?"

"No, it's not. We really do have a Wolf Lake."

"Okay," she said.

They turned and retraced their steps back to the horses.

Without thinking about it, he caught Grace around the waist and lifted her into the saddle. "I think I need a stool or something," she said, settling herself.

"Good idea." He wasn't about to mention how the feel of her in his hands was both pleasurable and unsettling for him.

They headed east, then cut sharply north and started to climb, zigzagging back and forth on well worn trails.

"We're going the back way so we stay away from any drop-offs," he said over his shoulder. "Just give your horse her head and she'll be good for you."

"Thank you."

They rode until he knew they couldn't go any farther on the horses. "We'll leave the horses here," he said, getting off and tying the reins to a gnarled tree near the rocks.

"Okay," Grace said, sliding down by herself, then handing him the reins. "Now, where's the lake?"

He pointed up. "Just a bit farther, but we need to do it on foot."

The narrow trail wound back to the west, then finally leveled out into an area about half a mile across and a mile deep, enclosed on three sides by slick stone walls that flowed up and into the mountains. A generous grassy section led to the ledge. He carefully steered Grace away from the direction of the open side, and made sure she was looking at the browned grasses that ran over the floor of the space. He motioned to her, out in front of them. "Wolf Lake," he announced.

She almost snorted. "Oh, come on, you said it wasn't a joke."

"It's not," he said, walking farther into an area of long grass that moved slightly in the mild breeze.

"No, no, no, you said there was a lake, period."

"No, I didn't. I said it's not a joke, and this is Wolf Lake."

She shook her head. "Sure, okay."

"No, really, when the moon is full, it causes an optical illusion that forms an odd shadow from the peaks above. It spreads across the grass and turns it dark, and when the moon creeps up over the mountains, it shines on the grass. If there's a wind, the shadow looks like dark, shimmering water. It's an optical illusion, and it only happens at a full moon. Even then it doesn't always work. Maybe six times a year it's perfect."

She exhaled heavily. "Why didn't you say it was just a trick of the eye?"

"Would you have come if I'd told you that?"

"Probably not," she admitted, but didn't turn to leave. She walked into the clearing, the crunch of dry grass under her booted feet. "I guess it could look like water if you narrowed your eyes and the moon was right, and the sky was dark, and…etcetera, etcetera, etcetera."

"You're being sarcastic, but it actually does look like a lake. I was up here a lot as a kid."

"At night?"

"That's the only time you can see it, around midnight, when the full moon clears the mountains."

She turned to him. "Let me guess, you used that line on girls when you were a teenager, didn't you. 'Come with me to see the secret lake?' and they fell for it, didn't they?"

She had him there. Again, he was glad he didn't blush. "Okay, I did, a couple of times." A powerful memory rose up in him. Robyn and him coming up here before he left for college. Sitting side by side, talking about their future, the one they dreamed they'd have. The house, the kids, each other.

He turned quickly, not sure what to do, and headed toward an opening in the west side of the rocky walls. He heard Grace coming after him, but he didn't look back. He stepped through the low opening onto a secondary ledge that overlooked part of the valley to the west. He crossed to the edge to stare out into the distance, knowing Grace wouldn't follow.

But she did. He could feel her presence, until, at last, her arm brushed his. "I thought you'd rather jump than be on a cliff like this?" he said without looking at her.

That made her chuckle. "I never said I'd jump."

"You said that heights bothered you."

"They do, but I can handle it as long as I look into the distance and not down."

"My brothers snuck out of the house when they were maybe ten and twelve and came up here after a rain. They ended up hanging from an outcropping about ten feet below here."

She gasped. "They fell?"

"No, they were climbing the face. It had rained and it was slick and they were idiots."

"What happened to them?"

"Grandpa had a feeling they were in trouble, not sure if it was something supernatural or if he just knew Adam and Gage and what they could get up to. He led a party of some friends to rescue them. The only problem they had was facing my mother and father afterward."

"They were lucky," she breathed.

Jack pointed to the northwest, to a blur of buildings with various shapes and angles. "See over there, about our height, against the low mountains?"

She looked. "What is that?"

"The Rez. It's the side view, the oldest

part. I never could figure out why the People started building there instead of in the valley. But they did, and that's where Grandpa was raised. His people were pretty dominant among the first comers. Lots of Wolfs and Wolf relations around."

"When did they settle there?"

"There are two stories, both passed down through the People. One is that they arrived after a massacre by soldiers in the late seventeen hundreds, and chose that location because of its good defensive position. The other story tells of them migrating off government land in Oklahoma by their own choice. I'm not sure which is the truth, but either way, they've probably been there a couple of hundred years."

"Wow," she breathed. "And you can trace your roots that far back?"

"If I wanted to, I could," he said. "But that's up to Mom. She's got that genealogy thing down pat."

"What about your father's people?"

"Irish, English, some German, I'm told. But he's not into heritage." He knew the bitterness he felt had edged into his voice.

"Never was, never will be—he can't understand why it's important."

"I can't trace my roots back more than two generations," she said wistfully. He moved then, to sit on the edge and let his feet hang over the side. Again Grace surprised him. He felt her hand on his shoulder, a bit unsteady, but she slowly sank down beside him, crossing her legs instead of dangling them over the edge.

"You surprise me," he admitted, still not looking at her.

Her hand moved from his shoulder. "I surprise myself sometimes. I never thought I'd be out here, on a ranch, and actually riding a horse." She exhaled softly, and the sound ran riot over his nerve endings. "But it's something you've done all your life."

"All my life," he echoed. "Ever since I could walk, I've ridden, and with my summers split between the Rez and the town and the old ranch with Grandpa, I've spent a lot of time riding and hunting and wandering the land."

"You're very lucky," she whispered.

Jack finally glanced at Grace. She was sitting up straight, her hands pressed to her knees, almost yoga style. As his eyes met hers, he thought he saw a trace of that wistfulness he'd caught in her tone earlier. He felt a powerful twinge of guilt for every time he'd led her on the roughest, hardest route or made this land seem unfriendly and harsh. That's when he realized that despite fully intending to discourage her from getting attached to the place, he hadn't made any headway in that direction at all.

She wanted a home here for her family. He knew her daughter was the most important person in the world to her, and this is where she wanted to raise her. He was starting to feel like a scrooge for trying to get the land away from her.

He turned from her, pushed himself up, knowing that he had to take a mental step back to get some balance as well as put some physical distance between them.

She got up with him, her arm against his for support, her heat seeping into him. She seemed oblivious to the contact and thankfully just as oblivious to his sense of loss when she moved away, and walked farther along the outcropping.

Jack stayed where he was, waiting, until she turned and headed back to him.

"I've never seen anything like this, and I've never been anywhere like this." She motioned around them and her smile came slowly, its impact on him growing stronger with each second that passed. "I can't imagine that I'm actually living here. It's like a dream, but a dream where I know I won't wake up and find it gone."

He turned away, unable to look her in the eyes. Scrooge was starting to look like a saint compared to how he felt right then.

"Time to go," he said, and Grace turned for one last glance, then nodded and they headed back.

Jack did something he hadn't planned on doing when they got to the horses. Instead of heading straight back to the old ranch, he veered onto a side trail where the riding was easy. The day was starting to warm, the sun climbing in the sky, but he wasn't very aware of the weather or the scenery. He was aware of the woman behind him.

"Jack?" Grace called to him.

He slowed, letting her approach on his left side. "What?"

"Is this the way to the house? Maybe I'm confused, but it doesn't feel like the right direction."

"It isn't," he admitted. "I was thinking, since this is our last ride, we can go to my folks' place, drop Lucy at the stables, then I'll drive you home." He was done trying to wear her down. If she couldn't make it on the ranch, it wouldn't be because of anything he did. He couldn't live with himself if he kept being devious with this woman.

She shifted in the saddle. "Okay, that would make things simpler for you, I guess."

"The Jeep's air-conditioned," he said.

That brought a smile. "Now that's really enticing."

They were on a trail that was wide enough to ride side by side. "This is the path we used to take from the big ranch to the lake. Well-worn over the years."

"Jack, just a minute," she said, and when he turned, she had her cell phone out of her pocket. "I need to call Mom."

He watched her press the keys, hold the phone to her ear, then smile a bit when it was answered on the other end. "Mom, can you get Lilly at the bus today?" She listened.

"Thanks, that'll work. I'll be home in a bit, but Jack needs to get his horse back." She nodded. "Love you, too." And she hung up.

"How's the school working out?" Jack asked as she pocketed her phone.

"Just great. Lilly's already made friends and loves her teacher, although she's starting to wish she had dark hair, instead of being a blonde."

"Being blonde is a good thing," Jack said, not even able to imagine Grace anything but.

"At six years of age, she thinks she wants to be dark-haired and have a name like Rose, or Swallow or Liberty."

Jack found himself laughing. "Oh, I see. Lilly doesn't cut it?"

"No."

"Well, having a mother named Lark, and two aunts named Willow and Swan, I have to say, you get used to the names. My mother always wanted to be called Victoria. She loved that name, but instead, she was Lark."

Grace smiled. "Lark is a beautiful name."

*So is Grace,* he thought, but didn't say it out loud. Instead, he changed the subject completely. "Where did you get your fear of snakes?"

She was thoughtful, as if she was trying to remember something. Finally, she said, "I saw a snake once in the zoo in San Diego, a huge, and I mean, humungous snake—it had to be twenty feet long. It was right by the glass and when I moved up to see it, it flung itself at the glass and I screamed. It was awful."

Jack recoiled from the thought that ran riot through him. If he'd been with her, he would have made sure she wasn't afraid of a snake behind glass. Protectiveness? Probably, but why? Grace was nothing to him, beyond a recent acquaintance and possible friend, but as soon as the thought formed, he knew he was wrong. There was something about her, something that touched him in the strangest way. Something that made him feel almost unfaithful to Robyn.

Going to the family ranch was out. She could keep the horse at her place. He would take her straight to the old adobe, then get out of there. These early morning rides were over for the two of them, but he knew he needed to head off by himself. Everything in his life had gotten horribly scrambled. His plans, his memories. A ride into the high country would give him time to think, to sort out his muddled thoughts He pulled his horse around to go south, breaking a new trail through the low, dead grass. If he angled across the sprawling pasture, he'd get to the old ranch in ten minutes.

GRACE SAW A look cross Jack's face that she couldn't explain. She wondered if maybe he was sick of her, of showing her the land, of her stupid questions. She could sense something had changed, and she gave him an out. "You know, I can walk from here. Why don't you take Lucy with you back to your parents' and I'll hike back to the house?"

He stopped and turned to her. His dark eyes raked over her. "You want to get away from me?"

She thought he was kidding, but he wasn't. "No, of course not," she said, and knew that she could ride all day with Jack and be happy. "Of course not," she said.

"Then what's with the idea of hiking back?"

"Making it easier for you," she blurted out. "You seem to want to get rid of me, and I was giving you a way to do that faster."

He stared at her. "You really think that I want to be rid of you?"

"Don't you?" she asked.

# CHAPTER THIRTEEN

JACK FELT AS if he'd been blindsided. Grace thought he wanted to be rid of her? She couldn't be more off base, but he wasn't about to explain that to her. He just needed to get away because of himself. To sort out what he wanted.

"No," he said truthfully, then proceeded to lie to her. "I forgot I have an appointment, and it's easier to get you to your place, than the big ranch."

She considered that, her lavender eyes intent on him. "Really?"

He forced himself to nod. "Really."

But she didn't let it go. "I'm so sorry about the land, about the mess this has caused. I really am."

"It's not your fault and it's not mine," he said. "So, don't be sorry. It is what it is."

That sounded so final, so awful for some reason. He hated her having to feel apologetic for her father's actions, as much as he hated feeling that way about his own father.

"You're really being great about all of this," Grace said.

He looked away, tugging at the brim of his cap, unable to speak. He was about to ride off when Grace suddenly screamed.

He turned to see a blur of yellow and black cutting through the grass. A snake, and it was coming right toward the horses.

Grace was staring at it in horror, then dropped her reins to grab the saddle horn. She had no idea the snake was harmless, and instinctively she kicked Lucy in the side. The usually placid mare took off, Grace holding on for dear life.

Jack took off after her and quickly gained on the smaller animal.

"Stop, stop, stop!" Grace was screaming, then he noticed the fence dead ahead of her. The top rail was broken, but there was no way Lucy could jump the lower two pieces.

He spurred his horse on until he was almost parallel with Grace. Pulling his horse even closer to the mare, Jack thrust out a hand and caught Grace around the waist. "Get your feet free now!" he yelled at her.

He could see her right foot slip free, and could only trust her left was also out of the stirrup. The next instant he jerked her toward him, swinging her up and over in a half circle until she hit his body, almost knocking the wind out of him.

"Whoa, whoa," he said slowly, and watched as Lucy made a sharp turn, taking off along the fence line.

Jack pulled Grace into his arms, setting her sideways over the saddle, on his thighs. She turned into him, sobbing, crushing his shirt in her hands, face pressed against his chest. He just held her, and didn't let go. He never wanted to let go.

GRACE FELT JACK'S heart thudding against her cheek, and his arms around her. She felt safe, and her relief almost made her giddy. She couldn't stop the tears, but now they were from knowing that the snake was gone, and she wasn't plunging headlong on a horse toward sure disaster.

"Oh, my gosh, my gosh," she gulped, her voice muffled against Jack's chest. "Oh, my gosh."

"It's okay," Jack said, his voice a rumble all around her. "You're safe."

Then she had a horrible thought. "Lucy, is she dead, or did she break her leg or something?"

"No, she's not dead," he murmured. "She's very much alive."

Grace let go of her death grip on his shirt, and made herself look toward the fence. Jack was right. Lucy was very much alive, her reins dragging through the dead grass as she cavorted in the pasture like a kid let out of school. "Thank goodness," she breathed, sinking weakly against Jack again.

He held her for a long moment, then eased back, managing to get out of the saddle and on the ground, taking her with him. Then he let her go, almost. His hands stayed on her shoulders while she found her footing, then when she was steady, he touched her chin, cupping it to make her look up at him. "What was that all about?" he asked softly, with no reproach in his tone.

She closed her eyes. "A snake, it was coming toward us, a huge snake."

"If you hadn't screamed, Lucy wouldn't have even known it was there."

"But, it was big snake, heading right toward the horse and me, and you, too."

He brushed at her hair, which had loosened from the ponytail. "That's a Desert King snake, Grace."

"Oh, okay, so it's got a name, but it was coming so fast through the grass."

He let go of her and stood back. "Time for a lesson. The Desert King snake is common around here and we try to encourage them to stay."

"Why on earth would you—?"

"They aren't venomous, and they eat rodents, lizards and small rattlesnakes. They're good to have around. They're also more afraid of you than you are of them. It probably didn't even notice us until the screaming."

A good snake? She shook her head. "That's what you think, but you can't know that they wouldn't bite someone."

"Gage had a Desert King as a pet and that thing would literally roll over and play dead when one of us got close." He laughed. "The thing is, once we thought it was dead, and when Gage flipped it over onto its stomach, the darn thing flipped back on its back and continued to play dead."

"Wow, I feel stupid," she said, although she'd never forget how the snake had seemed to come at them.

"No, it's not stupid to be cautious. You don't know about snakes, so how would you recognize if it was a rattler or not. We grew up around them."

Grace was shocked when something nudged her back and she turned to see Lucy standing there docilely. "Oh, there you are," she crooned, and reached out to stroke the mare's muzzle. "Good girl, very good girl."

"You've got the touch," he said as the horse moved closer to nuzzle into her. "I think Lucy likes you, despite the screams."

She found she could smile at that, and it felt good. Jack nodded to the horse. "You still want to hike to your place?"

"No, thanks," she said.

"Good, then get back on Lucy and let's get going."

"Okay." She rounded the mare and grabbed the horn with one hand, and the back of the saddle with the other. She pulled as hard as she could and pushed with one foot in the stirrup. Remarkably, she went up, almost sliding completely off the saddle, but Jack was there to balance her while she swung her other leg over. "I almost made it," she said, feeling just a bit of pride.

"You almost did," he said, then turned to remount his horse. The ride back was quicker than she thought, and by the time they reached the stables, she was amazed at how good it felt to be in the saddle. "Some day when you have the time, let me know and we can finish the part of the perimeter that we missed with our detour to the lake."

She looked at him, aware of how intense his dark eyes could be when he wasn't smiling. "Sure," she said. "That sounds fine." She hesitated, then surprised herself with her next words.

"Why don't you stick around and we can have some lunch. My mother's making chili for the first time, and I can't vouch for it, but everything else she cooks is very good."

Jack was silent, then shook his head. "Thanks, but I need to get going."

She wasn't prepared for the disappointment she felt at his refusal. "Are you sure?"

"I'm sure. Maybe another time." And with that he got down, and let Grace get off Lucy. He gave her the reins to his horse, and led

Lucy without looking back. "She can stay for another few days, until we finish the last ride," he called over his shoulder before he disappeared into the stables.

Grace stood there, waiting, until Jack was done and took control of his horse again. She could sense he wanted to be gone. But before he could start out, the front door to the house opened and Parrish came down the stairs. "Good ride?" he asked.

"He took me to see the lake," Grace said, and Parrish laughed.

"You do know that's a come-on line, sort of like 'come up and see my etchings,' don't you?"

Grace felt her face get hot, and she didn't look at Jack.

"Back in the day, that was a popular line for the teenage population," Jack said. "I just wanted to show her that Wolf Lake really does have a lake."

"Yeah, right on," Parrish said, then asked, "Is the little mare in the stables?"

"Yeah, I'm leaving her here for a few days," Jack said.

"Good, I'll go make sure she's settling down.

As Parrish moved off, a high-pitched squeal filled the air and Lilly dashing down the front steps.

JACK HAD REFUSED lunch at the ranch, because he wasn't sure he could get through it. The idea was appealing, but when he realized that was only because of Grace, he knew he had to get out of there as soon as he could. Now a child he knew must be Lilly was staring up at him.

It was as if Jack was looking at a miniature version of Grace. Lily was cute, petite and blonde, with those same lavender eyes.

He felt his heart lurch. A child like the mother. That was only right, the way things should be. He felt that familiar loss deep inside, the one that had been there since Robyn died. He knew he should leave, but he didn't. Instead he dismounted and watched as the child came closer.

Those large eyes looked him over from head to foot, then she pointed at his boots. "They're real dirty."

"Lilly," Grace said. "He's been out riding and hiking—boots get dirty."

"That man at the store said we had to keep our boots clean," she countered.

"Yes, but—"

Lilly turned and pointed at the horse. "He sure is big," she said, not going closer.

"He's a big one, okay, but he's only three years old," Jack said, not really sure how to talk with a child. Erin never said much when she was around.

"No," Lilly said. "You're kidding me, aren't you?"

"I'm not kidding. He was born and bred on my parents' ranch."

Lilly breathed, "Wow," then she said, "Jack, are you a real cowboy?"

"I guess so, at least, part time. Most times I'm an attorney, but I love to ride."

"I'm going to ride my horse soon. Mama said I could once I get taught. Then I'll ride Mosi over and see you, okay?"

"You do that," he said. "You get a few lessons, and I think you'll be a natural." She grinned at the compliment, and again, he could see Grace as a child. "I need to go," he said, more abruptly than he meant to.

Lilly said, "I got something," and ran back

to the house. She returned a minute later, holding something out to him.

He looked down and saw a large cookie in her hand. "Oh, I don't need a cookie," he said.

But that was the wrong thing to say. Her bottom lip jutted out and she moved the cookie closer to him. "It's for you."

He didn't want to hurt the child's feelings, so he reached out to take the cookie, then hunkered down in front of her. "Thank you very much."

Without saying anything, Lilly turned and ran back inside the house.

"Lilly doesn't share with just anyone," Grace told Jack truthfully.

He looked at the cookie and closed it in his hand. "I have to go," he said, then mounted his horse again, and with a nod, set off past the stables. Jack got down to the main road before he pulled the horse to a stop and opened his hand to see that he'd crushed the cookie into a gooey ball of chocolate and crumbs.

Memories he'd fought for so long were there, assaulting him, and he stayed very still. Why now, why those memories? The child and a cookie. Grace on the horse looking up at him. Brushing his arm, sitting by him. The feeling of her clinging to him when she'd seen the snake.

His stomach churned, and with a low groan, he threw the crumbled cookie into the brush and rode back to his parents' ranch. He didn't go up to the house. He went into the stable complex, got some supplies, then took off in the direction of the Rez. But halfway there, his cell phone rang, and he pulled it out of his shirt pocket. Maureen. He hesitated, then answered, knowing he owed it to her to let her know he wouldn't be in for a few days.

"Yes," he said into the phone.

"Good grief, man, I've been trying to find you for an hour!"

"What's so important?" he asked.

"It's your dad."

His hand tightened on the phone, and he closed his eyes so hard that he saw flashes of color behind his lids. He could barely get out the question. "What about him?"

"He knows how to get the land back," she said without preamble.

"What in the—?"

"Listen, I've talked to him, and he's told me about his idea, and, Jack, it's a good one. You need to talk to him right away."

Her words came to him, hardly making sense. An idea from his dad to get the land? He wasn't sure what he felt. But he knew that he didn't trust anything his dad said or did at the moment.

As if Maureen could read his mind, she said, "And if you're thinking of ignoring this because it came from your dad, don't do it. I know you're still hurt, but if this works, everything could be back exactly the way it was before."

He didn't know what he was thinking or what he felt. The answer to his prayers? Another scheme from the man who'd made the mess in the first placc?

"Thanks," he mumbled and cut off the call. When the phone rang again almost immediately, he glanced at the readout. Gage. He hit the ignore button. Before he could get the phone in his pocket, another call came in. Adam. He wanted to ignore it, too, but finally answered.

"What?"

"Oh, good, we've been trying to call you for an hour."

"What is it?" he asked.

He told Jack the same thing Maureen had.

But Adam ended with, "You know, it makes sense to me. I could work with it. This could all be over soon."

The lone ride he had planned disappeared. "Where are you?" he asked Adam.

"At the station covering for John. His son has a recital at school."

"I'll be there in half an hour." He hesitated. "You and me, and Gage if you want, but no one else."

Adam didn't argue. "You've got it."

Exactly thirty minutes later, Jack pulled up to the flat-roofed police station in his Jeep and got out. Striding through the swinging doors, he nodded to the deputy behind the low desk and headed straight for the chief of police's office. Pushing back the door without knocking, he found both of his brothers inside, waiting.

Adam sat behind the desk with its two computer monitors, stacks of files and a panel that serviced six separate phone lines. A red light flashed on one. The painted brick walls were hung with certificates for marksmanship and diplomas for the courses John Longbow had taken over the years. A picture of the chief's

family was front and center. Gage was oc-
cupying one of three chairs facing the desk.

Jack took the one closest to him, dropped
down heavily on the hard wood and sat forward, his forearms resting on his thighs.
"Okay, I'm here," he said.

The two brothers exchanged glances with
each other, then both turned to Jack. Gage
spoke first. "Dad called us this morning,
early, and we met at your offices. Maureen
was there."

Jack held up a hand to stop Gage. "I don't
care about that—just give me the basics."

Gage nodded, not offended, and started
right in telling Jack what he wanted to know.
"Dad had an investigator go to the place
where his game with Michaels was held and
asked around. Nothing for a bit, then the guy
hit on one of the other players. Bottom line,
that woman agreed to go to court and say that
Dad was totally drunk, out of it, and had no
idea what he was doing when he threw the
promissory note for the deed into the pot. Di-
minished capacity. And that Michaels knew
Dad's condition when he accepted the bet."
Gage spread his hands palms up. "Ergo, go to
court and sue for return of the property. Dad

said he'd testify about the blackouts and af-firm that he didn't even know what he'd done until you came after him. He's willing to go public about everything."

Jack stared at Gage, then turned to Adam. They both watched him, waiting. "Court, a drawn-out process, then pulling the deed, re-claiming the land and it's done," he muttered.

"Exactly."

"And Grace and Lilly and Grace's mom get evicted and sent on their way," he thought to himself, the idea making him sick to his stomach. "That's time-consuming and expen-sive," he said out loud.

"It might not be. Maybe the woman on the property...Evans, is it?"

"Grace," he said in a low voice.

"Okay, maybe she'll do the right thing and leave. Maybe not. That's her decision, but if you want to make it a bit easier on her, let Dad put up some money for her. A relocation fund of some sort. Maybe twenty-thousand." He didn't add, "That's the least he could do," but it hung between them.

"A relocation fund," Jack echoed.

"Yes, and that should grease the wheels. Maybe go higher if he needs to."

Jack swallowed the tightness in his throat, not sure why the image of Lilly running toward him at the ranch came to him in a jarring flash. Or why Grace's soft voice, talking about her awe at owning the land, rang in his mind.

"I don't know," Jack said as he sank back in the chair.

"What don't you know?" Gage asked. "Dad's dead serious about this. He's willing to take any fallout. He's doing it for you."

Jack frowned. "No, he's doing it for himself, so he can live with himself."

"You don't think it could work legally, no matter what his motive is?" Adam asked.

"No, it could work. It probably will work," Jack conceded.

"But?" Gage prodded.

"But, I don't know. I don't know."

Adam sat forward intently. "You don't want the old ranch anymore?"

Jack shook his head. "Of course I want it. I've always wanted it."

"Another but?" Gage asked.

A huge one. He wanted it, but Grace wanted it, too. In fact, he had a feeling that she needed it. As much as he did. He just couldn't make himself say, "Let's do it." Abruptly he stood and lied. "I need to check into this from a legal perspective."

Both brothers were on their feet. "Good," they said in unison.

Jack looked at both of them. "Two things?"

Both nodded.

"Nothing is done or said to anyone until I figure it out, and I don't want Dad involved in it beyond going to court to testify, if I decide to go ahead."

Both hesitated, then Adam said, "It's your call."

Jack left first, striding out to his Jeep. He drove by his office on his way through town. When he finally parked, he was out in front of the hospital. He made his way to reception, but passed the desk and headed for an office he knew well. Moses Blackstar was behind his desk, and he looked up as Jack walked in.

He sat back, nodded. "I was expecting you sooner or later."

Jack stood at the desk, ignoring the plush leather chairs. "You heard, didn't you?"

"Yes, I did, from Adam this morning." Moses motioned Jack to sit. "It makes sense," he said, "No matter where the idea came from."

Jack agreed. "Absolutely."

"Then what's wrong with it?"

He looked at his old friend and told him the truth. "I want the land, but I don't think that I can pay the price for it."

"What's the price?"

"Throwing Grace Evans and her family off it." He swallowed hard, his stomach knotting again. "I can't."

"Why not?" Moses asked, eyeing him steadily.

He couldn't answer his friend, because he didn't know that himself. Then again, maybe he did. Maybe he just didn't want to say it out loud. What he was feeling didn't make sense, and he didn't want to feel that way. He exhaled and finally sank down in the nearest chair. "I don't know."

Moses was silent for so long, Jack felt his nerves tightening. Finally, Moses said, "I think you should speak to Mallory."

"Why, she isn't part of this," he said quickly.

"I think she could be part of…whatever. She's smart and might help you out a bit."

Jack didn't understand what he meant, so he switched the subject. "That's not what I came here for."

"Oh?"

"It's Dad. He got the idea, and he's running with it. If you have any control over him, can you tell him to back off, to let me handle this my way?"

"Sure. That's what you came here for?"

Jack stood. "Yes, I don't want Gage and Adam to get caught between us."

A smile played at the corners of Moses's mouth. "And I'm expendable?"

Jack actually laughed. "No, never, just a good fighter, a smart fighter, and I think, after all the time you were with us growing up, Dad thinks you might be his son."

Moses laughed out loud. "I like that idea."

"Then take him," Jack muttered. "He's all yours."

# CHAPTER FOURTEEN

GRACE SORT OF expected Jack to call or come by the next day, but by midmorning he hadn't shown up, and she knew her disappointment was all out of line. Lilly was at school, and her mom had headed down to the stables after starting a pot of soup on the stove.

Grace sat on the porch, knowing she had a lot to do, but wanting to look at the pictures she'd taken over the past week. Lilly, her mother, the ranch, Parrish, Mosi the horse, the fat cat, the inside of the house. Jack. She'd only taken a couple of pictures of him, one while he was riding in front of her, and another by the windmill.

She missed him. It was that simple. Or maybe not. Nothing with Jack was simple. Her feelings certainly weren't. She shut off the camera, stood and looked around. She needed to go into town to speak to the owner of the restaurant she'd gone to with Jack to see about a job. If she didn't put in an application, they wouldn't call her.

But she couldn't make herself leave the ranch right then. The sun was warm, not hot, the air bright and clear, the land rolling off in both directions and the sound of birds chirping.

That sense of peace she'd felt the very first time she'd come here returned with a vengeance and she embraced it. She hoped she could make this work. She really did. The sound of laughter drifted up from the stables, and she found herself smiling. This was good. She sighed, then turned as she heard an engine approaching. Jack? She was surprised to feel her heart leap at the idea that he had come.

She stood, watching a huge black truck crest the rise and slowly drive up to the front of the house. But Jack wasn't behind the wheel. A woman who looked quite small in the big beast stopped the truck and smiled at Grace through the lightly tinted side window.

By the time Grace went down the stairs, the woman was stepping out of the truck.

"Hello, there," the woman said. "I'm Lark Carson, your neighbor to the west."

Jack's mother. Grace didn't know why she'd expected her to be tall and slim. Mrs. Carson was about Grace's height, with long, dark hair, just starting to streak with some gray. It fell halfway down her back in a single braid. Although Grace knew she had to be close to sixty, she didn't look it. Not with those bright chocolate brown eyes and a brilliant smile that revealed a duplicate of Jack's single dimple.

"I'm Jack's mother, and please call me Lark."

"Oh, right." Grace couldn't figure out why the woman was being so friendly when this used to be her family home, a home that she'd lost to Grace. But there wasn't a hint of phony emotion in her expression. "I'm Grace Evans."

"Well, Grace, I came to welcome you to Wolf Lake, and to this land. It's been a place of happiness and peace for as long as I can remember, and I'm glad that there's a family living in it again."

She couldn't believe what the woman was saying. What about her son, his stunning disappointment, his determination to get the land back sooner or later? This made no sense. And Grace found herself apologizing.

"I'm sorry this all happened the way it did, but I promise we'll take good care of this place."

Before Lark could respond, Gabriella came out of the stables with Parrish. "Mom, come and meet Jack's mother, Lark Carson."

She turned to Lark as Gabriella got close. "Lark, this is my mother, Gabriella Michaels."

The two women greeted each other, then her mom turned to Grace. "It's time to get Lilly. It's a short day today. Do you want me to go?"

"Lilly is your daughter?" Lark asked.

"Yes, she is. She's six, and she loves it here."

"I'm glad to hear that," Lark said. "I love her name. My Nana Wolf was Lilly Song Wolf."

"That's nice," Gabriella said.

"If you'd get her, Mom, that would be great."

Lark stepped in. "I have to go to town for a minute. Why don't you let me drive you in to pick up your Lilly and we can visit?"

"Would you?"

"Sure, come on. We'll get her and stop for an ice cream cone at Oscar's, if you don't mind?" She glanced at Grace for confirmation.

"Oh, no, she'd love it."

"Okay, then, let's go," Lark said, just the way Jack would have.

Grace wanted to ask Lark about Jack, where he was, but she kept quiet and watched the two older women climb into the monster of a truck and leave. As they drove out of sight, Grace stood there watching the deserted drive. Parrish must have gone back into the stables, because no one was in sight. She felt alone, not a bad feeling, even with an added restlessness that made her want to do something, but she didn't know what.

She went back to the house, got her camera, then wandered around outside taking random shots. An hour later, she was on the stone steps again, going over the new photos. She clicked back to the ones of Jack. Did he look sad in them, or was he just serious? She couldn't figure him out. One minute he seemed to want to be close to her, to spend time with her, and the next he was leaving with barely a goodbye.

If things were only different. But that really wouldn't change the situation. There was the whole issue with the ranch, and she had Lilly to think of. She'd made bad choices in the past and couldn't risk making another one. And it was obvious Jack still loved his late wife—not a great start for them to get to know each other. Maybe they could at least be friends. She'd like that, if that's all she could have from him. She'd really like that.

She was ready to go inside when she heard the engine, then the black truck was rumbling up to the house. Lilly jumped out of the passenger side, followed by Gabriella and Lark. The traces of chocolate ice cream were still on Lilly's face.

Gabriella came up to her granddaughter, took her hand, and spoke to Grace. "A good day at school and a better time at Oscar's, as you can see." She tugged Lilly's hand. "Come on inside and let's get you cleaned up. But first, thank Mrs. Carson for the treat."

"Thank you for the ice cream," Lilly said with great seriousness.

"We'll do it again, okay?"

"Okay," Lilly said, then her grandmother took her inside.

When they were gone, Lark turned to Grace, her expression serious now. "I think I need to say something to you, and I don't want you to take it in a bad way. But, no matter what you hear, or what Jack might say, I am very pleased that you and your family are in this place. It feels right to me."

That was the last thing Grace had expected to hear. "Do you mean that?"

"Yes, absolutely."

"Oh, thank you. Everyone in town's so nice, but you can tell they think I'm an interloper who doesn't belong here." She could feel heat in her face, and she added quickly, "I don't mean that they're unkind, but it's been a bit awkward, you know, and I really want to make a permanent home here for Lilly, like your boys had."

Lark came closer and hugged Grace. "Sure you do. A mother wants to provide that for her children if she can. This will be the best gift you can ever give her." Then she stood back.

"I just...." Grace bit her lip. "I hate the fact that Jack wants this so badly, and I'm keeping it from him because of...circumstances."

"Oh, dear, Jack wants this land, that's true, but it's not the most important thing that he wants. He wants a place to find an anchor, to rebuild his life." She looked incredibly sad for a moment. "You know about his wife?"

Grace nodded. "A little."

"He and Robyn, well, they were together from childhood on, then suddenly she was gone. It was like half of him dying. He's just trying to figure out how to live on his own, and he thinks this place is the answer."

Grace felt an ache deep inside her. "I can't imagine losing someone I love," she said softly. "If anything happened to Lilly, I don't know...it's unthinkable."

"Yes, it is," Lark agreed. "I came close to losing Jack's dad, a heart attack, oh, not a serious one, but it was terrifying for me. Despite all his problems, he's my life."

Grace knew that she'd never really found that sort of love with a man, not even close. "Well, I'm very grateful that we're here, and that you aren't angry that we are."

Her smile returned. "Not even close," Lark said. "I need to get back now. Tell Gabbie that I'll see her tomorrow, okay?"

Grace had a thought. "Can I hitch a ride to the mail box at the end of the driveway?"

"Of course, climb in."

Grace went around and opened the door, then grabbed both sides of the frame and used the running board to haul herself up. "This is huge," she said, sitting back in the soft leather. "Getting in is like trying to get on a horse."

"I have to use a step box to help me get on a horse, but not for this thing," Lark said, laughing.

When they reached the highway, Grace got out and Lark drove off for home.

Grace gathered the mail, just two fliers and a thick envelope from the post office, a "welcome" kit filled with lots of information about Wolf Lake. She turned to head back up the drive, but stopped when she heard an engine approaching from the west.

She thought Lark might be returning for something, or maybe the truck that was bringing their belongings from L.A. was finally arriving. Instead, a red Jeep came into sight and Grace stood absolutely still by the stone post at the gate. Jack. Her pleasure at the sight of him as he slowed to a stop was all out of proportion, but she couldn't help it. The passenger window rolled down. "I need to talk to you. It won't take long."

There was tension in his expression and it made her uneasy. "I've got time right now."

He motioned her to get in. "We can talk in here with the air conditioner running."

She hesitated, his obvious tension killing the happiness she'd felt moments ago. But she opened the door and climbed in. Jack sat back and let the car idle while the vents blew cool air.

"What did you need to talk to me about?" she asked.

"The ranch," he said.

Something in her had known this conversation was coming. The other shoe had just fallen. She didn't miss the intensity in his expression, the lines fanning out from his narrowed eyes. "Okay," she said, clasping her hands in her lap to keep them from shaking.

He turned, gripping the top of the steering wheel with both hands so tightly his knuckles grew pale. "If you weren't here, where would you be?"

That stopped her thoughts in their tracks. "Excuse me?"

"You said you'd give living here a chance, but if it doesn't work out, where would you go?"

"I don't know," she said honestly. She hadn't let herself make any plans, maybe because she hoped she wouldn't need to. She just wanted so much to stay here, make a life with her family. The man so close to her was the one who had shown her the uniqueness of the place, its beauty despite the hardships that came with it. And that feeling of peace that overwhelmed her at times, the feeling that she belonged here.

She took in his dark eyes, the set of his jaw, the strong hands that had rescued her when Lucy had bolted, and a thought came to her that jolted her. Maybe Jack was part of why this land seemed so right. His kindness to her, the help he'd given them with the two horses, riding the boundaries with her, teaching her about windmills and snakes. Maybe she owed more of her love of the land to him than she'd thought. And something in her stopped her from just telling him that she was here for good or bad. That she would never leave. She couldn't do that to him, and she didn't even want to try to figure out why she couldn't hurt him like that.

"I don't know," she repeated softly.

Jack turned from her. "Okay, that's none of my business."

"I would tell you if I knew," she said, not sure if she should get out of the Jeep now, "but I don't know." She couldn't say that there was no other place she wanted to be, so why bother choosing an alternative location unless she was forced to. "I *really* don't know. I mean, if someone asked you where you'd live if you didn't live here, what would you say?"

"Atlanta," he said in a flat voice.

She was shocked. "Really? Why?"

"My wife's brother, Robert, lives there with his family. I went there over Christmas and almost stayed." He exhaled. "But I didn't. I came back here. Honestly, I realized I didn't want to live anywhere else."

JACK WASN'T SURE why he'd told her all that. It was the past, his attempt to run away from here, to forget the familiar things, the places and people he'd shared with Robyn. But he was still running away, even here. He'd used the long, solitary rides into the high country to run away. He'd used work for a while, and maybe he'd started to depend on using this ranch. That possibility shook him. He felt

Grace looking at him, but he couldn't look back at her.

"Sometimes a change of scenery makes a person appreciate what they've always had?" she suggested in a soft voice.

"I guess, but that wasn't my case. I had to be here. It was stupid to think of leaving. This is where my life is, at least, the rest of my life."

"Your wife...?" Her voice faded for a moment. "She was a teacher?"

Her question was so simple, but it cut through him. And again, he found himself telling her about Robyn as if they'd been friends for life. "She loved kids and teaching just seemed as basic for Robyn as breathing." He felt the familiar tightness in his throat, but was shocked that his voice was so steady. "Kids were her life. But we waited...there never was a child. We'd just started talking about having one. Robyn wanted to, and I resisted for some reason. Then it was too late." He cleared his throat. "Would have, should have, could have, didn't," he muttered.

He wasn't prepared when Grace reached out and touched him. Her heat and gentleness grazing his bare arm, and for a split second, he felt a connection. An anchor. That made no sense. She was showing him sympathy, feeling badly for him, and he didn't want that.

"We all have regrets, believe me," she almost whispered.

He looked at her then, those lavender eyes touched by exactly that, regret. "You wish you hadn't divorced?"

She looked startled by the question and broke their contact. He hated the loss of that warm touch but at the same time knew it was probably for the best. "No, I mean, yes. I regret that I married someone I'd end up divorcing. Absolutely. But the divorce had to happen."

He wondered why any man would divorce this woman. "Problems?"

"One big problem. He didn't want to be married, and being a father was even further down his list of what he didn't want to be or do. So he left me before Lilly was born and never looked back."

Jack couldn't believe the disgust he felt for a man he'd never known. "His loss," he said without editing his response.

Grace shrugged and that action seemed to expose such vulnerability in her. "It's okay," she said without much conviction. "As bad as my decision was to marry him, I got a great gift from him—Lilly. I wouldn't give her up for anything, or change the past in any way, except for wishing she'd had a loving father. I'd change that if I could."

Jack studied Grace, taking in the slight unsteadiness in her jaw as she stared out the front window. "She's a great kid from what I've seen."

"Yes, she is."

Jack sat there, the urge to take her hand almost overwhelming. "And you want this place to be the home for your child?"

"Absolutely," she said without hesitation, and the tension in her face eased, almost giving way to a determined smile.

Jack figured he should not have come here. But he had, and right then, his life was messier than ever. His emotions were all tangled in the past, fighting for the present. The idea of getting his land back by taking Grace to court died a sudden death. He wouldn't do that. He couldn't. And he wouldn't even try to explain that to himself, much less to anyone else.

That was about the only solid thought right

then, everything else was up in the air. He couldn't get anything settled beyond that, and he needed to. Those lavender eyes were on him again, and he was so aware of the way she was nibbling on her bottom lip, as if unsure what to do about her thoughts. That same uncertainty echoed in him.

He shook his head sharply to refocus, but it didn't help. Nothing was making sense. He touched the gearshift, knowing he should let her get out so he could leave. But part of him didn't want to.

"Jack?" Grace said, cutting through his confusion.

"You don't need to tell me anything else," he said.

"It's not that. I just wanted to say that no matter what happens, I hope things work out for you."

That almost stopped his heart, and he closed his eyes for a fleeting moment before looking back at her. "Thank you."

"I understand about you wanting the land, maybe needing it, because I do, too. It's beautiful, and you've been here all your life. This is what you know, what you love. It's just, I've never had anything like this. I've never even lived in a house, much less one with all this land." Her eyes were overly bright for a moment. "You've got everything. You've got family and this town, and friends on top of friends. You're so lucky, so very lucky."

Her words almost broke his heart. And they were true. He had it all, except a reason to be here, to keep going, to find a life beyond his old one. If there was a woman like Grace in his future— He stopped that thought dead in its tracks. He couldn't think about that. "You're right," he managed to say, and if she hadn't touched his arm again, he would have ended it there. But she did.

He covered her hand with his, and the heat of her infiltrated him. The connection was so strong that it all but took away his breath. Before he understood what he was doing, or what he needed, he leaned toward her, lifting his hand from hers to cup her chin. Then his lips found hers, soft and slightly parted. Heaven help him, he didn't want to stop. He'd found the woman he needed. Grace. And he knew that he would never find a woman like her again.

No, he had had a woman he'd loved desperately, and the memory of her made him jerk back. He could barely focus on her face, the eyes heavy-lidded, her lips parted, and it took all of his will to pull away. Before he could embarrass himself by trying to apologize, she let him off the hook by turning away and grabbing the door handle.

"I need to go back to the house," she said on a slightly hoarse whisper. Then she was out of the car and walking quickly up the driveway. She didn't look back, but Jack couldn't take his eyes off her as she headed up the path.

Slim hips, slender legs, her ponytail swaying with each step of her determined stride. He watched until she was gone from sight completely, but even then, Jack just sat there in the idling Jeep, not moving. He faced the fact that it wasn't just his need for this land that was getting to him, it was the woman who now owned it.

Before he'd met her, she'd simply been the obstacle to his regaining possession of his grandfather's ranch, the person he had to convince to leave. But once he met Grace, it had never been that simple. He closed his eyes for a moment, but opened them again as the memory of the kiss hit him hard.

Heat and softness and need. He turned and jammed the Jeep into gear then took off in a squeal of tires. He'd lost all ability to deal with his life right then. He couldn't. And he couldn't face his family or his friends. They were all poised to do what his father had suggested. But he wouldn't do that, not ever. The land was lost to him. It was that simple, and he had to find a way to let it go.

Jack entered the main ranch on the service road, saddled his horse and rode off to the west, intent on bypassing the Rez and going up into the high country as he had planned before his father's "idea" had been put before him. This time he wouldn't stop until he got the taste of Grace off his lips and the thought of her out of his head. Hours later, he was on a high ridge, the sun dipping in the west, and he still didn't have any answers. Nothing made sense. Nothing at all. He'd go back. He'd forget about the old adobe, and he'd try to figure out where to go from there. He would. He had to. But one thing he knew, there weren't any answers for him up here. They had to come from inside himself.

He rode back slowly, and it was approaching dusk when he got to the ranch. He'd stabled his horse and was almost to the Jeep when his mother came hurrying toward him from the house.

"Oh, I'm glad I caught you," she said. "Your father just told me about his so-called plan."

Jack just stared at her.

"He's trying to make things right, you know that, but he can't let you do it this way."

He hadn't expected that. "What do you mean?"

"I mean, I met that girl and her child and her mother, and they're good, decent people who just want to make a good life out here."

She'd met Grace? "When?"

"I went by there to welcome them to the ranch and to town," she said firmly. "They're our neighbors now. We welcome neighbors."

"Or course we do."

"And?" she asked, frowning at him, waiting.

"Don't worry. I'm not going to take anyone to court or evict anyone." He heard the weariness in his voice. "I'm not going to do anything."

She sighed with obvious relief. "Good, good." She touched his arm. "Tomorrow, I'm going to ask Grace and her family over for the afternoon. I hope you'll be here."

"Mom, I don't think so."

She frowned, a sadness in her eyes. "You have to talk to your father," she said softly. "This is breaking his heart."

"Not now," he said in a rough voice, and headed back to his Jeep. But as he drove away, he realized he had nowhere he wanted to go. So he stopped at the first place he came to. The police station.

John took one look at him and said, "Come on in the office."

As soon as he'd closed the door and Jack sank down in one of the chairs, he said, "Okay, what happened?"

Jack told him about his father's idea, then leaned back with a long exhalation. "I can't kick that family off the land, even if I get a court order to do it."

"I didn't think you would," John said. "Not for a minute.

# CHAPTER FIFTEEN

GRACE TOOK HER mother and Lilly into town for dinner at the restaurant, partly to put in an application, and partly because she didn't want to sit around the house thinking about Jack kissing her.

Clare Money was at the reception desk, and greeted Grace as if she'd always been coming there. It felt good to be recognized, and not just another person wandering in the door looking for food. A young, red-haired waitress showed them to their table, took their drink orders, then Lilly and her mother picked up their menus.

Grace didn't touch hers. She excused herself to go back into the reception area. Clare looked up from the reservation log, and smiled. "I hope everything's okay in there."

"Oh, great. I just wondered, you know I'm new in town, and I thought I'd ask if you needed any other servers." Grace told her about her experience, offering to get references, and said she was available for any shift.

Clare studied her, then nodded. "You know, you came in just at the right time. The girl who seated you, Misty Nelson, just gave me her two weeks' notice." She reached below the counter and handed Grace a single sheet of paper. "Just fill this out and bring it back when you can. As it stands, I think I'd like to give you a try to fill Misty's slot."

She took the paper without looking at it. "Thanks."

"If you're as good as your experience, I'd love to have you on board."

"I'll fill this in right now, and drop it off when we leave."

"Perfect."

Grace hurried back to their table, another burden lifted. She slipped into the booth opposite her mother and daughter, smiling. "Whatever you want, it's on me," she said magnanimously.

Gabriella, looking more relaxed than Grace could ever remember, laughed. "You were buying anyway."

"Yes, but now it's steaks if you want."

She reached for her own menu. "Big, juicy steaks."

Lilly frowned, her pig tails swinging as she shook her head. "No, I want a hot dog," she said. Steaks had no allure for the child. *"Two* hot dogs."

"Two hot dogs it is," Grace said as their server, Misty, came back for their orders.

Before Grace could speak, Misty spoke to her. "I hear you're going to be doing my job in a couple of weeks?"

"It looks that way."

"Well, that's great! If you want to come in sometime this week or next, I can go over things with you. You know, regular customers, what they like, how we put in the orders. I'm here every weekday from three to eight."

"That's so nice of you. I'd be glad to pick your brain." She felt her mother watching her. "I'll be in soon."

"Good, now, what would you all like to eat?"

After Misty left with their orders, Gabriella leaned forward. "You got a job here?"

"Yes, at least a trial." She laid the application on the table and fished in her bag for a pen. "I just have to get this filled out and leave it before we go, but I'm hoping I don't get Misty's hours, more like mornings, so Lilly will be in school when I'm gone."

"That's great," her mother said, glancing around the restaurant. "It doesn't look like the staff dresses up."

A shirt and slacks, black and white. "No, the uniform's simple, and the food's good."

Her mother looked puzzled. "How do you know?"

She thought she'd told her mother about eating here with Jack, but then again, so much had been going on, especially with Jack. For a second, all she could remember was the kiss, but she quickly pushed that memory aside. "Jack and I ate here for lunch once."

Her mother lifted one finely arched eye row. "Oh?"

"I ran into him when I looked at the school, and he offered and I thought I could check the place out. Seems it was a very fortuitous decision on my part."

Grace rapidly filled in the form. One problem after another seemed to be vanishing. This was good, very good. When she'd finished, she set the form to one side, and sat back. She noticed two things at once. Misty,

coming from a side door with their plates of
food, and three people entering the front door.

She didn't know two of them, but Jack was
the third. He was with a man and woman. The
man wore a police uniform and the woman
was holding his hand. Grace turned away,
glad Jack hadn't noticed them.

Misty placed their food in front of them.
"Anything else I can get you?"

"Ketchup?" Lilly piped up.

"Absolutely, darling," Misty said, and went
to the next table to get a bottle. "Enjoy," she
said and left.

The steaks looked big and juicy, but Grace
found that her appetite was fading fast. Lilly
and Gabriella dug into their food with relish.
Grace stood and grabbed the application. "I'll
be right back," she said, and crossed to the
reception desk again.

Clare wasn't there, and the area was empty.
As Grace turned to retreat to her table, she
came face to face with Jack. He wore black
slacks and a coffee-colored shirt that was
open at the neck, and his midnight-black hair
was slicked back as if he'd showered recently.

"Hi," she said, feeling as awkward as a
teenager.

He looked past her, then met her gaze. "So, you're going to be working here?"

She didn't even ask how he knew. Misty was his waitress, too, she bet. "I hope so."

She heard him exhale, a sound that was very close to a sigh. Something was wrong, and she found herself bracing herself. "I was going to say something. I wasn't certain at first, but now I'm very sure about what to do."

"What?"

"It's about the ranch. I wanted to let you know that—"

A door opened and a large party of customers piled into the reception area. Clare appeared, smiling and greeting everyone, and their voices filled the small space. Jack didn't move, his eyes not leaving hers, but he stopped talking.

"Do you want to go outside, or something, to talk?" she asked, hating the question, because she had a gut feeling she didn't want to hear what he wanted to say to her.

"Jack!"

His head jerked to the left. A tall woman with dark hair shot with red highlights was smiling at him. She came toward him, a tiny girl with brilliant red curls clinging to her hand. Holding the child's other hand was a tall, dark man in jeans and a navy T-shirt, and as soon as he smiled, revealing a single dimple, Grace knew he must be related to Jack. "Gage, I thought you said you'd be off in Houston for a week?" Jack said.

Gage shook his head. "I scrapped the trip. We had some interviews in family court." He smiled down at the very somber little girl. "Another hearing done with." He glanced at Grace. "I'm sorry to be interrupting you two."

Jack quickly introduced Grace to his brother, his fiancée, Merry, and their little girl Erin. Jack had mentioned the adoption. Grace smiled, said the right things, but her mind was stuck on what Jack wanted to talk to her about. Finally, he said, "I'm here with John and his wife." He motioned with his head toward the dining room. "They'd love to see you two and especially Erin."

When the three had left, Jack looked down at Grace unblinkingly. "You know, your food's getting cold, and my party's waiting for me." He motioned vaguely with both hands, palms up. "Bad timing."

"No," she said, her nerves so tight she

wanted to scream. "No. What did you need to say?"

Jack hesitated. "Nothing that can't wait." He glanced over at Clare. "Tell John I had to leave?"

"Nothing's wrong, is there?"

"I just need to leave," Jack said, then looked back at Grace. "Enjoy your meal," he said, and walked away.

Grace watched the door shut behind him, then turned and headed back to her table.

GRACE WAS ON the porch at dawn, not expecting Jack to show up, but disappointed when he didn't. She'd been awake most of the night. She figured she knew what he was trying to tell her before he took off. He wanted the ranch, and had decided not to wait for her to fail. Maybe he had found a way to get the land back. He was an attorney, after all, but Mr. Vaughn had told her that her deed was binding.

It was Saturday, and the day dragged on, until Gabriella reminded her about their invitation to the Carson Ranch. Grace didn't want to go, but Lilly was so excited. By three o'clock they were at the ranch, in the huge stables, visiting with Herbert and Lark Carson. Jack's father was very like his sons, although not dark, and his waist had begun to thicken with middle age. But he was very friendly, and Lilly took right to him.

Herbert and Gabriella took Lilly outside, and Grace looked around the massive stables with Lark. The stall wings radiated out from a central hub, an area so big that stacks and stacks of hay and heavy bags of feed lined the walls, but barely took up a tenth of the available space. Grace had never seen anything like it.

Lark, dressed in jeans and suede shirt sewn with beads and glinting stones, smiled at Grace. "We have a Christmas party here every year, and the place is filled with kids and laughter and all things Christmas. You and Lilly and your mother will have to come. It's the best time of the year."

Grace nodded. "It sounds wonderful." But part of her mind was on Jack's decision. Lark had told her she'd asked him to come, and he said he would, but he still hadn't shown up. "It is," Lark said, then suggested she and Grace go up to the house. "Lilly will be fine with Herbert and your mother." Grace wasn't aware she'd hesitated, until Lark frowned. "It's okay, really, Herbert's doing fine now. I know what you've heard, and what you know. But he's a good man, working on his sobriety, and working hard on the ranch."

Grace couldn't imagine what the woman had gone through because of her husband's drinking, but she could see how strong Lark was, and how much she loved her husband. "I'm sorry. I didn't think…." She stopped the lie, a polite denial of the truth. "I trust you," she said, wanting to be sensitive but honest.

"Thank you," Lark said softly. "I know you've spoken with Jack a lot, and he's having a very hard time letting go of his anger at his father, but he's not a man to hold a grudge forever. He'll have one for a bit, then he'll think things out, and do the right thing."

Grace remembered the pain on Jack's face when he'd talked about his father and what he'd done. "I'm sure you're right."

Lark motioned them toward the exit that led to the pathway and up to the main house. "Let's go inside and see about a snack for everyone."

With that, the woman laced her arm in Grace's, and the two of them were soon standing in a large great room with tile floors and a huge, multisided fieldstone fireplace dead in the middle. Supple leather furniture had been arranged in three conversation areas, each with a view of the fireplace.

They settled on a sofa with a stunning view of the sprawling pastures with their miles of white fencing and the mountains far beyond. Grace turned to Lark and asked what she'd been wondering for almost an hour. "Do you think Jack will still come?"

His mother softly sighed. "Honestly, I don't know. He got here very early this morning and I assumed that he was getting the horse to go over to your place, but he rode north. I have no idea where he went. Since Robyn's death, he's taken to disappearing for a few days at a time, alone, riding up to the high country. I heard he's been at the Rez a few times, but mostly he's out on the land."

Grace realized that Lark's eyes were overly bright, and for a moment, she thought the woman was going to cry. But she didn't. "Jack's had a very hard time the past few years, but he's a strong person. I think he believes that he needs the old ranch to heal." She bit her lip. "No, it's not that exactly. It's just that he hasn't figured out how to heal himself without it, and he's grasping at straws."

"He must have loved his wife so very much," Grace said, her heart aching for Jack. She couldn't imagine loving a man that much, but she had a feeling that if she ever did, it would be a man like Jack Carson.

"Oh, he did," Lark said. "He did, and he always will. I wouldn't expect less of him, of any of my boys."

From deep in the house came laughter and the sound of rapid footsteps. Small, light footsteps. Lilly burst into the room, her face radiant. "Mama, Mama, can I ride a little horse?"

Gabriella and Herbert followed behind her.

"We have a small Pinto that's super calm and safe," Herbert said. "The kids from the Family Center in town come out here to ride and hike. They all love Buttercup. We have a helmet Lilly can wear, but I told her she had to ask you first."

Grace looked at her mother. "It's a darling horse," Gabriella said, "and she'll only ride around the arena by the stables."

Lark touched Grace's hand. "It's okay if you don't want her to right now. She can come back later, or bring her horse over. Herbert is a great riding teacher."

Grace looked at Lilly. "Okay," she said, "But do exactly what Mr. Carson tells you to do."

Lilly clapped her hands together. "Yeah, yeah!" she squealed, then turned and hurried back to her grandmother and Herbert. "She'll enjoy it," Lark said once they'd left. "And it will take Herbert's mind off Jack and things."

"Where exactly do you think Jack goes?"

"I don't know. He stays away for a few days, comes back looking exhausted, and all he'll say is, he was thinking." She frowned. "I don't know, these past few days, things have changed. I'm not sure what he's doing anymore. But he said he'd be here and now… I actually tried to call his cell phone. I never have before, but this time, I was uneasy. It went right to voice mail, but he never turns off his phone. As long as there's a signal, he should have answered."

Grace thought back to their time together, the perimeter rides, the kiss, the restaurant. Something had definitely been bothering him. She stood and went to the bank of windows, then it struck her. The lake. He'd said something about thinking up there, when he couldn't think anywhere else.

"I might know where he is," she admitted as she turned to Lark. "But I need to go home and get Lucy."

Lark hesitated, as if weighing the idea of her finding Jack, but she didn't argue. Instead, she stood and walked over to Grace. "Go ahead," she said quietly. "We'll make sure Lilly and Gabriella get home safely if you're not back in time."

When Grace arrived at the ranch, Parrish helped her saddle Lucy quickly, then she started out, wondering if she was crazy. She hoped she could find the trail she'd taken with Jack a few days ago. She soon recognized the way and realized Lucy seemed to know where they were going, although there was no sign of Jack.

Grace was about to give up after they'd made the strenuous climb. It was hot and she didn't want to risk either herself or the horse by staying out here alone. But just then a low whinny sounded, and when the path led them behind a particularly large rock formation, she found Jack's horse there, tied to a low shrub.

He whinnied again as they approached, and Lucy stopped right beside him. Grace slid off, tied Lucy to the same bush, then looked up. She tried not to think of snakes, good or bad, as she started the climb. There were no sounds beyond the low moan of an occasional breeze and the chirping of birds. Her boot dislodged a small rock and it skittered down the path behind her.

What was she going to say when she got to Jack? She didn't know, but she knew she wanted to find him. She had to find him. Her breathing was getting a bit labored when she finally climbed over the shale rocks and onto the ledge that led to the sea of grass.

She watched the rippling movements of the grass in the growing breeze, then noticed the crushed path where Jack must have walked earlier. She'd been right. He was there. She went to the low arched opening and stepped through.

JACK HAD BEEN achingly alone for two years, until the old ranch entered the picture. No, that wasn't totally true. The ranch had always been there. It was Grace who had come into his life. The rides they'd taken, the talks they'd had, then the kiss…. They'd all made him realize that despite his attempts to survive, he'd hit the end. He hated self-pity, and the old man's words came to him. "Live your own life. Only you can do that."

But what if his life right then was the best it would ever get? He had flashes of a future with Grace, things he rejected, things he hid from. Just acknowledging an attraction to the woman made him hurt, and seeing her child only added to the ache for what he'd never had and never would have. It was almost unbearable.

"Jack?" His name came like a soft whisper on the air, and for a minute he thought he was hallucinating, until he turned. His hallucination took the form of Grace in slender jeans, a cropped top and boots, coming toward him. He could see her eyes beneath the straw hat, the deep lavender, soft and gentle. And he could literally feel the loneliness he lived with lifting ever so slightly as she neared.

Without another word, she sank down by him, actually putting her feet over the ledge, keeping a foot or so of space between them. Her eyes were staring off into the distance.

He did the same thing, very conscious of her every breath.

"So, what did you want to talk about?" she finally asked.

He didn't answer. He didn't even know what to say about anything anymore.

After a few moments, she spoke again. "I am so sorry for all you've gone through."

That hit him hard. He hadn't expected that, and he didn't want her pity. Never. His voice was a hoarse whisper when he spoke, and the words were not planned. "Life happens," he heard himself say simply. "We had ours planned, everything to live for, then it was all gone. Just like that. Gone." He choked out the last word, and swallowed hard.

"When my father walked out," Grace said, barely above a whisper, "I made up this game, the 'What-If Game.' I even wrote the what-ifs down. What if he left because some bad guys were after him, and he left to protect us? What if he left to make his fortune so he could come back and get us? What if…?" She laughed softly, but there wasn't a whole lot of humor in the sound. "None of the 'what-ifs' prepared me for reality. Not one of them was about him being in a poker game and win-ning a ranch and giving it to me without ever having to see me. None of them."

Jack turned enough to see her hands clenched on her thighs.

Grace took a deep breath before continuing. "None of them were about him giving a huge opportunity to a grandchild he'd never met and never wanted to meet. But he did. That's my reality, and it's incredible. No more streets we can't walk on, where no one knows you or cares to know you, or schools where they have metal detectors. I'd felt for so long that I couldn't protect Lilly, couldn't provide her with the life I wanted to, and now I can, because of my father."

He let his gaze slide up the sweep of her throat, the delicate chin lifted just a bit. "I can't believe he left you."

She swallowed, then slowly turned to him. There were no tears, just an expression on her face that seemed resigned. "He did. He couldn't handle a family. He didn't want to handle a family, and that meant me. But even so, he gave me the one thing I really needed, probably because he simply didn't want it."

"What about Lilly's father?" he asked.

"I told you, he left well before Lilly was

born. He didn't even want to see her. The divorce was finalized by mail."

He put his hand over hers where it rested on her thigh. "He was a fool," he said. "To have it all and turn his back on it. A real fool."

Slowly, Grace turned her hand under his, and laced her fingers with his. It almost made it impossible for him to breathe for a moment. Her heat and softness. He wanted it. He needed it, but he felt so guilty. Robyn was everything to him. He couldn't just let that all go. He couldn't just turn his back and pretend that he was a whole man—it wouldn't be doing justice in a sense, but this woman was truly special to him.

But he didn't release his hold on her hand. He couldn't. Then he said something that he'd barely admitted to himself. "I almost can't hear Robyn's voice anymore." He stopped, feeling like a fool, and he would have pulled back from her if her hold on him hadn't tightened.

The connection overwhelmed him. He felt as if he finally had found a lifeline. No, maybe a mere thread to grasp, but it was more than he'd had before he'd heard her breathe his name. And the old man's words were there again. "It's your life to live, Jack, and only you can live it. What it is or isn't, is up to you." He felt a lifting of pressure, and he could actually take a breath into his lungs.

He stood, trying to absorb what was happening when Grace moved to stand by him. As if she understood it all, she reached out and went into his arms, hugging him tightly around his waist, burying her face in his chest. Both of them held on for dear life, for what seemed forever.

Until she stirred, moving back enough to lift her arms around his neck and gently pull him down to her. The kiss came from her this time, without hesitation, and as her lips met his, he could almost breathe in the taste of her. That was what he wanted, her, like this, and although it was insane, he cared for her, deeply. It couldn't be real love. That only happened once in a lifetime, but he also knew that whatever this was, he wanted it. He wanted her.

# CHAPTER SIXTEEN

GRACE KNEW THAT she'd become connected to this place, to the land, but she'd had no idea until yesterday that she was becoming connected to Jack. She could almost feel his pain, and she wanted to help him. But she couldn't. She'd thought she wanted a man like Jack to love, but she'd been wanting Jack all that time. He could touch her on some level no man ever had, but she couldn't let that happen. He was grieving for his lost wife, and she had no wish to be some "fill-in" for that loss.

She'd made mistakes, one huge mistake, and it had come from impulse and need. She couldn't let that happen again. Not to her, not to him, and especially not to Lilly. It was the hardest thing she'd ever done, to ease back from his embrace, to give up his heat and strength, and say, "We need to get back to your parents' ranch."

Jack reached out and cupped her chin with

his strong hand. "How did you know where to find me?"

"Your mother said you probably had to think a lot of things out, and I realized you'd be here." She tried to smile, despite his touch still on her skin. "I rode all the way up here on Lucy and didn't fall off. I didn't even know if I could find the place on my own, but I did."

"Yes, you did." His voice was rough, and he dipped his head to hers, his lips brushing hers with the ghost of a kiss this time. But it made her tremble and she moved to break the contact.

"We have to get back." She needed distance. It would be too easy to just act and not think. Far too easy.

He took her hand in his, leading her back through the opening, across the grass and down the path to the waiting horses. "You actually rode here all alone?"

She nodded. "Your mother was worried, and so was I."

He came to her, and for a frantic moment, she thought he was going to hold her again, but instead, he lifted her onto Lucy's back. Once in the saddle, Grace settled, and as Jack mounted his horse, she let him lead the way and Lucy fell in step behind him.

THEY RODE TO the ranch in silence, and Jack found himself starting his own "what-ifs." What if he could love again? What if he could let someone else become the center of his world? He understood one thing right then. Either he figured out what was happening between him and Grace, or he'd have to give her up.

"Jack?"

He glanced back at her. "You okay?"

"Yes, but maybe you should call your mother and let her know you're okay?"

He'd turned off his phone as soon as he'd left the ranch that morning. Digging into his jeans' pocket, he pulled it out and powered it up. "You're right," he said as the screen came to life.

He stopped the horse as soon as he saw a number of voice messages. The first few were from his mother, asking when he'd be back at the ranch. He smiled at Grace as she came up beside him on Lucy, but the next message made him freeze.

"Son, please turn on your phone. I need to find Grace right away."

The next message was more frantic. "Lilly's been hurt, and we're taking her to the hospital. Moses is waiting for us at the E.R. She needs her mother." He drew back, looked at the time and realized the last call was just fifteen minutes ago. He tried to think of what to say to Grace. But she understood something was wrong before he opened his mouth.

"Jack, what's happening?"

He didn't hedge. "Lilly got hurt at the ranch, and they're going to the hospital."

Her face blanched, and she reached over and grabbed him by the arm. "What happened?"

"Mom didn't say, just that Moses was waiting for them at the E.R."

She pulled away, nudging her horse to go, and he found himself riding behind her back to the ranch. He passed their horses over to a stable hand, then followed Grace at a run to get to his Jeep.

She sat rigidly in the seat, her hands clasped tightly in her lap, her eyes straight ahead. "Please, hurry," she said urgently.

Jack took off for the main road. He pulled

out his phone and put in a call to John. "Hey, I need a favor. I'm heading for town and going too fast, but I need to get to the hospital."

"Who's hurt?" the chief of police asked immediately.

"Grace's daughter. I need you to get me through town without any accidents."

"You got it." The line went dead.

Jack glanced over at Grace again. He didn't want anything bad to happen to her. If he could, he would make a law that nothing bad would ever happen to her, or to those she loved. Stupid. But he meant it, and he knew that whatever was happening between the two of them, it wasn't going away. The idea that he didn't want to make it go away stunned him.

Lights flashed ahead of them, then a siren wailed, as John pulled in front of them from a side road. Just minutes later, Jack was heading up the curved drive to the double E.R. doors. Before the car even stopped, Grace was out, running through the automatic doors.

Jack knew all too well where to go as he left the Jeep at the entrance and went after Grace.

# CHAPTER SEVENTEEN

JACK APPROACHED HIS MOTHER, who was standing at the first cubicle. He tapped her shoulder and when she turned, she hugged him fiercely. He glanced over at Gabriella nearby, noticing how pale and drawn she was.

"I just turned my back for a moment," Grace's mother said in a shaky voice, starting to wring her hands.

"She fell off the horse?" he asked.

"No, she'd already ridden and done well, but she got up on the fence to watch Walter, the trainer, working a horse and fell backwards. She broke her arm." Tears were coming now, and Lark reached out to gather the crying woman to her.

"It's a messy break," Lark told Jack, "not a simple fracture. Moses said he needs to get some input before attempting to set it."

Jack couldn't do anything in the E.R. cubicle, but he could make a call. "I'll be back," he said and jogged outside, through the security doors and waiting room to the spot where he'd left his Jeep. Taking out his cell phone, he put in a call to an old friend, Bryan Stater, a kid he'd gone through school with. Bryan had left Wolf Lake and become one of the top pediatric orthopedic surgeons in the country.

The phone rang three times before he heard his friend's voice, then explained the situation. He gave Bryan the number for Moses, then ended the call and went back inside.

His mother and Gabriella turned to him as he approached the cubicle. "I called Bryan," he said to his mother.

Right then, Moses's assistant walked up, pulled the curtain back and handed the doctor a house phone. All Jack was aware of was Grace hovering over the gurney that held her daughter, such a tiny thing on the huge bed. Grace was speaking softly to Lilly, whose eyes were closed as she made low sobbing sounds. Her broken arm was elevated on a pillow with an IV attached to her good arm.

Moses spoke into the phone. "Bryan, yes, that's about it. I ordered another set of X-rays for the angles." He listened. "Yes, anything at all. It's appreciated."

He got off the phone, and Grace straightened slightly to turn to him. "Why aren't you doing something for the pain?"

"She's getting pain medication through the IV, and we're going to fix her up perfectly," he said, then glanced over and nodded at Jack. "I'm consulting with the best pediatric orthopedist in the country."

Grace paled even more if that were possible. "Oh, I don't know if my insurance will cover that sort of thing." She shook her head. "I mean, I want the best, you know, I really do, but—"

"Don't worry. Bryan Stater is a former local. He knows a whole lot about setting a kid's broken arm and he owes me and a few people around here, a favor or two."

"Thank you," Grace said, laying her hand on her daughter's forehead.

Jack stood off to the side. He hated being in a hospital, especially in the E.R.—too many bad memories.

Moses spoke to Lilly. "I'll be right back to give you a ride." Then he looked at Grace. "I need to check with Doctor Stater, then we'll get her into an operating room." He hesitated. "No allergies, right?"

"None that I know of, but she's never broken anything before."

"That's great, very good," he said, patting Grace's shoulder.

Jack admired Moses' bedside manner. He was calming both Grace and the child. And that night in the past when Robyn had been brought in, Moses had been there too. He'd done all he could, both for Robyn and for Jack. A solid rock for Jack in the middle of a life suddenly destroyed.

Moses looked at Jack closely as he asked, "You okay?"

"Yes," he lied.

He wasn't, but he couldn't make himself walk away. He'd called Bryan to pull him into the case, and he should just leave, but he couldn't. He couldn't leave Grace. All he could do was stand there, feeling helpless once again

GRACE REACHED TO hold her mother. "It's going to be okay. She's going to be okay," she repeated, as much to convince herself of that fact as to convince her mother.

"She just slipped. I was right there, and she twisted and fell back off the top rail." Gabriella swiped at her face with a handful of tissues. "I grabbed, but I wasn't fast enough."

"Oh, Mom, you couldn't help it. Lilly's so quick." Grace patted her mother's back. "Dr. Blackstone is very good."

Lark nodded. "He's the best."

"See, Lilly's getting good care." Grace let go of her mother and turned to the gurney again. As she did, she caught sight of Jack just standing there, watching. Their eyes met, his dark with concern.

Moses came back in with a team who worked in perfect harmony, getting the bed higher, the IV strapped to the metal side. A nurse took Lilly's vitals, and someone from the hallway asked, "ETA?"

Moses looked at the clock on the wall. "Two to three. We're on our way." He turned to Grace. "You can walk with her to the doors of the O.R., if you want."

She'd go into the operating room with her daughter if she could, Grace thought. Instead she held Lilly's good hand as the gurney was pushed through the E.R.

Arriving at the O.R. was a blur. She kissed Lilly, promising to be right there when she woke up. The child's eyes were heavy, then she smiled faintly, and Grace had to force back tears until the team pushed Lilly through the doors and out of her sight.

Then the tears came, and she turned, almost running into Jack, who had walked behind her without her even knowing. He looked down at her, and she did what felt to be the most natural thing to her. She walked into his arms and let him hold her against him while she cried. There were no, "Things will work out," or, "Everything's going to be okay," platitudes that came so easily at a time like that. Just his strong arms around her and the sound of his heart beating steadily against her cheek…

Grace couldn't let go of Jack. She was afraid if she did, her legs wouldn't hold her. Thankfully, he shifted, pulling her against his side, and led her back to a waiting room. For three hours, people came and went, Lark, her mother, Mr. Carson, Mallory from the bed-and-breakfast, but Jack never left. He stayed right by her, holding her hand, not needing to talk. But he listened to her, to her guilt over leaving Lilly, at not remembering to take her own cell phone with her on the ride, anything and everything, and Jack just listened.

Then the door opened and Moses came in. He looked exhausted, but he managed a smile. "She came through it with flying colors. The fracture was complicated, but it should heal completely with no loss of mobility in the arm or the hand."

Grace felt the weight of the world slip off her shoulders. "Oh, thank you, thank you. When can I see her?"

Moses shrugged. "She'll be in ICU until she comes around. Why don't you go and freshen up, and I'll call you or a nurse will call when Lilly's awake."

"No," she said without a pause, "I'm not leaving. My mother can get me whatever I need."

"I didn't think you'd fall for that," Moses said with a smile. "Wait twenty minutes, then go to ICU and tell them I sent you. Lilly should be settled there by then."

Grace stood, her legs slightly wobbly. "I don't know how to thank you," she said to Moses.

"I didn't do it alone. Doctor Stater was on the line with me the whole time. I couldn't have done it without him."

Jack was beside her, not touching her now,

but so close she could feel his heat. She was grateful, so very grateful to so many people. Moses excused himself, and left.

"Oh, my," Lark said softly. "That is such good news."

Gabriella sat by her, nodding, but still looking pale. "That poor baby."

Lark patted her hand, then stood. "Let's go and see if we can find a toy in this place for Lilly when she wakes up."

Gabriella agreed, and the two women left for the gift shop. Grace looked at Jack. "Thank you so much for getting me back here, and…and for staying."

He turned to her and gently brushed her cheek with the back of his fingers. "I'm just sorry this happened."

"Kids," she said. "You can't keep up with them. Things happen, but I'm so grateful that Lilly is getting such good care."

Jack looked as if he wanted to say something else, but he didn't. Instead, he bent and brushed her lips with his. When he drew back, he just gazed down at her. Did she want a man like Jack Carson to love? Or did she want Jack Carson?

"I'm going to find where ICU is," she

said, not wanting to face the answer to that question.

He didn't go with her, but said as she went out the door, "Follow the yellow line on the floor."

"Thank you," she said. The ICU was in the west wing, two floors up. When she reached the admittance door, she ran into Moses. He held the door for her, motioned her to follow him and led the way to one of the glass-fronted rooms arranged around the nurses' station. Lilly was lying in a huge bed, tubes in her good arm, and her injured arm wrapped in something that looked like an Ace bandage. "She doesn't have a cast?"

"She will," Moses said. "She's up here until we're sure from the X-rays that everything's as it should be. Then we can make a cast that she can draw flowers on."

Grace held her daughter's limp hand, watching each breath she took, listening to the machines by the bed beeping softly in the background. "Are you sure she's just sleeping?"

"Half and half. She's sleeping, but she's also being sedated by medication." He looked at the machine with its bobbing graphs and multitude of switches and buttons. "She's doing very well. She's a strong little girl. We'll keep her here for a few hours, then get a regular room for her one floor down."

"When can she go home?"

He shrugged. "Let's play that by ear. Maybe as early as tomorrow, but it might be a few days."

As if he read her mind, he said, "We make concessions for parents so they can sleep at the hospital to be near their kids. Do you want me to set that up for you?"

"Oh, yes, please," she said. She wasn't going to go anywhere while Lilly was here.

When Moses left, Grace pulled a chair close to the bed and sank down on it, reaching for Lilly's good hand. Two hours later a tall man with a buzz haircut came into the room with Jack. He smiled at Grace. "Mrs. Evans?" he asked in a deep, resonant voice.

Grace got to her feet, glancing at Jack, then at the stranger. "Yes, Grace Evans."

"I'm Doctor Stater, Bryan Stater. Jack called me about your daughter, and when I got the X-rays from Moses, I decided it would be best if I just came out here in person."

He flew all the way from Atlanta? "Thank

you," she finally said, then motioned to Lilly. "She…she hasn't woken up yet, but the doctor said she needs to remain sedated for a while. They'll fit the cast when they know the operation was successful."

"That's right. I'm going to review the surgery, but first I wanted to see Lilly and meet you." He motioned to Jack. "I hear you're the proud owner of his grandpa's spread."

She nodded. "It's a long story."

"Then we'll have to make time to talk about it, but right now, Lilly is our most important business."

"Yes, yes, she is." Grace watched the doctor check Lilly and read the chart. The longer he looked and didn't say anything, the more nervous Grace felt.

Jack came closer, and slipped an arm around her shoulders. It took all her willpower to not lean into him. "Thank you for calling him," she said.

"Sure." His gaze turned to hers for a long moment. "How are you holding up?"

"I'm not important right now," she said.

"Oh, yes you are. You're the world to that child, and that makes you very, very important." He tightened his hold on her and she stopped fighting her need and leaned against him.

"I can't imagine not having Lilly in my life," she managed to get out in a choked voice.

"It's hard to watch someone you love so much be in pain. So hard. But I've got a feeling this is all going to turn out just fine."

She heard his words and knew he was talking about loving his wife so much and not being able to do anything to help her. "It has to," she said.

Doctor Stater stripped off the gloves he'd been using and walked around to where she and Jack stood. "I give you my word that your daughter will be fine. She's just going to need some therapy and time to heal, but the surgery looks perfect."

Grace felt almost weak. She turned into Jack and buried her face in his chest. She'd be okay. She'd need therapy, but Lilly would heal. Grace felt a hand on her back. It was Doctor Stater.

"I'll send them in to get the cast done, then get her in a private room and out of here."

Grace couldn't speak, but heard Jack say, "Thanks, Bryan."

"You know I'm there for you, and those you care about."

Then she heard the doctor walk out, his shoes tapping on the tiled floors.

Grace tipped her head back to look at Jack. He'd been terrific, and he'd never have any idea what it meant to her. But she owed him.

He touched her cheek with the tip of his forefinger. "You know, you need to find your mother."

"Oh, my gosh, I forgot," Grace said. She checked on Lilly one last time, kissed her sleeping daughter, then went with Jack out of ICU and in search of Lark and Gabriella.

Jack motioned to an arched doorway ahead. "She'll be in there," he said. "It's the main waiting room for ICU."

"Oh, thanks," she said and started toward it, immediately realizing that Jack wasn't going with her. Before she stepped through the doorway, she turned back and saw Jack leaning against the wall, his shoulders hunched, head bowed. Both hands covered his face.

She felt sick. Of course. This must be where his wife had died, in this same unit. In a way he must be reliving that time. Her heart ached for him when she saw the weariness in his body, that bow of defeat. Torn between going inside and going back to Jack, she closed her eyes.

"Gracie?"

She turned to see Gabriella coming toward her from the square waiting room. Her mother pulled her into a tight hug, with Lark and Herbert Carson right behind her. Behind them stood Parrish.

"Oh, Mom," Grace said, tears precariously close to the surface. But she wouldn't let them fall, not now, not when the news was so good. "She's going to be okay. Doctor Stater flew all the way here to check on Lilly, and he said that the operation was a terrific success. She might even be able to go home tomorrow or the next day."

The room was filled with hugs and smiles. Gabriella was talking about getting whatever Grace needed to stay at the hospital with Lilly, and Herbert Carson apologized over and over again. He said the same as her mom, that he never saw the fall coming. One minute she was on the fence, laughing and clapping. The next thing, she was tumbling over backward. Of course they would pay for all Lilly's expenses.

Grace smiled at Lark and Herbert. "It's no one's fault. Lilly's six and she's lively and curious. I know that. I'm just grateful that you all were there for her, and that you're here for me."

That seemed to do the trick. The tension in the couple eased, and Lark was smiling. "She's such a darling child. Maybe she and Erin will get along. They're about the same age. Erin is going to be taking riding lessons, and they could do it together."

Grace felt her stomach lurch at the idea, but was surprised when she didn't refuse it outright. "Maybe they can," she said. "Once Lilly's healed, I think she'd love that."

They all decided that Gabriella would go back to the ranch with Parrish to pick up the things Grace needed, and Lark and Herbert would go home for now, but be back in a few hours to check on Lilly. Grace wasn't going anywhere.

Once they'd left, and the room was empty, Grace stood very still, then hurried out. But the corridor was empty. Jack was gone. And Grace felt an emptiness that she couldn't bring herself to examine. Not there, not then.

# CHAPTER EIGHTEEN

Grace turned to go to the nurse's desk and ask about Lilly being moved, but before she got there, Moses came striding out of ICU. "Hey, Grace," he called and hurried over to her.

For a split second, her heart caught, afraid that Lilly had taken a turn for the worse. "What?"

"I just wanted to let you know, Lilly's on her way up to her new room."

"What room is she going to be sent to?"

"It's 255W. That's in the west wing, second floor. Private."

"Does my insurance pay for a private room?"

"No, probably not, but there isn't any insurance involved. The Carsons are paying for all Lilly's expenses."

"Oh, no, I can't let them do that."

"Please, let them do it. It's amazing how

guilt, whether real or perceived, can be assuaged by some form of payment."

"Do you really think I should?"

"Yes, absolutely. That whole family is so caring and generous. I can only imagine how horrible they felt when this happened. They have the special needs kids from the Family Center over to the ranch for riding and hiking, and they've never had an accident. It's just one of those things, but allow them to take care of it."

"Okay," she agreed, then had to ask, "Did you see Jack anywhere?"

He looked down, then back at her. "He's gone. He left about fifteen minutes ago."

"He didn't say anything."

Moses was sober. "You know about his wife and all?"

Grace nodded.

"Well, they brought her here, and Jack stayed with her until...." He shrugged. "I was surprised when he showed up with you. I never would have dreamed he could handle being here again. When Robyn died, he just seemed to lose his connection with life."

Grace swallowed the tightness in her throat. He'd lost a main connection when he'd lost the ranch. She knew that, and it brought an ache to her middle. He needed that land, but she loved it too. And she loved—

She must have gasped, because Moses was studying her.

"Are you doing okay?"

She was shaken by what she'd just realized. She loved Jack Carson. As insane as that seemed, she felt it deep inside her. And she didn't want him to be in pain, to be hurt. She couldn't stand it if she hurt him. "I'm okay," she lied.

"Good, Lilly should be up in her room by now. Why don't you head up and see how she is?"

"Yes, yes, I will," she said, and turned toward the elevators.

"Grace?"

Moses came hurrying after her, the huge bear Grace had seen earlier in the waiting room in his arms. "I'm assuming this is yours, or at least Lilly's?"

"Oh, yes, thank you," she said, taking it as the elevator panel chimed and the door slid open. "Thank you," she repeated as she pressed the button for the second floor.

JACK LEFT THE smell of disinfectant, the echoing of voices and footsteps on polished tiles. He hated them all. He hated the hospital, but he hated himself more. He'd thought he could be there, that he could stay with Grace, but when they'd stopped by the waiting room near the ICU he couldn't go any further. He could barely breathe.

He'd left, as quickly as he could, but didn't make it to his Jeep. He sat on a half wall just outside the hospital doors, unable to move. He had no idea where to go. There was no place, no part of the town or the ranch that he could go to and get rid of his guilt. And Grace was still back at the hospital.

"Jack?"

He looked up and found Mallory standing there, her face creased with concern. She studied him. "Oh, boy, you...." She bit her lip. "Do you want to come inside?"

"No," he said, he couldn't go in that place again.

Mallory sat down on the wall beside him. "You know, Jack, we haven't been really close. You were always ahead of me in school, and you were always with Robyn."

He felt cold, yet it was balmy outside.

Mallory kept talking. "I'm probably way out of line here, but you're doing what I did when Henry died."

Jack protested quickly, "It's not about…." But he couldn't finish the statement. "Moses called you to tell you that I'm acting crazy?"

"Oh, no, I mean, he called, but he's worried. He'd hoped you'd go back and talk to him." She seemed to brace herself. "I'm sure Grace was very grateful that you were there for her. Poor Lilly, hurting herself like that. It's sad, but also happy. She's going to be okay, good as new, so Moses told me."

Jack stared at her, waiting, knowing something else was coming and that he probably should brace himself for it.

"The thing is, Moses doesn't understand. He's totally compassionate, and sympathetic, but he never lost part of himself, part of the life he wanted to live. I have. Three years ago, now. Henry was gone. And I was here." She touched his arm. "And I was like you, scared and upset, and feeling guilty that I was alive and he wasn't. Then Moses came, and I fought it. I really did, but suddenly I knew that Henry loved me, and if he could come back for one instant, he'd tell me that he wanted me to be loved again, and to love again. And I do, Jack, I love Moses as surely as the sun rises, and it's real love, but it's different. Moses is different than Henry, but I love them both, and I always will."

Her hand was slightly unsteady on him, and he kept hearing her words over and over again, although she was watching him silently now. "Mallory, I—"

She looked down at his hands, and he realized he was twisting his gold wedding band around and around. "You feel unfaithful?"

He glared at her. She'd hit the mark and it hurt. "You don't?" he asked.

"I did. I really did, but what if you'd been the one taken, and Robyn was here alone. Is that what you would have wanted for her, to be alone for the rest of her life?"

"Certainly not."

"Then why do you have to be a martyr? I don't know if Grace is that special to you or not, but at some point you have to let go of the guilt and move on…start to live again."

Jack looked at Mallory and something inside him started to fall into place. Could it be that simple to love again? And the answer came with brilliant clarity.

Yes. If it was Grace whom he loved.

THAT EVENING, LILLY sat propped up in the hospital bed, using her good hand to color in a book Lark had brought in for her. She hadn't shown any signs of a fever, and the medication was working to dull the discomfort of a new, brilliantly white arm cast. Grace had already signed it, along with Lark, Herbert, Gabriella and Parrish. Moses had drawn a happy face on it and Mallory had drawn a remarkably accurate silhouette of Lilly near the wrist.

So far, the doctors were going with a release date of the next day by noon. Grace sat in a huge recliner that they'd supplied for her to sleep on. It lowered almost horizontal, and the TV in the room had cartoons on it.

"How could life be better?" Grace thought, then knew how it could. In the morning, she'd make it better, one way or the other.

Grace slept that night in the chair in Lilly's room, and when dawn broke, Gabriella was there with Parrish as Doctor Stater came into the room. He carefully checked Lilly, then backed Moses' call on the release. "Today by noon, you can take her home," he told Grace.

Before noon, she, Lilly and her mother were in the car driving to the ranch. They pulled up the driveway, crested the rise, and came to a stop in front of the porch steps. Parrish was there to greet them.

"Well, Little Lady," he said, opening the back door for Lilly. "Come on in." He expertly undid her restraints, then lifted her, managing to support her cast while he carried the child into the house. Gabriella followed them, and the last thing Grace heard was Parrish saying, "You know, that little Paint of yours needs a companion, one your grandma could ride."

The door shut and Grace felt the wind go out from under her. Slowly, she sank down on the top step and looked over the stables to the distant valley and the mountains beyond.

She wanted the ranch, this peace and quiet. The beauty. She wanted it for her family, but Jack needed it too. She knew that as certainly as she knew that she loved him. He'd lost so much, and a part of her didn't want to add this ranch to his losses. She didn't want to be responsible for any more hurt in his life. But she didn't know what to do.

By the time she'd gone inside and had lunch with Lilly, her mother and Parrish, who had started calling her mother Gabbie, Grace had a real need to just walk around the ranch. She kept telling herself that it was hers and she could do what she wanted with it. If that meant easing some of Jack's pain, she would. If she could just figure out how to do it and keep her family here as well.

She walked until late in the afternoon, then headed back to the house. She couldn't just go in, have dinner, put Lilly to bed, then go to sleep herself. An idea had come to her sometime during her walk. She was beginning to believe she might have an answer both she and Jack could live with. She had to do something about it right away, or she'd never sleep that night.

After going inside to let her mother know she had an errand to run, she got in her car and drove off toward town. But when she got to Jack's offices, he wasn't there. His assistant told her he hadn't been in all day.

Slowly, she went back out to her car, then drove back the way she'd come. But she didn't turn in at her driveway. She kept going until she was at the Carsons'. Stopping by the open gates, she almost turned and left, but she knew she had to do this. She drove up the long drive, spotted the red Jeep parked by the side of the house and pulled in beside it.

Walking over to the main entrance, she lifted her hand to grab the huge bull's head knocker on the dark wooden door, then let it fall with a thudding clang. There was no response, and she was about to turn and leave when the door finally opened and Jack stood in front of her. His clothes looked wrinkled, and more than a day's beard shadowed his face. He stood there, silently, just staring at her with those midnight-dark eyes.

She almost turned and left, her nerves so on edge that all she could think of was running.

Finally Jack spoke. "No one's here," he said flatly, as if that meant she should turn and go away.

"I came to see you," she managed to get out. "We need to talk."

He paused, then he stood back and let her walk inside. Closing the door behind her, he strode ahead of her through the great room, then up a staircase to the second floor. Quickly, Grace followed, and found herself in a library. The walls were lined with heavy wooden bookcases, and a huge desk stood in the middle of a thick Oriental carpet. Jack went around behind the desk and dropped heavily into a high-backed leather swivel chair.

"Moses told me Lilly went home today," he finally said as she sat awkwardly in a chair across from him.

"I need to tell you something—" Grace barely recognizcd her own voice, with its tremor and slight huskiness. "And please, don't interrupt me."

JACK LEANED FORWARD IN the chair. "What?" he asked cautiously.

"First, I need to thank you for bringing in Doctor Stater. He's so wonderful, and Moses is beyond great."

Jack wasn't sure how long he could just sit there, looking at Grace's delicate features, that smile, and her lavender eyes on him. "You said you needed to talk. Was it about the doctor? If so, I told you, we're old friends, and I've saved his butt more than once. He owes me."

She shook her head. "No, it's not about that, although I'm glad he owed you. It's about the ranch."

He held up both hands, palms out. "It's yours. Let's leave it at that and get on with our lives."

She looked stunned. "No," she said, sitting forward, pressing her hands on the edge of the huge desk. "No, it's yours. It's ours. I mean, I tried to figure out what to do, and I think that you should have the land. I can't run a ranch. I thought I might be able to, but I know now I can't."

She got to her feet, shifting her hands to rest flatly on the desk top, coming closer to Jack. "I think it could work, that you could have the land, you know, divide it or subdivide it or something, and Lilly, my mother and I will live in the house."

Jack watched her as she talked, the intensity in her eyes willing him to see things her way. "And you think that could work because—?"

"Because you love that land. I know, I know, the house is important too, but it would still be there and I'll promise to keep it the way it always was. You could come there whenever you wanted to and you could ride around on the pastures and run cattle or sheep or whatever."

He stood slowly, keeping the desk between them. "And you'd be willing to do that? Is this your back up plan?"

"No, I mean, I guess, but it's the best I can come up with. I just want…." Her words trailed off and she straightened, then hugged herself tightly and looked down.

"What *do* you want?" he asked, not taking his eyes off her.

Finally, she lifted her gaze to his, and he was shocked by the confusion he saw there. "I know how much you loved your wife, and you lost her. You love the land, and you lost it."

She bit her lip, then said in a rush, "I'm not sure I've ever seen real love, I mean, beyond what I feel for Lilly and my mother. But loving someone like you loved…." She bit her lip again and frowned. "That's something I never knew. I don't think my dad could have really loved my mother or me, and I don't think my ex-husband ever loved me, and I know, in retrospect, that I probably never loved him. I let go too easily when he left. Now, I can go weeks without thinking about him, unless someone else brings him up."

His stomach tightened and he clenched his hands, feeling the absence of the wedding ring he'd taken off last night. "Where's this all coming from?" he finally asked, slowly going around the desk to get closer to her.

She shrugged, and a single tear slipped out of her eye and rolled slowly down her cheek. She didn't seem to notice, until he lifted his hand and brushed at it with his thumb. "Oh, Jack," she whispered. "I'm in love for the first time in my life, and I know that it's all wrong, and it's tangled up with all sorts of things that make it impossible, but one thing I can do is let you have the land."

He wondered if he'd heard right, and his hand stilled on her cheek. "You what?" he breathed, not daring to move.

"I want you to…to have the…ranch." Her voice broke, and she had to swallow to finish the words. "I can do that for you. I want to do that for you."

He drew back, looking down into her upturned face. More tears came, silently, and she didn't bother to swipe them away. "No, before that. Before the stuff about the land. What was that?"

She grimaced and slowly sank back into her chair, hugging her arms around herself. "Please," she protested.

He hunkered down in front of her, but didn't touch her. "No, tell me."

The tear-bright lavender eyes slowly lifted to meet his gaze and he heard her swallow hard. "I'm in love for the first time in my life."

He let the words settle in, then he slowly lifted his hands and framed her face. "With me?"

Her tongue touched her pale pink lower lip. "It's crazy, I know, and it can't happen, and I didn't mean to tell you, ever."

"Why not?"

She shook her head, freeing herself, and pushed to stand, almost knocking him backwards. "Now, I have to…to go home and see about Lilly, and my mother, and figure out how to make this all legal, the land and house and all."

He steadied himself, but didn't move to let her pass. "No," he said, forcing himself not to touch her again. Not yet.

She blinked, her lashes wet with clinging tears. "What?"

"No, I've got a better idea. Grandpa just wanted someone on that land that loved it, that would care for it and build a family in the house. That's what he's got. And I'm okay with that."

"You are?"

"Well, almost okay with it. But I need to make one alteration in the setup."

She nodded. "Anything," He felt a lightness in him, a sense of the future and not the past. He'd finally managed to say goodbye to Robyn the night before. He'd always love her, but he knew that he could still love in this world, and he would.

"This is my plan. I'll take care of the land, make it work again, and I'd like to take care of the family, too." He paused, almost afraid to say the rest, but he went on. It had to work. "I want to build a family there, to make a real life."

Her face crumpled, and the tears came again. "No, no, no," she sobbed into her hands.

He grabbed her shoulders, pulled her closer, but not against him. Waiting for her to calm a bit, he finally saw his opening when she sniffled, then slowly lowered her hands. "I can't take Lilly away from here. I can't."

"You won't have to." He looked right at her. "I'm going to say something that I never knew I'd ever say again in this world. I loved Robyn, I always will love her, but that doesn't mean that I can't love someone else just as much. Maybe differently, but with all my heart."

She grew very still, the tears stopped, and he felt as if the world was waiting for him to step back into it and make it spin again. "Grace, I love you."

The words hung suspended between them, and the ensuing silence felt like an eternity. Then slowly, very slowly, Grace seemed to fall toward him, her arms holding on to him for dear life.

He could feel a trembling in her, and she moved back a bit, but did not let go of him. "Really?" was all she asked.

"Really. Things have been so tangled up and confused that I didn't realize that everything that was happening was happening because I love you. I fought it, I wanted it, I hated it, then I knew that I needed you more than I could ever tell you."

There was a wariness in her that he didn't understand. "I can't be a backup plan, Jack, I can't. I can't be just a way to get your land back. I'll give it to you, I swear I will. You don't have to say all this."

His smile came out of nowhere, and he said something he hadn't even thought about until that moment. "Grace, I love you, and I'm in love for the last time in my life."

She lifted her arms, clasping her hands behind his neck and standing on tiptoes to meet him in a kiss that didn't stop his world at all. It started it again, and that took his breath away. Moments passed, then both were breathing hard, still holding to each other, neither willing to let go.

He was grinning, and he knew it. He must look like some lovesick teenager, but he didn't care. Because he was in love, again, forever.

Could it be that simple? Could it be that miraculous? Both, he knew as he looked into lavender eyes that were filled with warmth and promise.

"I love you so much, Jack," she breathed, and he knew it was all true. His future had been there, waiting for him in the form of Grace Evans and a little blonde girl with pigtails. His second chance, his future.

AN HOUR LATER, Jack and Grace drove up to the old adobe, after promises had been made and a future laid out between the two of them. Her mother was there with Parrish and Lilly on the porch. The arm in the cast was supported by a bright red bandana, and the older man and little girl were playing a game of checkers on a tiny table between them.

Grace got out and met Jack at the front of his Jeep, then he took her hand and they headed toward the porch. Gabriella started to call out, "Things here are good," then stopped when she saw them holding hands.

She didn't say anything, but just grinned at them as they took the stairs together. "Mom, I need to talk to you."

"And I need to talk to you." She glanced at Parrish, who leaned closer to Lilly and said, "Why don't I get you settled in the house for a bit. We'll find you some ice cream."

"Sure," she said, and she went with Parrish inside.

Gabriella took the chair the child had vacated. "Sit," she said, "We'll discuss things as soon as Parrish gets back."

Jack and Grace rested on the top step, side by side, and once Parrish returned, Grace asked, "All right. So, what's going on?" Gabriella said on an exhale. "Parrish and I, we've been chatting, and it seems that he knew your dad."

Grace turned to the older man. "You knew him?"

"Back a while. He was on his way up north, Canada, and he was working on the same spread I was in Montana. He was a nice guy, actually, and he told me all about you two, and about Lilly. But he was going the wrong direction, and I told him he couldn't just leave family like that."

Grace was holding onto Jack's hand so tightly, she was afraid she was going to hurt him. "What did he say?"

"That he loved all of you, but he was broken, and he couldn't be fixed. He couldn't just sit in one place. He had to get out, but he'd taken care of all of you, and done it right. According to his thinking, this business with the land made up for leaving you all those years ago. He told me about this place and left a few days later. When I went into his bunk room, I found that box of photos that I put in the dresser. He must have forgotten it, but I took it and brought it here."

Gabriella stood and went closer to Parrish. "I told Parrish we understand about Charles.

And it was right that he brought the box here. He didn't want to intrude, but he heard about this job and took it, thinking he'd just stay a week or so to make sure we were okay." She touched his shoulder and he covered her hand with his. "He's not leaving. He's staying."

Parrish drew Gabriella from her chair and took her into his arms. "I can't figure out how Charlie let this all go. But I don't want to. I don't have much of a family, but always wanted one, and now, I want to stay here, with Gabbie and you all."

Grace felt Jack pulling her to her feet with him. He turned her toward him, cupping her face. "How about it, Grace? Grandpa would be smiling about this whole thing, I think."

Grace went up on tiptoes, kissed Jack, and then turned. "Absolutely," she replied, "with two conditions."

Parrish and her mother both seemed surprised at the kiss. Eventually he asked, "What conditions?"

"First, Parrish, you have to be in this for the long haul, no leaving on a whim."

"Absolutely," Parrish said.

"And secondly, Mom, you have to give Jack your blessing to marry me."

Gabriella smiled hugely, coming to her daughter and hugging her for a long moment. Then Lilly swung back the front door.

"Parrish, did you tell Mama about the kittens?" she asked.

Parrish looked a bit sheepish. "I did think that cat looked too fat," he said.

Their laughter echoed in the stillness of the day, sweeping over the land and toward the distant mountains. Grace beheld the people in her life, and knew she'd finally found that love, that connection she'd always dreamed of, and she smiled.

# EPILOGUE

*Thanksgiving*

FOR THE FIRST time every member of the Carson family was on the land Jackson Wolf had first claimed for his people. The land that had been lost to them was now restored, and Thanksgiving dinner was going to be set out in the main room of the old adobe.

Lark and Gabriella were busy in the kitchen, both refusing to use a catering service, and the children were in the stables, with Parrish. Adam and Faith had just arrived, the couple glowing with happiness, and Faith glowing in her second month of pregnancy. The secret marriage had barely raised an eyebrow, when the impending birth of a Carson grandchild was announced. Merry and Gage were celebrating their adoption Erin, and the little girl was smiling and t' ing more.

Lilly and Erin acted as if they'd l

each other all their lives. They were both scheduled to be flower girls at the wedding of Erin's new parents on New Year's Eve at the big ranch. Gabriella and Parrish were together most of the time, and Grace was pretty certain that Merry and Gage wouldn't be the only ones to get married in the near future.

Grace and Jack were hosting Thanksgiving dinner, but weren't anywhere in sight. The two had quietly walked away from the house. Jack had been edgy, unable to settle, and he needed to talk to Grace. With her hand in his, they crossed an irrigated pasture that was greening up nicely.

They didn't speak until they climbed a rise that overlooked the newer ranch. They stood for a long while, Jack's arm around Grace, then he spoke.

"Finally, alone," he said, pulling Grace against him and kissing her temple. Her hair was loose and he loved it that way, a curtain of pale gold. Jeans and shirts had become her clothes of choice and she was wearing her fourth pair of boots. She was still a city girl but the country girl was there too. "I love you," he whispered, and kissed her again.

Grace cuddled into him, out over the view. "Why are we here?"

Jack hesitated. "I'm tired of going home to the loft, and I want to live at the house with you and Lilly...and your mom and Parrish."

Grace moved back enough to look up at him, and her lavender eyes twinkled. "So, you want to move in?"

"Absolutely. Enough of empty nights, and missing time with you and Lilly."

"Okay," she said. "So, what's your solution? I don't think you can just move in and have it go unnoticed in Wolf Lake, let alone by your parents and your brothers and the kids. The kids! What kind of thing is that to do with children around?"

He grinned, and she reached up and touched his dimple with her forefinger. "Exactly. You said it."

"So, what did your very brilliant criminal mind come up with?"

He grew serious, his heart hammering. "I told you that I'm in love for the last time in my life, and I don't want to waste any more of it living apart."

"You sound like you're ancient," she said, her finger slowly tracing the line of his j

"...ve learned...." He had to stop

"N...allow to clear the threatening tight-
and...
...s in his throat. "I mean, time isn't made
to waste. Right now is all we've got, and I
want that time to be with you and Lilly. It's
that simple."

"And...?"

"And...." He pulled her to him, kissing her
with a hunger that echoed in her. When he
drew back, he looked into her beautiful eyes
and whispered, "Marry me, marry me now,
as soon as we can work it out. Tomorrow, next
week. Just soon."

She studied Jack, then snuggled into his
chest, but she didn't say anything. He rested
his chin on her head, held her close and
waited.

Finally she stirred, but didn't let him go.
"Yes, yes," she whispered. "Yes."

He closed his eyes tightly, a feeling of joy
flooding through him. "Do you want a big
wedding?"

She shook her head no. "Just you and me
and Lilly and Mom and Parrish, and your
mom and dad, and—"

"Family," he interjected to stop the list-
ing.

"Exactly."

"When?"

"In a week, here, simple. And when the ceremony is over, you won't leave. You'll stay here with us."

He hugged her tightly. "Yes!" he said, feeling as if he should be pumping his fist into the air. "Yes!"

Grace drew back, her smile beautiful. "A week," she said.

Jack reached into his jeans pocket and tugged out the small box he'd been carrying for two weeks. He held it up to Grace. "Grace Carson. I like the sound of that." He placed the box in her palm, but she didn't move to open it. "What's wrong?"

"Oh, nothing, love, absolutely nothing," she said.

"Then open it."

"A one carat diamond surrounded by local turquoise and set in antique silver?"

"How did you know?"

"Well, Mallory saw you go into Maureen's new jewelry shop and then leave, and Mal lory was going there to have her engagem ring from Moses resized, and Maureen slip that you'd just bought a ring, the biggest sale she's had so far."

"Oh," was all he said.

"Then Mallory let it slip to Oscar, and Oscar's grandson Aaron told my mom about it, and my mom told Parrish and—"

Jack cut her off with a quick kiss. "Enough. I get it." He took the box back from her, took out the ring she'd just perfectly described, and held it up for the sun to catch the glitter of the stones. Without another word, Grace let him slip it onto her finger.

"Oh, Jack, it's perfect."

"I wish it had been a surprise," he said.

"It was...when Parrish let it slip."

They looked at each other and started to laugh. "Small town gossip has been fine-tuned in Wolf Lake," Jack said.

"A blessing and a curse," Grace said as she kissed his throat.

Jack shook his head. "A blessing." He slipped his arm around Grace and they headed for the old adobe house.

"Do we even need to announce our engage-ent?" she asked.

They stepped down into a dry creek bed. held her hand in his and laughed again.

"Why, they'll probably know all about the wedding before we even get back."

Grace stopped and turned to him. He could tell she was thinking of something besides their upcoming marriage. "What's on your mind?"

"Your dad. Where is he?"

It had been hard to have a talk with his father, to hear the promises, the hope, and him finally saying it was over. The past was the past. This was their future, and he wanted his dad in it with him.

"He'll be here. He just had something to do first."

They started walking again. "What did he have to do on Thanksgiving Day?" she asked.

"A meeting. He goes every day, early in the morning. He'll be done in time for dinner."

"Thank goodness," she said, squeezing his hand.

They continued on in silence until they stepped up and out of the creek bed into the clear day. As they got closer to the house, they could hear voices and laughter, and sniffed the smell of turkey in the air. In unison, they stopped, watched the activity at the house from a distance, then resumed walking.

"What a perfect Thanksgiving," Grace said.

"Grandpa would be right in the middle of all of this, smoking his turkey, shucking the corn." He missed the man fiercely, but found himself smiling. "But most of all he'd be in the middle of the family, his heritage."

They got closer and saw Willie G. on the porch, shucking the corn. Parrish was with him, laughing at something Jack's father, seated on the stone step with them, was saying.

"Our heritage," Grace said with a touch of awe in her voice. "Our family."

*"And your father's legacy to you,"* he wanted to say. Despite his past mistakes, Charles Michaels had sealed the future for everyone at the house. He wished he could thank the man, but knew he'd never have the chance. The one thing he could do was love his daughter and granddaughter forever.

Jack Carson put his arm around his love, and headed with her into their future. It was right here in front of them on the land where it had all begun...in Wolf Lake.

\* \* \* \* \*

# LARGER-PRINT BOOKS!

## GET 2 FREE LARGER-PRINT NOVELS
## PLUS 2 FREE MYSTERY GIFTS

*Love Inspired*

**Larger-print novels are now available...**

# *ReaderService*.com

## Manage your account online!

- Review your order history
- Manage your payments
- Update your address

---

*We've designed
the Harlequin® Reader Service
website just for you.*

---

## Enjoy all the features!

- Reader excerpts from any series
- Respond to mailings and
  special monthly offers
- Discover new series available to you
- Browse the Bonus Bucks catalog
- Share your feedback

*Visit us at:*
**ReaderService.com**